DEATH
UNDER THE
MOONFLOWER

DEATH
UNDER THE
MOONFLOWER

A PETER BOUNTY MYSTERY

Todd Downing

Coachwhip Publications

Landisville, Pennsylvania

CONTENTS

Introduction
Curtis Evans

"Mr. Downing is a born detective story writer."
—Edward Powys Mathers ("Torquemada"),
review of Todd Downing, *Vultures in the Sky* (1935)

THE RICHNESS AND DIVERSITY of American genre writing during the Golden Age of mystery fiction (c. 1920 to 1939) is much under-appreciated today. Golden Age mystery readers could choose from a wide variety of literary dishes, be it the tough stuff of the hard-boiled boys (most famously Dashiell Hammett, Raymond Chandler and James M. Cain), which has long received the lion's share of the attention that scholars have granted American Golden Age crime writers; the psychological suspense (or HIBK—Had I But Known—as it was once disparaged) of Elisabeth Sanxay Holding, Mary Roberts Rinehart, Mignon Eberhart and Leslie Ford; the ur-ban sophistication of Rex Stout, Patrick Quentin and Rufus King; the madcap humor of Phoebe Atwood Taylor and Craig Rice (the latter making the tail end of the Golden Age); the eccentric extra-vaganzas of Harry Stephen Keeler; the police procedurals of Helen Reilly; the courtroom dramas of Erle Stanley Gardner; or the mag-nificent baroque puzzles of S. S. Van Dine, Ellery Queen, Anthony Abbot, John Dickson Carr, C. Daly King and Clyde B. Clason.

This listing of authors just scratches the surface of American mystery writing in the years between the two world wars. So many accomplished mystery writers from the period have undeservingly fallen into obscurity. One such individual is Todd Downing, the Golden Age chronicler of fictional murders in Mexico.

Todd Downing was born in 1902 in the town of Atoka, Choctaw Nation, Indian Territory (soon to be Oklahoma). Though one-eighth Choctaw and, like his father Samuel (Sam), an enrolled member of the Choctaw Nation, Todd Downing had what in many ways was a traditional, early twentieth century small town American upbringing. Both Todd's father Sam and his mother Maud were staunch churchgoing Presbyterians and Republicans and Todd was brought up according to the proper precepts of these two orthodoxies.

Yet the Downing family of Atoka was unusual in its great love of reading. From an early age Todd Downing could be found in nooks and corners of the family's two-story foursquare house with his nose buried in books. He particularly loved romantic tales of adventure, played out in settings around the globe. Beginning with Sir Walter Scott's and H. Rider Haggard's colorful sagas of derring-do, Todd moved on, in his teenage years, to crime and mystery, in the form of the short story collections of Arthur B. Reeve, creator of the virtuous scientific detective Dr. Craig Kennedy, and the novels of Sax Rohmer, creator of the diabolical criminal mastermind Dr. Fu Manchu.

After Todd became a student at the University of Oklahoma in 1920, he soon discovered Edgar Wallace, the awesomely prolific English king of the thriller. Todd devoured Wallace shockers at a prodigious rate. (His library of books, bequeathed at his death in 1974 to Southeastern Oklahoma State University, included sixty-five Wallace novels and short story collections, as well as Wallace's autobiography and biography.) Yet as the 1920s progressed, Todd, like many bright people in his day, became increasingly interested in fair play detective fiction, where the point is not emotional jolts but cerebration: the reader tries to solve the mystery for her/himself through clues provided within the text by the author. Over the decade of the twenties Todd purchased detective novels and short story collections by Anthony Berkeley, Earl Derr Biggers, Lynn Brock, G. K. Chesterton, Mignon Eberhart, Rufus King, Marie

Belloc Lowndes, Baroness Orczy, Mary Roberts Rinehart, T. S. Stribling and S. S. Van Dine.

Between mysteries Todd managed to find time to qualify for his B.A. and M.A at the University of Oklahoma, as well as to take classes in Spanish, French and anthropology during summers spent at the National University of Mexico. In 1928 OU hired the young Atokan as an instructor in Spanish. (Todd was fluent in five languages: English, Choctaw, Spanish, French and Italian.) In addition to teaching his OU classes and conducting summer tour groups in Mexico, Todd continued voraciously reading both detective novels and crime thrillers; and in 1930 he began reviewing mysteries of all sorts in the literary pages of Oklahoma City's *Daily Oklahoman*. Especial favorites of Todd's in the mystery line were Agatha Christie, Dorothy L. Sayers, Ellery Queen, John Dickson Carr, Dashiell Hammett, Mary Roberts Rinehart, Mignon Eberhart and additional worthy writers who likely are less familiar to many today: Anthony Abbot, Rufus King, H. C. Bailey, Eden Phillpotts and Anthony Wynne (for more on Todd Downing's mystery fiction reviews see my book *Clues and Corpses: The Detective Fiction and Mystery Criticism of Todd Downing*).

Encouraged by an older colleague at the University of Oklahoma, Professor Kenneth C. Kaufman, Todd Downing wrote his first detective novel in 1931, not long after he had begun contributing mystery fiction reviews to the *Daily Oklahoman*. Eventually published in 1933, *Murder on Tour* introduced Todd's most important series detective, United States Customs Service agent Hugh Rennert, who would appear in seven detective novels between 1933 and 1937. (A Hugh Rennert novella, probably written by Todd in 1932, was published in 1945.) Besides *Murder on Tour* these are: *The Cat Screams* (1934), *Vultures in the Sky* (1935), *Murder on the Tropic* (1935), *The Case of the Unconquered Sisters* (1936), *The Last Trumpet* (1937) and *Night over Mexico* (1937). All six of these later novels now have been reprinted by Coachwhip Publications.

The Hugh Rennert detective novels are primarily set in Mexico (the one exception being *The Last Trumpet*, where the action ranges from Cameron County, Texas to the Mexican state of Tamaulipas). Todd Downing's authoritative and fascinating use of Mexico as a setting in his detective novels makes him one of the most important regionalist mystery writers of the Golden Age and is his most significant contribution to the genre. Additionally, the Rennert novels are graced with teasing fair play puzzle plots, stylish writing and interesting characterizations. Hugh Rennert himself is a notable detective, modest, middle-aged, self-reflective and somewhat melancholy, yet resolute and determined. ("A good kind man," one character calls him in *Night over Mexico*, and he is.) Hugh Rennert is fascinated with Mexico and *vacilada*, the mirthfully stoic attitude of the country's people toward life and death; and over the course of the series Todd Downing explores what might be termed the metaphysical relationship of Rennert and Mexico in interesting ways. We learn a lot about both a man and a country.

After 1937 Todd Downing wrote two more detective novels, both with a different series detective (Texas sheriff Peter Bounty, introduced in *The Last Trumpet*): *Death under the Moonflower* (1938) and *The Lazy Lawrence Murders* (1941). He also published the work which he considered his crowning achievement as a writer, a non-fictional study of Mexico, *The Mexican Earth* (1940; reprinted by the University of Oklahoma Press in 1996). Sadly, Todd's attempt in the 1940s to write a mainstream historical novel about Mexico came to naught. Todd had resigned as an instructor at the University of Oklahoma in 1935 in order to devote himself professionally to writing, but after 1941 he would never publish another novel—indeed, after 1945 he never published any fiction of any kind again. In the 1940s Todd found employment as an advertising copy writer in Philadelphia. One of his ads, the tongue-in-cheek mystery homage "The Case of the Crumpled Letter," was chosen in 1959 as one of the 100 greatest advertisements.

In the 1950s Todd returned to the teaching profession, taking posts at schools in Maryland and Virginia, but after the death of his father in 1954 he returned to Atoka to live with his octogenarian mother and teach Spanish and French at Atoka High School, from where he had graduated thirty-five years earlier. After the death of Todd's mother in 1965, Todd lived on alone in the old family home until his own demise in 1974. The professional highlight of his later years was his appointment as Emeritus Professor of Choctaw Language and Choctaw Heritage at Southeastern Oklahoma State University (then Southeastern State College). Reflecting Todd's continued interest in his Choctaw heritage were his series of lessons in the Choctaw language, *Chahta Anampa: An Introduction to Choctaw Grammar*, and his historical pageant play about the Choctaw Nation, *Journey's End*, both of which were published in 1971, forty years after he penned his first detective novel.

Todd Downing is buried beneath a simple headstone in Atoka, the place of his birth. Fittingly, his writing lives after him.

1

IF EVER A VOICE had honey in it, South Texas honey, it was the voice at the other end of the wire.

"Sheriff Peter Bounty speaking."

"Sheriff?" Mallory Winters pressed the receiver to her ear and turned to face the open window, whose curtains were beginning to ripple in the breeze from the Gulf of Mexico which everyone in Las Palmas seemed to spend the day anticipating.

"Yes, sheriff of Hesperides County. You're in Hesperides now, you know."

Mallory didn't know. "There's some mistake. This is Mallory Winters at the Sutherland Hotel," she said distinctly, wondering what flower it was that spiced the breeze so.

"The young lady who arrived on the eight-ten train from Corpus Christi last night and met the nine o'clock plane from New York?"

"Why—yes."

"Good. I'm sending a deputy over to talk to you. Right away, if it's convenient."

"But what about? I'm a total stranger here."

"I know." The voice's honey had acquired a tang. "My deputy will explain. Thanks, Miss Winters. Bert—" Mallory hung up, too, with suddenly lax fingers, and stood listening for sounds from the adjoining room. If Fred had gone out he would have steered his course to the nearest bar. He had been on edge all day and snappish, what with the heat, idleness and her unwelcome presence.

But if he had got into trouble the sheriff would have asked if she were Fred's cousin, not about her arrival in Las Palmas.

On the telephone stand was a directory on whose cover was printed "Las Palmas, Cameron County, Texas." Mallory stared at the words for an instant, waiting for meaning to resolve itself out of them. Then she hastily opened the book and turned the pages, to the Bs and Cs and Ss. A section at the back was devoted to advertising, and she found several land companies' maps of the lower Rio Grande Valley, from Laredo to the Gulf. She slapped the directory shut, took up the receiver again and with difficulty made the liquid-voiced operator understand the name Fred Winters.

Two men went along the corridor, their musically slurred foreign speech coming in through the ventilating slats of the false door. The Spanish one heard on all sides here wasn't the Spanish Mallory had studied in school. It gave point to a feeling which had been growing in her since from the train window she had first sighted palm trees: a feeling of utter isolation, and in her own United States. Everything down in this Magic Valley had an exotic stamp, too tawny or too vividly colored. And on the map it looked like the jumping-off place, with rail, air and ship lines converging here to shoot vaguely off the bottom of the paper. . . .

"Yes?" Fred's voice was a breathless little hiss in her ear and she knew for a certainty that he was up to something, that he was expecting a call.

"Fred, did you get some man to call me up and say he was the sheriff?"

"Did I do wha-at?"

Mallory repeated the conversation, listening for a snicker which didn't come. "Tell me the truth now, Fred. Because I know this is a joke. No one named Bounty is listed in the directory. This isn't a county seat and there's no sheriff's office here. What's more, my smart cousin, there is no such county as Hesperides!"

The silence at Fred's end was profound. It was a full half minute before he laughed weakly. "I don't know anything about it, Mal," he said in a tone which sounded convincing enough. "Honest. I've been resting. One of the local cowboys must be getting playful. Sure he didn't ask for me?"

"I'm sure, Fred. But how could he find out so much about me? I don't know what to think. Can you come in? I want you with me when I see this man."

"Soon as I get some clothes on."

Mallory snapped on lights, smoothed down her white sharkskin suit and glanced askance at the mirror. After those days on the beach at Corpus Christi her face looked shrimp pink and shiny from the various oils which people had recommended. Most of the curl was gone from her blonde hair. The squint the sun had forced on her blue eyes seemed permanent.

Hesperides. By the door was a wicker table whose sole purpose was to hold a huge beribboned basket of fruit, a plate of green Mexican pottery and a silver knife. Every time you turned your head that cornucopia was replenished, with fruits that were familiar and fruits whose skins were familiar but whose pulp was strange. The Mexican maid that morning had tried to teach her the names of some of them. Kumquats, shaddocks, citranges. Pomelos, tangelos, mandarins. . . .

Fred lumbered in and to her surprise carefully closed both doors. He wore no vest, and braces rather than a belt, so that his gray trousers, pleated at the top, showed how his waist-line had bulged in the past year. He was losing his blond hair rapidly. His large-featured face was no longer firm-fleshed but puffed, with a coarse and grainy appearance. His mouth looked as if he had a bad taste in it all the time. Fred's general dilapidation had shocked Mallory when she met him at the airport the night before. Something in his manner now, something secretive behind his bluffness, was a renewed shock, the greater because she had suspected its presence at once and, unable to account for it, had been trying to close her eyes to it.

"You say this guy asked about last night, Mal," Fred said. "Well, what happened?"

"Not a thing. I merely took a taxi from the railway station to the airport. I didn't speak to a soul except the driver. But"—Mallory hesitated—"you may be right. One of the town bloods came into the waiting room at plane time. With his servant. I shouldn't be surprised if he's trying to get acquainted. He must have followed

us. I saw the servant down at the desk this morning, probably getting my name from the register. I absolutely won't see him."

"What did he look like?"

"A black panther. An American but dark as a Mexican. Fred,
you have to go down and get rid of him. He'll be here any minute
now."

"All right, I'll go shoo him off. I want to see if there's a message
at the desk anyway. Then we'd better be thinking about having dinner sent up. I want to eat in my room again."

"Why, Fred?"

Mallory followed him to the door without getting an answer.
"While you're down there," she said then, "send Sue a wire, won't
you? So she'll get it before bedtime. Tell her you're here and something about what you're doing. Please, Fred."

"To hell with Sue! What she doesn't know won't hurt her." He
asked from the hall: "You sure there's no Hesperides in Texas?
Seems to me I've heard of the place."

"Not in Texas, Fred."

Alone in a room which was cool, clean and pungently cool,
Mallory wandered to the window; that perfume, heavy, cloying, like
and yet unlike tuberose, muddling her thoughts about Fred and
Sue and a marriage which was in the process of going to pot.

Fred was a consulting engineer, always at loose ends, and from
one place and then another Sue, who had been her senior room-
mate in college, had kept Mallory posted as to their bickerings,
Fred's increasing surliness and philanderings. Their present address was New York. It was a telephone call from there which had
interrupted Mallory's vacation in Corpus Christi with Minnesota
friends. Out of a clear sky, it seemed, Fred had announced that he
was catching the next plane to South Texas. His evasiveness at
departure had aroused Sue's suspicions. That plane made an overnight stop at Las Palmas, on the border, then continued on to
Mexico City. A friend had been talking about Mexican divorce mills,
and Sue had got it into her head that Fred was going to cut loose
from her, on terms of his own making. A telegram had come to his
office, she had learned. Hence she was convinced that he had a

rendezvous with a woman. She implored Mallory to intercept him at Las Palmas and worm the truth out of him.

Against her better judgment and in disgust at the commonness of it all, Mallory had come, getting a scowl of exasperation for her welcome at the airport. She was going to make one more attempt at peace-patching tonight, then wash her hands of the affair and depart in the morning, with nothing gained from the experience but profound disillusionment and the decision to enter forthwith upon some career. She had seen enough of the blessed state of matrimony. . . .

The phone rang. It was Fred, speaking in a hurried undertone: "Listen, Mal. You'll have to talk to this fellow. We'll meet you on the mezzanine. Sort of string him along, see? From his looks he's big-mouthed and dumb. And, whatever you do, don't say a word about anything that ever happened to me. Just leave me out of the conversation. For all you know, I never was inside a hospital in my life."

"Fred, a hospital!"

He was gone and the odor of that flower was a drug to be fought against, because it stupefied and threatened to leave you helpless when you had to have your wits about you.

As she put on her black straw breton hat and went up the hall to the elevators, Mallory was seeing Fred and his actions in a new and coldly disturbing light. Last night she had had to accept his vague offhand allusions to a deal which must be kept under cover at all costs. Today, when he had stayed close to his room with the explanation that it was Sunday and no business could be transacted, she had told herself that she wasn't deceived: he was engaged in some shady enterprise and was biding his time until she left. Now she had to shift everything into another pattern. She recalled their conversation of that morning, about the newspaper article, and her astonishment at the heartlessness and egoism which Fred had manifested, his promptness in changing the subject.

Before the elevator completed its drop from the fifth floor she had grasped the significance of the quantities of food which Fred had been consuming all day, the bottle after bottle of milk which he had ordered when whisky would better have suited his taste.

The doors slid open and Mallory had the sensation of looking up and up a shaft of mahogany, trimly clad in brown tweed, to a pair of large and suddenly alert brown eyes.

Fred was beside him, stunted. "Sure enough it was the Big Bad Wolf!" Fred announced. "Mallory, this is Mr. Larrick. Bert Larrick. He *is* a deputy sheriff, with a badge to prove it. And, believe it or not, he says we *are* in Hesperides."

The clean mahogany became very much alive, a hale young giant with the well-proportioned brawn of a basketball player. "Well, I certainly am glad to know you!" he exclaimed with too much emphasis, in a voice which had a slight drawl. "I had no idea what you'd be like."

"Naturally not. I didn't know what to expect myself."

"We're blocking traffic," Fred said. "Let's sit down."

The lobby of the Sutherland was a glass-roofed patio, with pillars supporting the projecting balcony of the mezzanine. Palms and mirrors and lights with cocoa-brown shades gave this last the effect of extending back into dim cool regions where the bustle of the lobby would never reach.

"Your cousin told me what you thought when Peter Bounty called," Larrick said as they went toward an isolated couch of deep red leather. "You looked in the old directory. They haven't had time to get out a new one yet. You see, when these border counties were formed hardly anybody lived down here, so they made 'em big. But the population has increased so that now you can't always tell when one town ends and another begins. Recently they shifted the lines of Zapata, Starr, Hidalgo and Cameron and organized a new county, with Las Palmas the seat. Peter Bounty was the Cameron sheriff but he moved over here. Said he didn't want to sit all his life in the same chair."

He grinned as if this were very funny indeed, and Mallory had to grin back as she took the middle of the couch.

Larrick lowered himself beside her as if he were afraid he might break the springs. He crossed then uncrossed his long legs, laid his smart and not too wide-brimmed Stetson across his knees and resumed his contemplation of her. Mallory had been able to meet the probing look of that fellow last night, but before this intense, different gaze she found herself following instead the sweep of his long, strongly hinged jaw and satisfying herself that his skin's warm, even coloring wasn't innate but acquired by years of exposure to the sun. If ever sun faddists required a testimonial to the soundness of their doctrines, they need only point out this healthy specimen, whose lightly worn earnestness made him seem younger, less than ever an officer of the law.

"I love the name Hesperides," she said, since conversation seemed to be in order.

"You do? I never thought much of it myself. I wanted 'em to call it Citrus County."

"Oh no."

"No?"

Fred cleared his throat meaningly but, once launched, Larrick didn't seem able to stop.

"I've got an idea I know who's responsible for that name. The Chamber of Commerce had a contest. Whoever sent in the winning name was to get a cash prize and a free trip to the eastern fruit markets on a special boosters' train. Hesperides was an anonymous entry. Nobody knew what it meant at first. They looked it up and found 'delightful gardens at the western extremity of the world.' Not much point to that, of course. But somebody's kid had a schoolbook where it said the Hesperides raised oranges that the poets called golden apples. Oranges are one of the big crops here, so they announced they'd chosen the name for that reason. Then one of the judges got tight at a banquet and let the cat out of the bag. The real reason they picked Hesperides was because there wouldn't be anybody to claim the prize and they'd save money."

"Say, Larrick," Fred broke in, "you don't have a cigarette on you, do you? I meant to get some but I thought you were in such a hurry that I didn't stop."

"Sure." The deputy dug into a pocket and brought out a package. "Just keep those. I don't smoke much. Oh, pardon me. Will you have one, Miss Winters?"

"Not now, thank you." Mallory bit her lip as she watched the cigarettes disappear into Fred's pocket. Fred always had been a moocher. She turned her head. "Won't you relieve my curiosity, Mr. Larrick? I can't imagine why the sheriff called me."

"I'm sorry. I shouldn't have been so long." Larrick, getting back his self-possession, crossed his legs and folded his arms. "Maybe you've read of Jimmy Norcott," he said, "the nineteen-year-old boy who's in the John Belton Lack Hospital here, suffering from a streptococcus infection?"

Springs creaked and Fred barked out a little cough. The smoke of his cigarette was all at once a disagreeable cloud about Mallory. Her eyes smarted with it and she put a hand to her forehead to hide her bemused state from Larrick's steady gaze. She nodded. "The young man they're trying to find blood donors for."

(Corpus Christi papers had headlined the case and news commentators on the border radio stations had made the most of its dramatic aspects, somewhat cheaply she had felt. Reading feature stories about the Norcotts, she had wondered how greatly they were exaggerated. It was difficult to accept nowadays these families who lived "like feudal barons" on fenced-in estates of twenty-five thousand acres, who dominated politics and played rex with trespassers.)

"Jimmy's in a bad, bad way," Larrick continued gravely. "The only hope of saving him is transfusion. But the trouble is, it takes a certain type of blood, and the person who gives it must be immune. That is, must have recovered recently from the same kind of infection. *Streptococcus viridans*, it's called."

Mallory cast a swift sideways glance in Fred's direction. He sat far back in his corner, seemingly interested only in the antics of his smoke. She said deliberately: "According to the papers, it's type B that's needed. Is that correct, Mr. Larrick?"

He nodded with an air of authority. "There are four blood groups. O, A, B and AB, they're usually classified. Eighty-five per cent of white people have O or A. Only about ten per cent have B. So you see how that limits the field. Roger Norcott, Jimmy's uncle and guardian, has broadcast appeals and got lots of volunteers. But not until today was one found that was suitable."

"They've found a donor, have they?" Fred spoke up. "Who is he?"

"John Joseph Hieronymus. We haven't got much of a line on him. He's from up North somewhere. Came to Brownsville, then on here this spring. For his health, he says. He owns—or did—a little fruit store on the road between here and Mercedes. Lived in the rear."

"What do you mean—lived?" came quickly from Fred.

"The store was blown up last night."

"Hieronymus—hurt?"

Larrick smiled knowingly. "No, he wasn't hurt. We're positive he was at the airport when the explosion took place. That's why I'm here: to find out if Miss Winters saw him and can identify him."

"Why come to her?" Fred shot out.

"Well," Larrick grinned, looking at Mallory, "she seems to have attracted all the attention there last night. Because she was in the waiting room so long before plane time, of course. The ticket agent and the porters can't swear about anybody else being there but they can describe her. It was easy to locate the taxi driver who brought you to the hotel, to call and learn the name of the good-looking young lady who registered at that time. You don't mind, do you, Miss Winters?"

"Why no, I don't mind. But go ahead and tell me about this man I'm supposed to identify."

"A seedy old fellow, in a hard straw hat and a suit that once upon a time was white. He wears thick-lensed glasses that give him a walleyed look. Something's wrong with his mouth, so he seems to be smiling all the time. Remember him?"

"Yes," Mallory said at once. "I remember that smile. I thought at first he was getting ready to beg. But I saw it never changed."

"Good! Now tell me exactly what he did, will you?"

"He came in the waiting room about"—Mallory paused, aware that one of her auditors was hanging just as intently on her words as the other—"five or six minutes till nine. He stood looking around a moment, then went into the telephone booth. He was in there until nine, when the New York plane landed. He ducked out the front door then and was standing just outside when Fred and I left.

You remember, Fred. While we were waiting for the taxi to pull up you went back and asked him about hotels."

Fred disgorged the smoke of a second cigarette. "Um-huh," was his answer.

Larrick snapped his fingers. "Absolutely perfect! More than we hoped for—that you'd be able to swear he put in a call at five minutes till nine."

"Wait, Mr. Larrick. I couldn't swear he put in a call. Only that he went in the booth."

He threw up his hands and pretended to slump down on the couch. "There you go! I thought your testimony was airtight and then you had to stick a pin in it. Oh well, a man doesn't spend five minutes in a phone booth unless he's phoning. And you can redeem yourself by identifying Hieronymus."

"Tell us what this is all about first," Fred said. "You can't ask the girl to commit herself without knowing what she's getting into."

"Sorry." Larrick straightened. "You see, I'm rather new at this sleuthing."

"You need tell me only what the sheriff expected you to," Mallory interposed. "He said you'd explain, but there are probably things you have to hold back."

"Oh, it's all right to tell you folks. A little after nine last night Peter Bounty got word that there'd been an explosion on the Mercedes road. He went out and found this store blown to smithereens. A lot of cars had stopped and the highway patrol had taken charge. He stayed till it was certain there was no trace of a body. No trace of a live owner either, and no car in the garage. A man by the name of John Joseph Hieronymus lived there, that's all the neighbors knew. This morning an arson expert came, looked over the remains and said nitroglycerin had been used. Probably exploded by means of an electric iron left in circuit. Peter inquired in town and soon discovered the building had been insured. In the meantime there was an alarm out for Hieronymus, of course, but nobody thought of it being anything more than a petty insurance swindle. It wasn't till this afternoon that I knew about it. Peter never calls the undersheriff or me out at night or on Sunday if he can handle the case himself. He wouldn't have let me help at the scene of the explosion anyway. He wants me to be a surgeon some-day and is always riding me about taking care of my hands."

An audible puff from Fred disrupted a smoke ring and Larrick shifted position self-consciously.

"This afternoon the Las Palmas police finally stretched, yawned and came to life enough to give Peter some information. Roger Norcott had notified them of a telephone message he'd received during the night."

"Is Norcott staying in town?" Fred asked.

"Yes, here at the Sutherland. Since his nephew's case has been spread all over the newspapers a regular horde of grafters and cranks and fake healers has been trying to get to him. To protect himself he has a special operator on the switchboard downstairs, to weed out incoming calls. Those about blood donors she con-nects with Chris Hand's room. Chris gives out all statements to the papers as well, since Doctor Lack is poison to reporters. Doc-tor Lack is Jimmy Norcott's physician."

"And who's Chris Hand?"

"Christopher Hand. Oh, he's a dumb ox who acts as a sort of glorified errand boy for Roger Norcott. Well, it seems Chris was away when a call came for Norcott about five minutes till nine. The girl decided it was important enough to put through to him. A man, who refused to give his name, said he thought it his duty to warn Norcott of a plot to intimidate donors and keep his nephew from getting blood transfusions. He went on to say that a resident of the county, a stranger to Norcott, was known to have recovered from a streptococcus infection and to have the right blood group. He'd been ready to give a transfusion but his life had been threat-ened and he was afraid to go to the hospital. The man on the phone said he'd try to help the donor slip into the hotel that night. Norcott was to give orders to admit him and to be making up his mind how much he was willing to pay him for taking the risk of a transfusion. The man warned Norcott to keep mum, then hung up. Norcott didn't put any stock in the conspiracy part, I'm sure, but thought it barely possible that the much-talked-of 'one donor in a thousand' was getting ready to gouge him. Nobody showed up, though, and he was going to forget about it when he heard of the explosion. And what socked him right between the eyes was the fact that a man named John Joseph Hieronymus was on their list of eligible donors."

"What's that?" Fred's voice was sharp. "Where'd they get a list of donors?"

"From a hospital in a suburb of Chicago. They had a streptococcus case there a couple of months ago and Hieronymus donated blood. But to go on, Norcott had Chris report that call to the police. Not, mind you, to our office, though Hieronymus' place was outside the city limits. Chief Tanner was reading the funny papers or something and couldn't be bothered to do more than pass the word along to Peter Bounty. But, believe me, Peter pushed the search for Hieronymus! It was the undersheriff, Gus Broddus, who covered himself with glory, though. Gus' feet hurt, so Peter stationed him in an easy chair down in the lobby, on the chance that Hieronymus might come to call on Norcott. And sure enough he did. At least he was downstairs about six this evening. Gus spotted him from the description and took him to our office. A dumb stunt, of course. He should have tailed him and seen where he went."

"What did Hieronymus have to say?"

"He pretends ignorance of everything. Says he went to Brownsville on business long before nine last night and stayed in a tourist camp. As for the explosion, he hints it's the work of racketeers but hasn't given us any definite information. His car was outside, with a lot of clothes and things in it, and he had about five hundred dollars on him that he hasn't explained. He admits he gave the transfusion in Chicago but claims he never reads the papers and didn't know Jimmy Norcott needed one. He stalls about giving one now. Says he's not sure he's physically able and we've got to turn him loose and let him see about his affairs first. He has gone so far, though, as to consent to let Doctor Lack give him an examination tonight and test his blood to see if he's still immune to streptococcus."

"Is he under arrest?"

"Only held for questioning so far. Before I came up here we were beginning to think there might be something to this talk of intimidation after all. We took him to the airport but couldn't find anyone who'd seen him. Now we have a case against him cinched." Larrick looked at his watch and turned to Mallory. "This identification will be simple. Peter has Hieronymus at the office. That's in the courthouse, on the other side of the park. I'll call him when we're ready and he'll bring Hieronymus through the lobby. The desk clerk and elevator and bellboys who were on duty last night and this afternoon will be on the lookout. We're catching them as they change shifts. We want to know for sure if Hieronymus has made an attempt to see Norcott. You'll be sitting in the lobby, just like anybody else. You take a look at Hieronymus and tell me that it's the same man. There won't be any embarrassment connected with this, I promise you. You'll do it?"

"What'll happen to Hieronymus if she does identify him?" Fred asked before Mallory could make a reply.

"With her evidence to prove that Hieronymus himself phoned Norcott—"

"That he was in the phone booth."

"Oh well, it's the same thing. Peter will put it up to him that we can't force him to give a transfusion but we can prosecute him for arson and attempted extortion. If he claims he was frightened away but will donate his blood now, we'll guarantee him protection. Also I'm sure we can get the promise of the insurance company that no charges will be filed so long as he doesn't try to collect from them. But we figure his original plan was to kill two birds with one stone: to cash in on the insurance and to put the screws on Norcott by pointing to the explosion as evidence his life was in danger. We think he got cold feet last night but is trying to get up his nerve to carry that plan through now. If he does, we'll call Norcott in and turn over to him what cards we hold. There's no telling what the result will be. Norcott's canny and closefisted and is known for driving hard bargains. On the other hand, while no other donor shows up, Hieronymus has Jimmy's life to dicker with." Larrick made a wry face. "Can you conceive of anybody being so low as to do that?"

"Oh, I don't know." Fred jingled coins in his pocket. "Grocers boost food prices when they can, whether people are starving or not. Norcott pays the doctor and the hospital. Why shouldn't he pay for a man's blood?"

Larrick looked confused. "He intends to pay, that's understood. Fifty dollars a transfusion. Though if I had the right type of blood and all, I'd feel cheap taking that."

"Fifty dollars! Isn't he the richest man down here?"

"Well, he's been considered so till recently. His money's all tied up in land though. Shall we go down, Miss Winters?"

Mallory failed to catch Fred's eye. "You'll go with me, Fred?"

"I might if there were some inducement. Larrick, you ought to know where a man can find a bottle of something to drink around this town on Sunday night. I feel the need of a little bucking up."

"Let's see." Surreptitiously Larrick put a hand against one of his own pockets but produced the slightest of jingles. "Oh, I know!" he exclaimed. "Peter has a pint of whisky in his desk at the office. The Cameron County sheriff gave it to him but he'll never drink it in a month of Sundays. I'll have him bring it over and leave it at the desk downstairs."

"Now you're talking," Fred said, rising. "This Doctor Lack," he pursued as they walked toward the elevators. "What about him, Larrick? Does he have money?"

"People say he's a multimillionaire. At least he has more than Roger Norcott."

"John Belton Lack, you say. A white-haired fellow?"

"No, redheaded, freckled. He came here from the East, built a fine home and gave the county its hospital."

"A philanthropist, eh? Does he have any relatives with white hair?"

"He's a bachelor without any relatives here. He's supposed to come of an old New England family."

"From Boston?"

"No, from someplace called Beacon Hill."

Mallory halted and caught Fred's arm. "Mr. Larrick, I'd like to speak to my cousin a moment, if you don't mind. We'll join you in the lobby."

"Sure. I'll call Peter and tell him to start the parade." Larrick cocked his head to one side and looked at her keenly. "You mustn't let all this disturb you. There's no plot against these blood donors. Others will keep showing up and Jimmy Norcott's life will be saved. That's the way it has to be. Because you're in the Magic Valley now, where no one ever dies."

2

"KER-PLUNK!" Fred blew out of one side of his mouth as the elevator doors closed on Larrick. "Want his badge, Mal? He'll take it right off and give it to you."

"Don't, Fred!" Mallory drew him back beside a pillar.

"Huh!" He cocked his head at her as Larrick had done. "Two ker-plunks."

She shook his arm and said, "I've got to know what's going on here, Fred. You had streptococcus this spring. You're one of the donors they're looking for. This morning you said you didn't remember what group your blood belonged to and were too busy to go to the hospital and find out. But you've known all along. You've been getting ready today for a transfusion. I think you came here for that very purpose. You had a reason for pumping that deputy the way you did. I want to know if you've had a hand in any of this. If you've been keeping still because somebody threatened you, I want to be told."

"Calm down, kid," Fred said, fidgeting. "Sure I've got what they want. But I'm not saying anything about it yet. And you aren't either. I'm going to lie low till I see what's what. There's some monkey business here. I can't figure it out. Listen, tell High Pockets you're not sure whether you recognize Hieronymus or not. Then make the lad take you to dinner and keep him on the hook this evening. He's better than a newspaper."

3

THE ELEVATOR DOORS slid open and Mallory, stepping into the lobby, had the sensation of looking up a block of ebony that strained at the seams of white flannel trousers and blue coat to a pair of dark and surly eyes which had fastened upon her in recognition.

The young man with Bert Larrick was an inch or more shorter than the latter and proportionately thicker and heavier. He had a heavy-boned, flat-checked, Dutchman's face. It was closely shaven, probably massaged, and powder hadn't dulled enough the bluish gun-metal luster of his powerful jaws.

"Hello," Larrick said lightly, his eyes alive with what looked like malicious amusement. "Miss Winters, may I present Mr. Hand? Mr. Winters, Christopher Hand."

The fellow swept off his Panama with his left hand and stuck the other halfway out, jerking it back at the instant when Mallory, who had had no intention of giving him hers, started automatically to come to his aid. Back went hers and out came his again.

"Keep pumping, Hand," Larrick chuckled. "You'll get water."

With the heel of a palm Hand rubbed back a lock of dark hair which had swayed like a tendril over his forehead. "Glad to know you," he said thickly. "I think I seen—saw—"

"We can't wait for you to seesaw, Chris. We've got things to do." Larrick took Mallory's arm and drew her in the direction of the desk, while he surveyed the lobby, under whose shaded pillar lights were grouped Mission chairs of deep red leather, most of them occupied. "Now of course," he said, "I can make anybody here get up and give you his place, if necessary."

Mallory glanced back. Christopher Hand hadn't stepped into the elevator yet but was staring after Fred, while he blew upon a ring and polished it against his coat sleeve.

Fred was occupied with another cigarette. "Say, Bert," he said as he tossed away the match, "wonder if you'd do me a little favor?"

"Why, sure—Fred. What is it?"

"I'd like to get a check cashed before dinner. It's on a New York bank, so I expect they'll want an endorsement."

"Of course. Come on."

Fred made a backward gesture of the head. "That was Roger Norcott's errand boy you introduced us to?"

"Yes, I couldn't very well help it."

"A friend of yours?"

"Not of mine. He was telling me they'd located another blood donor for Jimmy Norcott—maybe."

Fred stopped stock-still and the cigarette slipped from his fingers. "Who?" he asked as he ground it out with the sole of his shoe.

"The Man in the Moon." Larrick turned to the cashier's window, between the elevators and the desk, and said airily: "Mr. Winters wants to cash a check. I'll endorse it."

The cashier might be a Mexican; Mallory found it hard to tell down here. Looking as if he had suddenly acquired a headache, he passed behind the desk clerk, lifted a flap and crossed the narrow corridor to a door which Mallory could see bore the legend: PAUL PALLADAY, MANAGER.

Not at all disconcerted, Larrick said: "Go ahead and fill 'er out, Fred," and moved so that he could look down the rows of chairs which flanked the space between them and the front door.

Fred followed, frowning and studying Larrick's face. "You wouldn't kid us, would you, Bert?" he asked with a little laugh.

"About the Man in the Moon? Well, there's some kidding going on, I'm afraid. A reporter had been talking to Chris, wanting to know the same thing. Seems he'd just been upstairs interviewing a specialist Doctor Lack has here. He asked about blood donors and the doctor said, yes, he knew where one was: on the moon. The reporter took it as a joke at first but later he wasn't so sure. And neither was Chris. He's going to ask Doctor Cotillion just what he meant."

"Doctor Cotillion?"

"Yes. Unusual name, isn't it? He's the Chicago specialist who had a streptococcus case this spring. He flew down last night to consult with Doctor Lack."

"Is he staying here?"

"Yes. Chris was on his way up to get him then. Cotillion and Lack and a couple of other doctors are having dinner in Norcott's suite. Bet it's a skimpy meal."

"Will Doctor Cotillion be in the lobby when Hieronymus comes in?"

"No, there'd be no point in that. Hieronymus admits he's one of Cotillion's donors. Ho-ho!" Larrick's face broke into a grin. "I know a way to get you a seat, Miss Winters. Excuse me half a second."

As he hurried toward a freckled bellhop Mallory went back with Fred to the cashier's window. "Fred," she whispered, "is that check going to be good?"

He exaggerated Larrick's "Sure!" and looked at the elevators. Christopher Hand had gone. "What did that fellow start to say to you?" he asked.

"He's the one who was at the airport last night."

"He was?" Fred frowned quickly and scrutinized her face. "Then the man with him must have been one of Norcott's servants. Find out from High Pockets. I smell a rat somewhere about that Norcott outfit. And about this Doctor Lack too. A wharf rat there."

"Fred, I'm not going to take advantage of Mr. Larrick. Don't you, please."

"There may be a diamond ring in it for you, little girl. Careful, here he comes."

Larrick was shaking with suppressed laughter as he rejoined them. "See that man sitting in front of the first pillar to the right of the door?"

Mallory looked at a large solid individual who wore the sombrero which in her mind's eye she had seen all men wearing in this border country.

"That's E. Matthew Rone, the hotel detective. A big windbag. Used to be Hidalgo County sheriff. When Hesperides was formed he established residence here and ran against Peter Bounty. Didn't get to first base. And in the meantime somebody else had nabbed the Hidalgo office. So E. Matthew was left holding the sack. They pay him in cigars here, I think."

The cashier had returned. "How much is it for?" he asked, eying the check which Fred was tearing from a full book. "Fifty dollars," Fred told him.

The man shook his head. "We do not have that much."

"Forty?"

Another negative. "I am sorry. We have been very low on cash today."

"You sure must be," Larrick said impatiently. "How much can he make the check for?"

"Not more than ten dollars. And he will have to wait a few minutes before I can cash it."

"Will ten do, Fred?"

"It'll do." Fred proceeded to fill out another check.

While he was at it, Mallory, standing between the cashier's window and the desk, heard a man ask the clerk in a somewhat apologetic tone: "Will you be kind enough to give me the number of Mr. Roger Norcott's room?"

"Your name, please?"

"Ainsworth. Doctor Hugh Ainsworth."

"Do you have a card?"

"A card? No, I don't."

The cashier had turned his head. "O.K., Lequire," he called. "That's Doctor Ainsworth. Good evening, Doctor."

"Sorry I didn't recognize you, Doctor Ainsworth," the clerk said. "You understand how careful we have to be in giving out Mr. Norcott's number. But you're expected." He lowered his voice and Mallory heard only: "Mezzanine floor."

"Thank you very much." The man who was coming toward them had "old-fashioned country doctor" written all over him, Mallory thought. He wasn't a large man, and the stoop of his shoulders served still further to diminish his stature. He smiled at Larrick and laid a hand on his arm as he passed. "Hello, Bert."

"Good evening, Doctor," the deputy said respectfully.

"How's your mother?"

"Just fine, thank you." Larrick took the pen which Fred had laid down, signed his name with a flourish on the back of the check and flipped it over the counter. "You can join us as soon as you get your money, Fred. While I think of it, Peter Bounty's bringing that whisky. I told him to leave it at the desk for you."

Fred was looking after the physician, who stood in front of the elevators. "That one of Norcott's doctors?" he asked.

"He's the regular Norcott physician, but I don't think he's having much to do with this case. It's all Lack's show. Norcott's having Doctor Ainsworth to dinner to meet Cotillion."

"A regular medical convention up there."

"Four doctors, Chris said. Cotillion, Lack, Ainsworth and Angelo."

"Angelo?"

"County physician and head of the John Belton Lack Hospital." Larrick took Mallory's arm again. "Let's walk down toward the door," he said to her. "Slow. Watch E. Matthew Rone."

The freckled bellhop had been keeping an eye on Larrick. "Call for Elmer Matthew Rone!" he began chanting, moving off toward the side entrance of the lobby. "Elmer Matthew Ro-one!"

The big man heaved himself to his feet and as he passed them, either not seeing or ignoring Larrick, his teeth were clamped upon his cigar.

"Ready to bite nails," Larrick sputtered. "Nobody's supposed to know what the E. stands for. Quick, get his chair."

Then Mallory was deep in a very warm chair, Larrick was perched on the arm and they were watching, while pretending not to, the return under full sail of Mr. Rone. He stopped abruptly, looked from her to Larrick with hard little china-blue eyes, turned and made his exit from the scene past a potted palm.

"You shouldn't have done that, Bert."

"Aw, he didn't like me anyhow, because I'm Peter Bounty's appointee. And, by the way, when I called Peter I suggested that the sheriff's office ought to stand its witness a dinner. Up on the roof garden, where there's an orchestra. He said it was a good idea. What about it? I know from what your cousin said you haven't had dinner yet. I'm including him, of course, if he wants to come."

Mallory looked at Fred, who was leaning against the ledge outside the cashier's window, blowing smoke through his nose and watching them with a little smile, as if he had heard Larrick's words. "No, Mr. Larrick," she said firmly, "I'm going to have to say good-by as soon as this is finished. I'm getting ready to leave in the morning."

"Leave! Why, you just got here."

"I know, but I must. Now here's something more I want to tell you about last night at the airport. You wanted to know exactly what this man Hieronymus did. You'll think my imagination has been at work. Maybe it has. But when I got up to go meet Fred at the exit from the landing field, at nine sharp, Christopher Hand and another man entered the front door. Hieronymus left the booth just then and saw them. It certainly seemed to me that he tried to keep from being seen by them. He sidled to the door at once."

Larrick's face needed yet more toughening by sun and wind, if he wished, as he plainly did wish, to hide his agitation. "What did the other man look like?" he asked.

"I took him to be Hand's servant."

"That would tickle Chris: to know you thought he had a servant at his beck and call." He tried unsuccessfully to put pleasantry into it. "What gave you that idea about the man?"

"His looks and manner. The way Hand acted toward him, especially when he gave him some money. He was smaller and older than Hand. He wore black clothes, with a stiff shirt front and collar and black tie. He was dark-skinned like Hand."

"Not that dark, was he?"

"Maybe not. All you men down here look so dark to me. Come to think about it, that's why I have to describe people by their clothes. I'm sure of those, when I'm not about ages and faces and—character. The tan gives everybody a mask, so you look very much alike at first sight. Not very complimentary, is it?"

"It's not complimentary to be told you look like Chris Hand."

"But you must notice in this lobby how an untanned man like Fred stands out. Or that one going there."

Mallory wished at once that she hadn't called his attention to the broadly built man in dark gray clothes and Panama who was going past with a rather waddling gait. He couldn't have heard her, yet his eyes switched to the left and he slowed his steps to let his gaze travel leisurely and insolently up to her face. His eyes were black and soft and slightly almond-shaped. With his small black mustache they accentuated the whiteness of his moonlike face.

"Good evening, Doctor." Larrick spoke with a slight and rather perfunctory note of deference. "Darn him," he added in an under-tone when the other looked his way without apparent recognition and moved toward the desk. "He'd better not act so high-hat around this town. That's David Angelo. Doctor Lack knew him in the East and got him the job as head of the hospital. Only Lack's influence has kept him from being kicked out long ago. You don't mean to say you like pasty-faced men like that? Angelo never gets out in the sun. Lies around and sleeps all the time. That's why he's put-ting on weight."

"No, after being in the Magic Valley I'll always think a man's lacking unless he has a coat of tan. But Angelo—that's a Mexican name, isn't it? Strange I picked a Mexican as the whitest man here."

"Angelo's not Mexican. Well, maybe he is partly, too. I think he's from Mexico City originally, of some family of Southerners who left the States after the Civil War. But don't judge Mexicans by him. Or Southerners either." Larrick was thinking about some-thing else, Mallory knew. "That man you saw with Chris Hand," he said. "Did he have white hair?"

"I couldn't tell. He wore a hat. A derby."

"Of course. We'll watch and you'll probably spot him as he comes in. That must have been Beck, Doctor Lack's valet, body-guard or whatever he is. Nobody but he and his boss go in for boiled shirts and collars in the summertime here. Though if he's got a coat of tan it's been since I saw him last. Doctor Lack's due at Norcott's dinner, and where he goes, Beck has to bring up the rear. But listen, are you sure Beck and Chris Hand were together last night?"

"They came in together and looked at the Chicago bulletin board. The Chicago plane and the one from New York, that Fred was on, are due in at the same time, you know. The Chicago plane was late. The valet turned and—since you're laying so much stress on that telephone, I remember he went straight to the booth that Hieronymus had just left. He came back and got some money from Hand. Then he went across the room to a vending machine, got a package of cigarettes, brought them to Hand and lighted one for him. Then he went back to the booth and closed the door."

"That was after nine though, was it?"

"A minute probably, when he was at the booth the first time."

"Did he put in a call then?"

"I'm not sure, but I don't think he had time."

"What did Hand do?"

"He stood and looked—at the people in the waiting room and at the passengers from the New York plane. Fred came then and I didn't notice either of the two again."

Larrick's eyes had narrowed. "So that's what Chris was trying to say when he got tongue-tied! He saw you. And Fred told me when he met me that you thought some masher was calling you. Did Chris—uh . . ."

"No"—Mallory had to smile—"he didn't."

"Well, that mug needs to be put in his place. He and I went to school together, and it wouldn't be the first time I knocked his big ears down. I'm sorry I introduced him. If he so much as looks your way again, let me know, will you?"

This was anticlimax for Mallory. It was too much like school-boy chest-thumping, and she wondered if Larrick weren't trying to brazen out something within himself. "I don't think you need worry," she said. "I haven't seen anything of him all day. I did see the valet this morning though. When I was on my way to breakfast he was there at the desk."

"With anybody?"

"No."

"What time was that?"

"A little after nine."

"Good Lord!" Larrick exclaimed. "This is getting complicated. I think I know what Chris and Beck were doing at the airport. Doctor Lack must have sent Beck to meet Doctor Cotillion. Of course Chris would have to tag along, to bask in the reflected glory of the man who gets to see John Belton Lack, M.D., with his coat off."

"That's supposed to be something, is it?"

"In Chris' mind. He's the worst kind of snob. He probably couldn't help throwing his weight around a little, to give the impression he gave you. He never smokes. He was just putting on airs. That's odd, though, about Beck getting money from him. Maybe Beck didn't have anything but hundred-dollar bills. This morning—let's see. I suppose Beck came to see Doctor Cotillion about something, maybe to take him to the hospital or to Doctor Lack's. That clears everything up, doesn't it?" Larrick gave a fillip to his hatbrim. "You didn't get the idea, did you, that Hieronymus was—well, afraid of Hand or Beck last night?"

"That's exactly the idea I got."

"He was merely afraid of being seen. He must have known one or both of them by sight. Naturally he wouldn't want anybody connected with Norcott or Doctor Lack following his movements." A slight crossness was gone from Larrick's voice as he said: "Do you notice what a good air service we have here? Better than Brownsville. A new company's come in to compete with the Pan American Airways."

"May I ask a question? You haven't said so, but I judge Mr. Norcott traced his call to the airport. How does it come then that you didn't know either Christopher Hand or Doctor Lack's servant were there?"

Larrick hesitated. "Well, Norcott didn't trace the call. We did. And Peter thought, since Norcott hadn't seen fit to ask our assistance, we'd better get the lay of the land before we barged into his private affairs. Not that we suspect—"

Mallory's hand touched the back of Larrick's. She tried to withdraw it but found it imprisoned between both of his.

She hadn't seen the two men come in.

One was the skulker of the airport, still in his faded yellow straw hat and baggy linen suit. With the light on the lenses of his spectacles he appeared sightless and rather meek and cringing. The rictus at the corner of his mouth became what it had been last night, a wistful pleading smile, and Mallory was suddenly reluctant to add weight to the evidence which Larrick said was bearing down upon him.

Hence, when she gave her attention to the man who had him in charge, she wasn't altogether unbiased.

Sheriff Bounty himself, if that were he, would stand out among Valleyites because of his comparative fairness, his complexion evidently being one of those which will take no more than a bit of toasting from the sun. His face was finely featured but doped, so to speak, by a faintly sleepy, dissolute look. His frame was heavily muscled but slight and lithe rather than stocky. He was thinly clad in unpressed blue serge, worn so shiny in places that, watching his walk with its suggestion of stalking, Mallory thought of him as a sleek-coated animal.

Neither spoke as they went to the desk, and only there did they seem to attract any particular attention. Discipline was relaxed and groups of uniformed boys crowded in closer, agog with excitement. Beside the clerk had appeared the plump little man, the manager evidently, whom she had noticed last night because of the queer scarred look of the lower part of his face. E. Matthew Rone was in evidence again, at one end of the desk. His hands were in his pockets and he was teetering back and forth as he looked the newcomers, Bounty as well as Hieronymus, up and down. On the other side Fred still leaned against the counter, doing an imitation, Mallory decided, of a poker-faced gentleman crook of fiction.

Under the clock, whose hands were nearing the seven forty-five position, the pair paused. Bounty took a package from under his arm and laid it on the counter. The manager spoke to him and beckoned to the cashier, who came and presented the sheriff with a slip of paper. So absorbed did Bounty seem to become that

Mallory couldn't determine whether or not he noticed the long look which passed between Fred and Hieronymus.

Larrick certainly didn't see it, or the little shrug which Fred gave to the shoulder which was turned away from the lobby, for he was bending over her and whispering: "Well, Miss Witness, that's the man, isn't it?" When she hesitated his voice had a catch of dismay in it. "What's the matter? Don't tell me Hieronymus isn't the one you saw!"

"Yes, he's the one. But I *didn't* see him use the phone. Remember that, please. The doctor's servant was in the booth too. And I'm positive this man was afraid of Christopher Hand."

"I know." Larrick pressed her hand. "You feel sorry for Hieronymus. So did Peter for a while. He does seem a harmless old codger at first. But we've caught him in an out-and-out lie now."

"That's the sheriff with him, the man you work for?"

"That's Peter Beauregard Bounty in person."

"You—like him?"

"Sure, Peter's a good fellow. Everybody likes him."

"Bert, I think he has the cruelest face I ever saw. There's something silky and vicious about him. I wish—"

"See here, little girl, you must be looking at E. Matthew Rone. Peter's about as cruel as a nice old pussy cat stretched out by a fire."

"That's just it, Bert. He's like a cat. With claws. Isn't this enough? I'd like to go to my room."

"Wait a minute. You'll attract too much attention if you go now."

Hieronymus had turned and was looking over the lobby, his thin neck stretching gooselike out of his overlarge collar as his eyes went from chair to chair. Mallory had a revulsion of feeling toward him now. He had recognized Fred and was searching her out. She shrank back and covered the lower part of her face with a handkerchief but continued to stare at him in fascination. He was pale, that was it; his skin had the gleam of oiled parchment, and among these men he looked unhealthy. Like an old scar.

"They're leaving," Larrick whispered. "I'll move back so he won't be so likely to notice you. No use letting him know who identified him."

Suddenly Mallory leaned forward, wadding the handkerchief in her hand. The sheriff had been looking at the register. Now he was looking at Fred, who stood in front of the window, taking a bill from the cashier.

Both of them missed Hieronymus' first signs of sagging. As Mallory's gaze shifted and as Peter Bounty grabbed at him he sank to his knees, folded his arms across his stomach and fell over on one side.

People jumped up from chairs then and blocked her view, but she heard his piping little cry: "Get me a doctor. Quick!"

4

MALLORY TAPPED ON Fred's door and felt as if she were beating on a drum that sent its reverberations up and down the long deserted corridor. This hotel, with its Spanish-castle atmosphere, wasn't the picturesque and cheery place it had been by day. Those brass lamps suspended by chains from the ceiling helped shadows to stir and stretch in corners and doorways.

"Fred!" she called. "Are you in there? Answer me."

A key turned in the lock, the door was opened a few inches and Fred said hoarsely: "For God's sake, get in here and shut up!"

Mallory slipped inside and watched him lock and bolt the door, cross the room and sink into a chair. He was shaking and his eyes looked large and glassy as he stared at one of the empty milk bottles which stood on the table. The fingers of his right hand were tight about the handle of a fruit knife.

The sight of his panic steadied Mallory. "I saw you run up the stairs," she said. "I don't blame you for being scared, but you might have waited a moment on me. Bert Larrick took time to put me in an elevator."

"He wouldn't have if he'd been in my shoes. Somebody was after Hieronymus. He'll be after me now—if he finds out I'm here. What happened downstairs? Did you see?"

"Hieronymus simply crumpled up. When I left they were getting ready to carry him into the manager's office, I think. It's a madhouse down there." Mallory took a cigarette from a package on the table and lighted it. "Fred, you and I are going to stay in this room until Bert Larrick comes. He said he would as soon as he could. You're going to tell him everything you know about what's been happening. You've been up to something crooked but you're going to tell him that too."

"No, I'm not. Not yet anyway. He talks too much and I'm afraid he'd crumb the deal sure enough. But if I can get a gun from him—" Fred started to his feet. "What's that smell in this room? Is that poison gas?"

"It's only a flower, Fred."

Hard knuckles thumped on the door. Mallory looked in that direction and up at the closed transom, then at Fred, whose breathing was a succession of little snuffs in the stillness. He shook his head.

She waited, thinking that if this were Bert Larrick who had followed her up so quickly he would knock again and call when he got no response. So thick was the carpet in the hall that she couldn't decide whether their visitor had walked away or was still standing there.

5

FOR ALL HIS FORTY-ODD years of knocking about the Mexican border, Peter Bounty felt weak in the knees as he stood at the foot of a black leather and chromium davenport in the private office of Paul Palladay, manager of the Sutherland Hotel. It was all very well, he had seen, for Sutherland guests to be given the illusion that they were living like Spanish grandees, but for himself Mr. Palladay, now cooling his heels in his own anteroom, preferred modernity.

Hazel dominated blue in Bounty's eyes as he watched his deputy straighten and stand with his hands on his hips, frowning down at Hieronymus.

"*I* can't tell what's the matter with you." Larrick spoke crossly. "Why in the dickens don't you want us to call the hospital for an ambulance?"

"I'm not going to any hospital here," reiterated the man on the davenport, turning on Bounty the blank panes of his spectacles and that carved smile which, if he were the shifty rogue that the sheriff thought, stood him in such good stead as a mask. "I'm afraid to."

Larrick glanced quickly at Bounty then demanded of Hieronymus: "What're you afraid of?"

"Get me a doctor. I've been poisoned."

"Well, darn it!" Larrick's self-confident front was crumbling. He looked at Bounty again. "There's a roomful of doctors upstairs. Lack, Angelo, Ainsworth and Cotillion are having dinner in Roger Norcott's suite. Doctor Cotillion is that Chicago specialist. I suppose we couldn't very well ask him. But maybe Doctor Lack would come."

"Lack?" Hieronymus repeated, twisting a little. "I'm afraid of him. Get Doctor Cotillion. He's from out of town. He's safe. And he took a transfusion from me once. I'll trust him."

Bounty took a hand. "What about Doctor Angelo?" he asked quietly. "The county physician."

"No, I'm afraid of him too." One might as well have searched for expression on Hieronymus' bald egglike head as on his glabrous face.

"And Doctor Ainsworth?"

"I tell you, I won't have any of those doctors."

"What makes you afraid of our town doctors?"

"Doctors can furnish poison. And somebody's been at it for days, poisoning me slowly. That's why I went to Brownsville, to get an out-of-town doctor to look at me."

"Did you consult one there?"

"It was Saturday. And I saw in the paper Doctor Cotillion was here. I came back to see him."

"Why didn't you tell me this at once?"

"If I can't trust the doctors I can't trust you. I told you to turn me loose and let me attend to my own affairs."

Bounty ruminated on the end of a match and decided that the cylindrical upright chocolate bar in the corner between the head of the davenport and the south window was a water cooler. "Call and see if you can get Doctor Cotillion," he instructed his deputy. "Just tell him it's a former patient of his. Maybe the news hasn't reached Norcott yet. If it has, say I'll be up for a talk later."

As Larrick went to the telephone on a desk which resembled an oblong chocolate bar, Bounty took a turn about the office, ascertaining that there was no means of exit (or, incidentally, of entrance) save through the anteroom. A second door opened into a small bath. The place was air-conditioned. Outside the closed windows, giving on the court and a side entrance to the court, were substantial bars of iron grillwork.

Bounty tightened his belt and advanced toward the huge shadow on the glass door of the partition between office and anteroom.

E. Matthew Rone was planted squarely between that and the outside door, chewing on a dead cigar. In one of a pair of springy black leather and chromium chairs sat Mr. Palladay. Mr. Palladay looked odd, and, talking to him across the desk, Bounty had had to repress a smile. His face was that of an overly nourished cherub, which fact had been disguised when he came to Las Palmas by an impressive golden beard. It hadn't taken him long to discover why Valley men are beardless, but he had held out until summer set in in earnest. Now he was clean-shaven, but the lower part of his face was still white, whereas the upper had the pink and blistered look which was the penalty of his first incautious exposure to the sun.

As Bounty closed the door Palladay sprang to his feet, his reedy voice high-pitched and quavery: "Sheriff, I must ask you to remove this man immediately. By the back way. It is a policy of the Sutherland—"

"I know, Palladay: to pretend such things don't happen in the Valley. I'm more sorry than you that it did happen here. Now your clerk told me a while ago that the man I brought over was in the lobby, near the desk, about nine forty-five last night. You were so interested in that darned check I didn't get a chance to ask you if you'd seen him then or this afternoon or any other time. What about it?"

"I never saw him before."

"And you, Mr. Rone?"

Rone's bushy brows were drawn together, burying his eyes more deeply than ever in flesh. He tilted his cigar up, then down, and said: "I saw your undersheriff, Broddus, pinch him this afternoon. About six. That means you had him in your office an hour and a half."

"Never mind that. How long had Hieronymus been in the lobby when Broddus took him in custody?"

"He'd just come in. Looked in good health too."

Bounty turned back to Palladay. "Now, Mr. Palladay, I'm going to need this anteroom. Why don't you go on out and let your guests see how calm and unconcerned you are? You know, the way a ship's captain does when panic threatens. And you might see if the bellhops or elevator men have anything to report about this man's movements." Bounty held open the door into the corridor and flapped a hand. "Just go right on out and take Mr. Rone with you."

"See here, Bounty!" Rone boomed. "You can't get away with this. A prisoner faints after you've been questioning him in your office. We all know what that means. But when you try to keep it up here—"

"So that's it, is it?" Bounty's voice was soft, but his eyes were like little agates as he looked at the hotel detective. "Quick thinking, Rone. Better go sit in the park now and rest your brain. Somebody might hear you if you make speeches like that here. And I know you wouldn't want that."

Mr. Palladay had backed across the threshold. "Lummox!" he cried as the closing door forced Rone back and onto his trimly shod toes. "Watch where you're going."

Bounty was frowning as he turned to his deputy, who had come out of the office. E. Matthew Rone had been too abstracted to watch where he was treading: a man in the grip of an idea.

"I got Doctor Cotillion," Larrick said. "He's on his way down. Norcott answered. He said Chris Hand had just called from the lobby but he hadn't found out for sure yet that it was Hieronymus who'd collapsed. I had to tell him it was. Lord, Peter, this throws everything out of kilter, doesn't it? Listen, nobody got near enough to Hieronymus out there in the lobby to poison him in any way, did they? I wasn't looking at him just before he fell."

Bounty shook his head ruefully. "Neither was I, son. But I don't think there're any darts from blowguns in this case." He went to a chair, tilted back and locked his hands behind the sleek flaxen hair whose excessive oiliness should have concerned him but didn't. "I'm afraid," he said, "this is one of those cases where we have to work on checking up matters like this: Hieronymus was here at the hotel about nine forty-five last night. That was while the guests from the Chicago plane were registering and the clerk was too busy to pay much attention to him. But he thinks Hieronymus looked at the register and then went to the elevators. Now he wouldn't have got Norcott's room number from the pages that were open, and the clerk doesn't think he turned any pages. So we'll have to do a little study there. I've been thinking of that money he had on him and of his return to the hotel this afternoon. Does that give you any bright ideas, son?"

"No," Larrick said, "that doesn't give me any ideas."

Bounty bit into a match. "What were you looking at me that way for, son? It's the same old face."

Larrick was at the door, playing with the handle. "You need a haircut," he said.

"Do I? I'll get one tomorrow. Tell me about this blonde at the airport. Keep your voice down. Did she recognize Hieronymus?"

"Yes, she saw him go into the telephone booth about five minutes till nine." Larrick spoke soberly. "Peter, that call to Norcott was before nine. You're sure of that, aren't you?"

"No, Bert. The operator marked it down as of nine. When I jogged her memory she said she was several minutes making the connection with Norcott and wasn't positive whether her record was of the time the call first came or of the time it went through to him. Also she admitted that anything a little on either side of the hour would go down as straight up nine. She finally decided the line was occupied the five minutes before nine. But a lawyer could shake her testimony to pieces. Why, son?" Bounty asked, eying his deputy shrewdly.

"Oh, I just wanted to make sure. It looks as if Norcott would have traced that call, doesn't it?"

"He did trace it. As soon as the man hung up. That's how I was able to get on to it. The girl at the switchboard remembered giving Norcott the number it came from."

"And Norcott didn't tell you he'd traced it?"

"No."

"Well," Larrick went on reluctantly, "I saw Chris Hand out in the lobby tonight and told him where the call came from. It was news to him, I'd swear. That means Norcott held back on him too. And I think I can tell you why. Chris was at the airport at that same time."

"You're sure, son?"

"Miss Winters saw him there. I didn't ask Chris tonight, but I'm sure he went to meet Doctor Cotillion. Norcott would know where he was and when he found out his call came from the same place—well, you see what he must have suspected."

"I see, son."

"It's a rotten business," Larrick said, opening the door. "I'm going out and receive Doctor Cotillion. Peter, don't chew on those matches while you're talking to him. Please."

"I won't, son."

There was pride in Bounty's eyes as he watched the door close on enough brown tweed to make a suit and a half for him. It wasn't so long ago that he had had to hale a defiant young sport named Bert Larrick into the sheriff's office for questioning about a drunken roadhouse brawl. Their session had been a lengthy one but he had got through Bert's defenses, found the trouble and devised at least a temporary antidote. The lad had just completed his premedic work at the state university when the death of his father, a member of the Border Patrol, had interrupted his studies and thrown him upon his own, to drift in the bitterness of his disappointment into the company of the town's ne'er-do-wells. Within a week Bounty had pinned a deputy sheriff's badge on a swelling chest. The best day's work he had ever done, he thought now, knowing that he ought to think about the seamy side of human beings.

Bert had something on his mind and Bounty had an inkling of what it was. This was his first case and he was finding it difficult to keep an official viewpoint on people whom he had known all his life. To be specific, on Christopher Hand. . . .

Bounty got to his feet and his match disappeared as Larrick opened the door, ushered in a robust figure in gray herringbone and said over his shoulder: "Wait out there just a minute, Red."

Bounty's ideas concerning metropolitan blood specialists derived largely from newsstand fiction, hence he had expected Dr. Cotillion to present at least a black Van Dyke and pince-nez. Instead Bert was holding the Oxford-gray hat of a hard-bitten businessman. Better still, an army surgeon in mufti, one who has lost his illusions dosing men in outposts with quinine. He had a gritty-looking, slightly puckered chin, and deep lines slanted from his nostrils to draw down the corners of his mouth and throw his full sensuous lips into prominence.

"Doctor Cotillion," Larrick said with a formality which Bounty didn't know was his, "this is my superior officer, Sheriff Bounty."

"Good evening, Sheriff." No, Cotillion didn't possess even a silky voice, but one which was gruff and homespun. There was considerable iron-gray in his hair and that hair could do with a bit of trimming as well as Bounty's.

Bounty shook hands and wished that John Belton Lack had this much of the flesh about him.

"Right in here, Doctor Cotillion," Larrick said, going to the door of the office.

"One moment, young man." The gray-brown eyes which still were taking stock of the sheriff were rather jaundiced-looking; their lids had the familiar inflamed and granulated appearance that comes of too much sunlight or of inexperience in meeting the sun. "Your deputy tells me this is one of the blood donors in my recent streptococcus case and that he seems to be suffering from some sort of poisoning. Let me ask just how you came to call me."

Bounty had his reply ready. "The hotel physician is on his vacation. I learned that you and Doctors Lack and Angelo and Ainsworth were upstairs. Naturally the man preferred that I call you."

"Doctor Lack didn't come to our dinner. But no matter. How long have you had this donor under arrest?"

"He's not under arrest. But he has been held by our office for questioning since six o'clock."

"What has he had to eat or drink during that time?"

"About seven—an hour ago—I ordered sandwiches and coffee for him. And for myself, I'd better say, Doctor. I noticed no symptoms at all of distress in him while I was with him at the office or while I was bringing him over here in my car. In the lobby he suddenly fell and called for a physician."

"I'm really not prepared for this emergency. My case, with what it has in it, is at the hospital. But I'll look at the man. I expect I'd better see him in private."

Larrick was opening the door. "I'll go in and turn on some more lights for you and show you where the washroom is," he said in a hushed voice. "Peter—Mr. Bounty, there's a bellhop out in the corridor who says he has something to tell me. You might talk to him."

Bounty opened one door as Larrick closed the other. "Howdy, Red," he drawled, grinning. "Come on in."

He knew the freckled bellhop as the kid brother of a pal of Bert's and wasn't prepared to see the boy's eyes bulge at sight of him.

"Where's Bert?" Red asked in a small voice and edged toward the lobby.

"He'll be out in a minute. What's the matter? I haven't taken to biting."

The boy stared at him for a time. "They're sayin'," he blurted, "you did something to that prisoner of yours. That's why he fainted and you had to get a doctor."

Bounty's face stiffened a little. "Tell 'em they're mistaken, if you want to, Red. You *have* been standing up for me, haven't you?"

"Well, yes, Mr. Bounty. But they're all a-sayin' it."

"That makes it hard to do your own thinking, I know. Well, don't go away. Bert won't be long."

Bounty closed the door and blew his nose.

Larrick emerged from the office with disappointment written on his face. "Hieronymus told Doctor Cotillion he wanted me put out of the room," he said, going to the stand in the corner where he had hung Cotillion's hat and taking it down to read the manufacturer's stamp in the crown. "I have a textbook of his on physiology at home," he informed Bounty reverently.

"Better brush up on it while he's here, son," Bounty said, trying to remember just what physiology was. Glancing over the morning paper, he had come upon a write-up, emanating from Dr. Angelo and the pages of Who's Who, of Clive Cotillion. Just what he was famous for Bounty hadn't fully comprehended: something to do with the blood stream. Neither had the sheriff heard of the Chicago suburb where he lived nor of the college in which he taught. Cotillion was a college professor; maybe that was why he didn't sport a Van Dyke. . . .

"Son, Red's waiting out there. He didn't want to come in till you were here. You might sort of put in a good word for me, if you will. He's been listening to E. Matthew Rone blacken my character, I'm afraid."

"Aw, it doesn't make any difference what a kid like that thinks of you," Larrick said and opened the door.

The boy entered at once, expanding his chest. "Say, Bert"— he spoke importantly—"I've been doin' a lot of work for you. Had a hard time too. Mr. Palladay's mad as hops and Mr. Rone said none of us was to come near you-all. He's still sore about bein' paged as Elmer."

Larrick, with his boxes and shelves of athletic trophies, was the hero of every small boy in Las Palmas. And had the proper hero's indifference to their worship. "What'd you find out, Red?" he asked, straightening his tie.

"Well"—the bellhop gulped, then his words tumbled over one another—"that man with glasses on came in the lobby last night. After nine-thirty, I know it was. Because people were already in from the New York plane—it was on time—and were comin' from the Chicago plane—it was late. I didn't like his looks so I kept an eye on him. He went to the desk, then got in the elevator—"

"Oh, we know all that, Red."

"But I know what floor he got off at!" the boy said triumphantly. "Jack Simmons— You know him, Ed's brother. Well, he was runnin' that elevator and I asked him. He says he's forgot now but I remember what he told me then. It was the fifth floor. And I saw that man leave too. In about half an hour. By the side door. He just scooted out as if something was after him. That's all. I got to go now." Red stood on one foot and then the other.

Bounty took a half dollar from his pocket. "Thanks, Red. You've helped us a lot. Here." Seeing the boy's hesitation, he tossed the coin to him.

"I wouldn't depend on *that*," Larrick said when the bellhop had caught and pocketed the money and bolted out the door. "Jack Simmons is a dumbbell. And Red sends in breakfast-food labels for G-man badges."

"We'll see, son. Sit down now and tell me in more detail what this Winters girl saw at the airport."

"Don't speak of her that way, Peter. Miss Winters." His tone and a sight of the young lady made Bounty certain that he had another job of chaperonage on his hands. He was like a watchdog in this regard, leery of each new object of. Bert's affections lest the boy form a permanent attachment which would hold him back when a way was finally found to boost him on up the ladder.

Larrick roamed about the room as he talked, with Bounty, sleepy-eyed, following his every move. You learned as much by watching Bert sometimes as by listening to him, and Bounty wondered if big people who are high-strung don't have a harder time of it than runts like himself.

"A little more slowly, son; what she said about Christopher Hand and Doctor Lack's man."

Again that almost desperate defensiveness where Hand was concerned which had been so obvious all afternoon. "You know how girls are," Larrick concluded. "And I must have made it all sound too scary, because Miss Winters got rather worked up. When she remembered Hieronymus didn't want to be seen she just imagined he was afraid."

Bounty's forehead was pursed one instant, smooth the next. "What do you know about this fellow Beck?" he asked.

"Well, a lot of my dope comes from Chris Hand. He goes with Carrie Ainsworth, Doctor Ainsworth's daughter, you know. She started in as Doctor Lack's assistant. Of course Carrie never has had much to say about Doctor Lack or his affairs." Larrick was silent for a moment, and Bounty knew that he was hankering to say more in this connection. He thought better of it, however, and went on: "But Chris is always soaking up news of Doctor Lack. And since the doctor examined his father—"

"I think I talked to his father on the street once. Jacob Hand, a garrulous old codger?"

"Yes. He has a bad heart. After Doctor Lack took Jimmy Norcott's case Chris brought the old man in to the hospital, and I suppose Lack couldn't very well help looking him over, though he doesn't go in for general practice. That meant he had to notice Chris."

"But Chris and Beck, are they buddies?"

"No. I think what it amounts to is that Chris gets a—what do you call it?—vicarious kick out of associating with Doctor Lack's servant whenever he can. Too, he's working hard to get the country out of him. He buys expensive clothes but they never look right on him. He hopes to get pointers from Beck. Beck falls heir to all the doctor's clothes when they've been worn a few times. The two of 'em are the same size. And Lack orders all his stuff from Brooks Brothers in New York. I don't suppose that means anything to you?"

"Not a hell of a lot, son."

"But," Larrick said emphatically, of a sudden recollecting himself, "I'm sure Chris and Beck don't see each other once in a coon's age except when Beck's with Doctor Lack. Now I don't know Beck. He looks to me like the meekest sort of person, though he had that run-in with the police about that robbery in Doctor Angelo's apartment. But you can take it from me that it's ridiculous to suspect Chris of being mixed up in anything underhanded. You know how I hate that guy. But I've got to give the devil his due. He's perfectly square. Anyway, he's been acting as Jimmy Norcott's bodyguard ever since Jimmy came back from school. They've been driving all over hell's high acre alone. If he'd wanted to harm Jimmy he wouldn't have gone at it in this roundabout way."

"Why a bodyguard, ever hear?" Bounty had soon learned that his deputy was a repository of information, or gossip at least, about every strata of Las Palmas society.

"Well, maybe I shouldn't say bodyguard. Chris says he's Jimmy's companion. He may be trying to get on the good side of Jimmy, as he is with old Roger. It's not long till Jimmy's twenty-one, you know, and takes over his half of the Norcott estate." Larrick checked himself and sank his teeth into his lower lip. He looked at his watch and said: "Miss Winters will be wondering why I don't call. I promised her I would as soon as I found out what had happened. Where's Gus tonight, Peter? At home all tired out from his afternoon's sitting?"

"His mother-in-law's still here, and Mrs. Broddus ordained that Gus had to stay home one night and be sociable." Bounty hesitated. "Son, you didn't make that dinner date for us with Miss Winters, did you?"

"For us?" Larrick laughed. "Why, I have a sort of halfway date with her. But when I said the sheriff's office ought to take her to dinner you didn't think I meant—"

"No, no, son." Bounty laughed too. "Of course not. I was meaning—well, I was meaning I'd help pay for it. Here." He got up and tucked a ten-dollar bill into a pocket of the tweed vest. "A little extra for helping me today. I've sure appreciated it. You go on whenever you want to."

"Thanks," Larrick said, patting the pocket. "That's what I meant too."

Bounty sat down and fussed with a shoestring. "Son, who is this Fred Winters?"

"Mallory's cousin. He's down here from New York on some kind of business. I'm not sure what. Oil, I suppose."

"Yet you endorsed a check for him?"

"How'd you know about that?" Larrick demanded quickly. "Oh. That's what you and Palladay were talking about at the desk just as Hieronymus had his spell."

"Yes. I told him it was all right to cash it. But you want to be a little more careful, son."

"Listen!" Larrick scoffed. "You haven't met the Winterses. If you had, you wouldn't be so suspicious."

"I was only speaking generally, son." The opening of the office door gave Bounty an excuse to postpone again the lecture which he was always on the point of delivering to Bert about money matters.

On Dr. Cotillion's face, as he went to a chair and dropped heavily into it, was the expression of one who has the taste of quinine in his mouth. He looked at Larrick, rather than at Bounty, in a way which prompted the latter to say: "Doctor, my deputy and I take things together. Also, he's going into your profession. So he'll probably understand what you have to say better than I."

"A doctor in embryo, eh?" Something about Cotillion's continued scrutiny of Larrick, accompanied by a hardening of the muscles of the jaw, made Bounty wish he hadn't stuck his oar in. "Keeping up with your studies this summer, young man?"

"Not very well, sir," Larrick answered self-consciously. "I—I have your book, of course. I study it."

A smile worked at the corners of Cotillion's mouth. "That answer proves you've been to college, at least. Well, you're going to hear a masterpiece of a diagnosis. I don't know what's wrong with that man in there."

"Is anything wrong with him?" Bounty asked quickly.

The physician seemed to go off into a brown study, staring with wide bleary eyes at Larrick's right hand. To Bounty it was an odd and aggravating hiatus. When he exchanged glances with Bert he knew that the latter was no less puzzled by it than he.

"Yes," Cotillion made deliberate answer, "I should say that he is frightened half out of his wits."

Bounty scrutinized the other's face, slightly olive-tinged at close range, as he asked: "Did he tell you of whom he is frightened, Doctor?"

"He has been afraid of poison," the physician went on as if he hadn't heard the question. "He believes he has poison of some kind in his system now. And from my brief examination I can't say definitely that he hasn't. I wish you hadn't called me, Sheriff."

"Hieronymus asked for you, Doctor."

"I know." Cotillion passed a hand across his eyes. "He has put himself under my protection."

"That's satisfactory as far as we're concerned, Doctor. Will you take charge of his case and give him a thorough examination?"

Cotillion glanced quickly at Bounty and then away. "You realize the situation you're putting me in, Sheriff." There was sarcasm in his tone.

"Not fully, I don't," Bounty said.

"I told the man he ought to be in a hospital. He said it would have to be one out of your jurisdiction."

"Did he explain why?"

"Not in so many words. I told him at once that it was impossible for me to leave Las Palmas at present. I came to consult with Doctor Lack on young Norcott's case. That's my first and only concern. Of course anything affecting a blood donor affects Norcott. But—callously—after looking at that man in there, I believe I'd be of more service at Norcott's bedside."

"You mean you won't be able to use Hieronymus for a transfusion?" Larrick said in consternation.

"Not so long as there's a possibility of poison being in his blood stream. And that's a question it may take some time to settle. If the worst comes to the worst, of course, we might take the risk."

"Well, Doctor, what would you suggest we do with Hieronymus?" Bounty asked.

"He agreed to go to a hospital here if I would look after him. I don't know what all is included in that commission but I'm willing to accept it, temporarily at least. On the condition, Sheriff, that I be given full particulars of his case."

"We'll have to do some detective work before we can give full particulars. But I promise you all the information we have if you'll take charge of him." Bounty watched Cotillion's face as he asked: "Are there any objections to the John Belton Lack? It's our best hospital. In spite of its name it's a county, not a private, institution."

"Even if I hadn't been through it today that name would carry its own recommendation."

"Call the hospital, will you, Bert? Tell them to send the ambulance to the rear and bring the stretcher through the patio. And notify Doctor Angelo." Bounty gave his attention to Cotillion again. "I wonder if our county physician is still up in Mr. Norcott's suite?"

"He was when I left." Apparently Hieronymus had revealed nothing to arouse distrust in Cotillion of the hospital, of its head or of the man who had given it its name. "You might ask Doctor Angelo to stop for me here, if he's ready to go," the Chicago man said to Larrick.

"I have a car outside, Doctor. I should be very glad to drive you."

"Won't I be keeping you from an engagement?"

"No sir."

"Very well then." Cotillion rose. "While you're at the phone I'll step out to the cigar counter."

Larrick opened the corridor door for him, then remarked to Bounty as he crossed the anteroom to the office: "I'm ashamed to make Doctor Cotillion ride in that old runabout of mine."

"Want to use my car, son? It's out front."

"Well, it's some better."

"You might drop in Norcott's rooms when you get back," Bounty told his deputy as he tossed him his keys. "I'm going to beard the old lion in his den."

Larrick returned first, looking a little more like his usual self. "Angelo wasn't upstairs," he said. "He'd just been called to the hospital. I rang it again but he hadn't got there yet. I want to be the one to give him orders. He tried to high-hat me tonight while I was with Miss Winters. I called her, too, while I was at it, told her I'd be up after while. She was in Fred's room and said she certainly was glad to hear my voice. They must think they're in the Wild West. Somebody has been to Fred's door a couple of times and knocked but they're afraid to open up. He wants me to bring him a gun."

Bounty frowned. "You aren't going to do it, son?"

"I thought I'd stop at the office on my way back from the hospital and get one."

"Use your head, son. These people are strangers."

"It's my gun."

"No, it's not. It belongs to Hesperides County."

"I have an automatic at home. I'll give Fred that."

"Bert, what's got into you this evening? I admit that Miss Winters helped us out and you ought to take her to dinner. But it seems to me you're doing enough for her cousin if you endorse his check and furnish him with liquor. I left that pint at the desk for him, as you asked me to. Gus had taken a swig out of it, that was all."

"I've got it here." Larrick tapped the inside pocket of his loosely fitting coat, where Bounty hadn't noticed a bulge before. "You can have it back if that's the way you feel about it."

"Please, son, don't let's squabble. But listen. And don't go up in the air. How many people did you tell that Miss Winters was identifying Hieronymus for us?"

Larrick's back had been turned. He pivoted about slowly and stared at Bounty with widening eyes. "Nobody but Chris Hand," he answered. "Peter, surely you don't think that's it: someone is trying to get at her because she's our witness?"

"I don't think so, son. Honestly, I don't."

"Well, she's safe enough until I get there anyway. Fred's with her. And we arranged how many times I was to knock to let them know who I was. It sounded foolish at the time. Oh hell, I know that couldn't be it."

"I might stop and see her while you're gone."

"No, no," Larrick said quickly. "Don't."

"Why not?"

"I'd just rather you didn't. I—I don't think you and she would get along very well."

"All right, son. I understand," Bounty said as the outer door opened and Doctor Cotillion came in.

The physician had a Chamber of Commerce brochure in his hand. "Takes football tactics to get through that lobby," he said, his first glance for Larrick again. Why in the deuce, Bounty wondered, did he keep looking at Bert in that probing way?

"Doctor," Larrick asked hesitantly, "were you joking when you told that reporter you knew where another blood donor was?"

Cotillion sat down with a grunt. "No, I was telling him the literal truth. I answered his question without thinking and then decided I'd better let Mr. Norcott or Doctor Lack dispense the news, if they saw fit. So I left the donor on the moon, without specifying that Moon Island, where he is, is one of the Aleutians."

"The Aleutians?"

"You know, son," Bounty spoke reprovingly. "The Aleutians are the islands that separate Bering Sea from the northern Pacific."

"Oh yes. Who is he, Doctor?"

"Miles is his name. I got my information about him from Doctor Lack. I turned it over to a private inquiry agency I knew of that has a branch in Chicago and operates up and down the West Coast. I had this reply from them this evening."

The physician took a telegram from his pocket and handed it to Bounty, who read aloud for his deputy's benefit the message from a nationally known agency. It informed Dr. Cotillion that Justin Miles, Seattle blood donor, was a member of the University of Washington Ethnological Field Expedition, with base on Moon Island in the Aleutians; that communication with him had been established; that his reply would be forwarded as soon as received.

"This is the only donor besides Hieronymus you're in touch with?" Bounty asked as he returned the telegram.

"Yes, and you can see that he might as well be on the moon so far as tomorrow's needs are concerned."

"Whom have you told of him?"

"The gentlemen who were at Mr. Norcott's dinner."

"Norcott, Christopher Hand, Doctor Ainsworth, Doctor Angelo. That right?"

"Yes, Sheriff. They were all interested parties and it was up to Mr. Norcott to take at least part of the responsibility for getting the man here."

"He did?"

"Oh yes, although he seemed a bit dismayed at thought of the expense."

"He would be," Larrick put in.

Dr. Cotillion looked up and then down at the brochure. "I picked this up in the lobby," he said as he unfolded it. "It reminded me of a question I've wanted to propound all day. I notice you people down here boast that your climate is so healthful that no one ever dies. I understand your cemeteries aren't recognizable as such: flat meadows with grass and flowers. But how does that attitude toward death affect your attitude toward men of my profession?"

So abrupt was the change of subject that Bounty thought the doctor was shying away from further discussion of Roger Norcott's well-known parsimony. "I don't know that I ever considered it," he said. "If anything, I'd say physicians are more highly valued here than elsewhere. You help us hold the fort against death."

"There's no hostility toward us, then?"

"Hostility? No, it's true we disguise our undertakers and their calling. Pick out the most beautiful house in town—with the exception of Doctor Lack's—and you have the morgue."

Cotillion switched his eyes to Bounty's face and in them was the emotionless look of a surgeon seeking a place to probe. "Then I wish you'd explain a remark made outside my door last night. 'This is a healthy place for some folks, but not for doctors.'"

Bounty stared at him sleepily. "Tell me more about the circumstances, Doctor Cotillion."

"That's all there was to it. My plane got in at nine-thirty. Mr. Hand met me and brought me here to the hotel. I registered and went to my room to wash before he came to take me down to meet Mr. Norcott. The bellhop hadn't much more than left me when I heard those words, spoken very distinctly, in the hall. As I remember, I was a bit startled. But it wasn't until today that I gave serious thought to them. And to the possibility that they were meant for me. I've hesitated to say anything about the matter. It sounds so melodramatic. But then, everywhere I've turned today I've run into something that sounds melodramatic."

Bounty's chair swung slowly forward. "Where is your room, Doctor?"

"On the fifth floor. Five-twenty, I believe, is the number."

"Hieronymus!" Larrick exclaimed. "But that doesn't make sense. Did it sound like his voice, Doctor? He was on that floor about that time."

"He was?" Cotillion looked at him for a moment, then shook his head. "I wouldn't recognize the voice. I'm treading on delicate ground here, I suppose, but at the time I took it for a Negro's voice. Today I've noticed the same softness of speech in everyone who seems to be a native here. It's my first experience with the Southern accent."

This was too much for Larrick. "We don't have Southern accents, Doctor," he said defensively. "And we don't sound like—"

"Call it the old Texas drawl and remember the Alamo," Bounty interposed. "Was there anything in yesterday's papers about Doctor Cotillion, Bert?"

"I didn't see anything."

"What people here knew the hour of your arrival, Doctor?"

"My only communication was with Doctor Lack. He kindly made reservations here for me. I know he notified Mr. Norcott of my coming, because Mr. Hand met me. I believe Doctor Angelo was also notified."

"Doctor Lack didn't send anyone to the airport to meet you then?"

"I talked to Doctor Lack over the phone last night. He said he had sent a man to meet me but the fellow hadn't been able to wait for the late plane."

"Mind telling me who saw you after you registered?"

"Only Mr. Hand and Mr. Norcott. Hand came for me about ten-fifteen. We went to Mr. Norcott's room and I stayed half an hour or so. I was in bed by eleven."

"Did Mr. Norcott have a caller while you were there?"

"A caller? Why, no."

The ambulance siren whined in at them then and, as always at the sound, Bounty went tense. Deputy and undersheriff never guessed what squeamishness their superior had to fight down, not at contact with the fact of death, but with its ugliness.

"Bert, go meet these men with the stretcher, will you?"

When the door had closed Bounty said quietly: "Why don't you tell me, Doctor, exactly what Hieronymus told you?"

Cotillion gazed steadily at the floor. "It was what he didn't say, rather than what he said, Sheriff. Most of his talk consisted of pleas to save his life and protect him. He said he was sure he was being poisoned, he didn't know how. I asked him whom he suspected and he promised to tell me if I would get him away from you and your men."

"Why from my men and me?"

"You asked me that once and I answered that he didn't say in so many words. My inference was that he was afraid of you."

"I thought so." Bounty rose. "That's the reason you've been interested in my deputy."

"Not altogether, Sheriff. I'm always interested in seeing what the next generation of physicians is going to be like."

"In that case you may not veto my suggestion. You've stepped into the midst of alarms and excursions, Doctor, and frankly I don't know what it's all about. But if I reserved a double room here, or two connecting rooms, would you consent to move, without saying anything to anyone, and let my deputy enjoy your companionship during your stay? We won't call him a guard."

"I'll be glad to, Sheriff," Cotillion said as Larrick swung open the door. "Though I'm afraid it will mean shattering his illusions."

Larrick had let in two white-garbed youths who carried a stretcher jauntily, as if they were half intoxicated by the odor of night-blooming cœreus which entered with them.

"Hello, Mr. Bounty!" one sang out. "Full moon tonight."

"Snake cactus in bloom," the other added.

"And not a thought in town fit to go into print," Bounty contributed, happy at a kind word.

Larrick wasn't having any of their frivolity. When he had opened the inner door he brought his own and the Oxford-gray hat and inquired: "Shall we go, Doctor Cotillion?"

The physician was removing the tinfoil from a plug of ordinary chewing tobacco. "Here's what I went to the cigar counter for," he said. "I felt in the need of it. Hope you don't mind, young man."

Larrick looked at Bounty. Bounty had a brand new match in his mouth.

"Say!" came the cry from within the office. "Where did you tell us to take this bird?"

Larrick stepped to the door. "To the John Belton Lack Hospital."

"Hospital, hell! You mean the morgue."

6

"You can't keep me away from my son."

At the turning of the stairs on the third floor of the John Belton Lack Hospital stood Jacob Hand, his head lowered like that of a bull at bay. Dr. Angelo, the little group of nurses and orderlies in their stern white uniforms—these were his adversaries in no personal sense. He was ready to charge blindly at all that this spotless, regulated world had for him of the occult. About his neck he still wore the ball of asafetida which had been there when he came to the hospital. He was a squat hulk of flesh and bone and muscle which the light lounge suits that Christopher bought for him couldn't be made to fit. Not such an old man, although there was gray in his rank black hair; not an unprepossessing man, thanks to the eyes that enlivened his dark, earthy face.

Now that she knew who he was, Susan Ray, the nurse from the chart desk who had seen him corning up the stairs and who had given the alarm, was beginning to get over her scare. For a few minutes there it had seemed that the dark and hellish monster who climbs staircases in hospital melodramas at last had visited the John Belton Lack.

"Moley" Angelo ("Moley" because of the moles that rumor said were all over him) was scared, though. He kept the nurse and the orderly from the first floor a little ahead of him as he said: "No one is trying to keep you from your son, Mr. Hand. Your son's not up here." He turned to the orderly: "Take him to the elevator and down to his room."

He had given that command twice and each time Bingham, the orderly, had looked Hand over and shrugged helplessly, as he did now.

"Well?" Angelo demanded. "Aren't you going to do it?"

"Not until I grow a little," Bingham answered.

Angelo mopped perspiration from his white round face. "Brownlee," he said to the nurse, "call the Sutherland Hotel and see if you can reach Christopher Hand."

"I just called, Doctor. Christopher Hand is not in his room. I left a message for him. And I called a friend of his. She said she'd be right over."

"First day since I been here Chris ain't come to see me." Hand was moving slowly toward the stairs that led to the fourth floor. "'Tain't like the boy to forget. I know what's the trouble. It's Roger Norcott's doin'. That scrawny old jay bird. He never had it in him to beget a family his own. So he comes tryin' to steal Chris away from me. Well, he can't do that, for all the money he's made sweatin' the folks as work for him."

"Now, Hand, I wouldn't talk about my private affairs when so many people can hear." Dr. Angelo stood at the foot of the stairs, one hand on the newel post, the other on the wall, and eyed the distance between them. Orderly and nurse had deserted him, one sliding along the wall, the other retreating to the fourth tread of the stairs.

"I got a right to talk. It's time folks was hearin' what Norcott's done to me. Shut me up in this here sick-house, so I'd catch a disease an' die an' he could have Chris to hisself."

Susan Ray had noticed a Western Union messenger boy hanging on the outskirts of the excitement. He had started several times toward Dr. Angelo but always had lost his nerve and fallen back. He came up to the desk by which she was standing and said in a shrill whisper: "Gee! Is that a loony?"

"No, son. He's just an old man with a weak heart. They don't want him to climb those stairs. You have a telegram for Doctor Angelo?"

"For the hospital. He came in just ahead of me. I tried to catch up with him but he was goin' so fast I couldn't."

"Mr. Norcott had nothing to do with your coming here, Hand. Listen to me!" Angelo succeeded in making his voice more authoritative but he gave himself away by taking a step up the stairs. "You cannot go up to the fourth floor. You know very well a boy there is on the point of death. Unless you go to your room at once—"

"Don't want me to know what's goin' on up there, do yuh, Doc? I think you got Chris up there, doin' somethin' to him."

"I tell you your son is not in the hospital."

"Yuh ain't foolin' me, Doc." There was a rumble beneath the words. "Somethin' unnatural's goin' on. If it's what I think it is, I'm gonna put a stop to it. The Norcotts always were a poorly race. There's a blight on 'em. It ain't gonna be Chris who saves 'em from peterin' out." Hand put forward two fingers, hooked at the button which held Angelo's coat tight about his fat middle. The button broke and the claw caught the belt buckle.

Down the hall one of the student nurses screamed.

"Tell me he ain't a loony!" said the messenger boy to Susan.

Effortlessly Hand was drawing the doctor down to him, shaking him with his own shaking. "Yuh been helpin' Roger Norcott with his jay-bird devilment. Don't do it no more. Yuh let Chris alone with them knives o' yourn. He's my flesh an' blood."

"Father Hand!"

At the clear, controlled cry Hand released Angelo and turned, rubbing his palm on his trousers, to the girl who was coming from the elevator. He smiled timidly and muttered: "I wasn't doin' nuthin', Carrie."

Carrie Ainsworth, of course. A dark-haired, dark-eyed girl of the athletic type whom Susan Ray remembered seeing with Christopher Hand.

"Of course you weren't," she said, taking the old fellow's arm. "But what in the world is Christopher going to think when he comes to your room and you aren't there?" She turned to Angelo and smiled. "He'll be all right now, Doctor. Let me talk to him awhile."

Angelo's face was beginning to work, with anger Susan Ray thought. He had his mouth open to say something when the messenger boy approached him. He signed the boy's book with trembling hand, took a telegram from him and tore it open.

Carrie Ainsworth and Jacob Hand had started down the stairs, very slowly, the girl talking in an undertone about Christopher.

Susan Ray looked back at Dr. Angelo. He had turned down the hall in the direction of the elevator. His hands were busy and she thought he was tearing the telegram to pieces.

7

CHRISTOPHER HAND STOOD staring down into the lobby when Peter Bounty stepped from the elevator onto the mezzanine floor of the Sutherland. The young man's heels were together, his hands were gripping the railing, his heavy body was thrown slightly forward, so that he appeared to be gathering strength for some prodigious acrobatic stunt.

Bounty had the population of Hesperides pretty well pigeon-holed by now, but this was a notorious character whom he hadn't been able to fit into any compartment, high or low, small or large. In fact, if he made use of "notorious" in an unfavorable sense, he was fair enough to admit that he had always seen Hand through the clouded spectacles which Bert Larrick put before his eyes. And it had taken this experience to show him (and to show Bert, too, perhaps) what latent friendship was between these two traditional rivals of Las Palmas' younger set.

Bounty approached slowly, studying him. Hand's blue coat and white flannel trousers were those of the young man about town but, as Bert said, they didn't look right on him. At his ease in cor-duroy and boots, he might have cut a handsome figure. An inferi-ority complex was at work here, undoubtedly, with consequent aping. Whereas Roger Norcott, Bounty remembered, wore unob-trusively a single small but probably perfect diamond in an old-fashioned setting, his protégé had a ring on each hand: big 10-carat gold rings, one set with initialed imitation onyx, the other with a tiger-eye cameo. You could tell by the way he held his fingers that he was conscious of them, proud of them, unaware that to Bert and his critical friends they set him apart.

"Hello, Chris," Bounty said companionably. "The excitement's finally dying down a little."

Hand turned. "How do you do, Mr. Bounty." He spoke, as always, as if from a congested chest. "You want to see Mr. Norcott?"

"In a moment." Bounty stood beside him and looked into the lobby. "Anybody standing here could have seen the whole show, couldn't he?"

"I guess so. They say Hieronymus fell right in front of the desk."

"The center of the stage. Bert and I carried him back to Mr. Palladay's office. How much would you say Hieronymus weighed?"

"How would I know? I never saw him."

"Why, yes, you have," Bounty said, resting a hip on the rail and turning to Hand.

"When?"

"At the airport last night."

"Oh." Hand bent over again, hunching his pugilist's shoulders. "Bert told me tonight you'd traced Mr. Norcott's call there. And found a girl who saw Hieronymus make it. That must have been just before I went in."

"You and your friend Beck."

Hand stiffened and raised his square chin. Blood darkened his face even more, and behind the ear lobe turned to Bounty was a little flutter, like that of a fish's gills. "Beck?" he repeated, as if trying to place the name.

"Doctor Lack's man."

"Oh, that servant. Yes, he was there awhile. Doc sent him to meet the same plane I was meeting. But when Beck reported it was late, Doc had him come home."

"How did Beck report to Doctor Lack?"

"Phoned him."

"And you stayed and met Doctor Cotillion?"

"Yes. Mr. Bounty, I saw Bert and Doctor Cotillion go through the lobby a while ago. Where's that girl—that Miss Winters—Bert was with?"

"Looking at the moon till Bert comes back, I suppose. What did you do after you brought Doctor Cotillion here?"

"I saw that he got registered. Then I went in and told Mr. Norcott he'd come. I went and got him about ten-fifteen and introduced him to Mr. Norcott."

"And after he left?"

"I went to bed." Hand straightened and turned on Bounty. His face remained stolid but, looking at his dark surly eyes, it was easy to believe Bert's stories of an ugly temper. "What're you trying to do?" he demanded. "Check up on me?"

"What would be your guess, Chris?"

"Well, you can go straight to hell. You and that grinning ape of a deputy of yours."

Bounty looked at him steadily. "We're letting that pass this time, Chris. As spoken just between us fellers. But hereafter remember this: Bert and I are commissioned by this county to investigate a murder case and to send someone to the electric chair."

Hand stared past him into the recesses of the mezzanine, perspiration gleaming upon his metallic face. There was no movement there, but by shifting his head a little Bounty could see that gill-like fluttering behind each car lobe. "Murder," Hand repeated thickly. "Then this blood donor has died?"

"Died, Chris. And I understand taking Mr. Norcott that news is equivalent to taking him news of his nephew's death."

Hand's eyes moved slowly to Bounty's face, and the sheriff was puzzled by the puzzlement in them. "Unless we have another donor tomorrow," Hand said, "Jimmy Norcott will die. Anybody who knows of another ought to tell us."

"Granted."

"Call for Christopher Hand!" rose a bellboy's cry from the lobby.

"I'll get that in my room," Hand said, turning toward the east side of the mezzanine. "Mr. Norcott's in here, if you want to come in. It seems to me he has a right to know what's going on. He's the biggest taxpayer in the county—"

"Save the speeches till next election," Bounty said, going along with him.

Hand came to a standstill a few feet from a door, with a key held ready to slip into the lock. "Mr. Bounty"—he spoke haltingly—"you'd better go slow about accusing me—or anybody else—of scaring off these blood donors. There's a racket connected with this somehow. And I don't need a racket to make money. But I know—and everybody in town knows—how bad in need of money Bert Larrick is this summer—"

"Careful, Hand."

Hand's laugh was hard, with a sneer in it. "Not so much fun when you're on the receiving end, is it? But Bert didn't sprout any wings when he put on that badge, Mr. Bounty. Now don't get me wrong. What I'm saying I'm saying for his own good and you ought to thank me for doing it. I'm sure under no obligation to Bert. All his life he's gone along owing money and spending money and getting by with it because everybody likes him. While some of the rest of us poor devils have been working and paying our way and not going to all the dances. Now it's my turn to laugh. Bert's in a hole and wishes he'd saved something. But I know he'd never in the world do anything dishonest to get out of that hole. That's me saying that, understand. But I've heard people wondering about Bert tonight. People who aren't so sure. The first thing you know, Mr. Bounty, the county commissioners will be wanting to know a few things that you may be too blind to see. What I think's happened is this: Bert's let himself be roped into something. And now that he sees what it is, he'll want to back out. Get the truth out of him, Mr. Bounty, then send him away. For a trip over into Mexico. I'll pay his expenses. And I'll fix things with Mr. Norcott. Because Bert's father was a friend of his. But make Bert tell you what he's been up to. That call. Come on in."

Bounty went unsteadily into Roger Norcott's sitting room. He had stepped into Rio Grande quicksand once and experienced panic, the sort that brings heartburn, not unlike this. It wasn't that he had any suspicion of Bert or believed that anyone else had. But his deputy had been remote from him that evening. And somewhere in Bert's words or actions had been something whose significance he had let elude him. . . .

It was a high-ceilinged room where adherence to a formal Spanish décor hadn't been allowed to interfere with comfort. There were doors in the side walls, and at the rear wide-open casement windows through which the breeze brought the odor of night-blooming cereus to mingle with the fragrance of Roger Norcott's thin black cigar.

"Good evening, Sheriff," Norcott said in a noncommittal tone as he rose and automatically extended a leathery, big-knuckled hand. "Christopher, the hospital has been trying to get you. They asked for you when they called Doctor Angelo. Better see what it is right away."

Bounty had a glimpse of Hand's face as the young man turned and strode to the door on the left. Stolidity was breaking and Bounty thought the expression that was about to appear must be like that which he himself was trying to hide.

"Have a chair, Sheriff," Norcott said and sank back into his place by a table with a parchment-shaded lamp. His "Smoke?" and his nod at the humidor were ritualistic.

"No, thanks," Bounty said, crossing to the chair which he had selected out of range of the window. Cereus always made him lackadaisical and at peace with the world.

There was silence while he and Norcott studied each other through smoke, in the time-honored manner of men of their breed. Poker in their generation and maybe parleys around Indian camp fires in another had made of this preliminary quiescence a thing to be respected.

There had been a sapping of Norcott's constitution since Bounty last had had occasion to observe him closely. The plain gray business suit was looser on his spare frame. His wide shoulders sloped now. His crown was almost completely bald and the sparse hair which encircled it was grizzled. His strong lower jaw seemed to have sagged, giving his weather-beaten face a more equine appearance than ever. His small steel-gray eyes had lost some of their keenness while the sun-etched wrinkles at their corners had deepened.

Norcott shot a quick glance of inquiry at Hand as the latter came out, pushing back that dark Medusa lock which any movement of his head seemed to disturb.

"It was about my father," Hand said, looking at the crown of his hat. "They want me to come over."

"Anything serious, Christopher?"

"No sir. But I haven't been to see him all day. I thought if you didn't need me here . . ."

"Of course not, my boy." Norcott rose and laid a hand on his shoulder as he went with him to the door. "Two old war horses like Bounty and me aren't going to have any trouble. Give your father my regards. I'll try to stop by and see him tomorrow myself. Pardon us a moment, Sheriff."

They passed outside and Bounty felt sure that they left the vicinity of the door to talk. When Norcott returned, some three minutes later, he had his watch in his hand. He looked at it, then at Bounty and said as he sat down: "Christopher tells me this donor Hieronymus has died."

"Yes," Bounty said, free here to chew on matches as he pleased. "He died a few minutes ago, down in the manager's office."

"Well?"

Norcott wasn't a man to show his emotions but he was taking this too lightly. Altogether too lightly, Bounty felt, for a man whose nephew's life hung in the balance.

"Here's the full story, Norcott. From six to seven forty-five Hieronymus was in the custody of our office and showed no symptoms of poisoning. Then, down in the lobby, he fell and wanted a doctor and claimed he'd been poisoned. I called Doctor Cotillion, as you know. Cotillion examined him and couldn't determine what was wrong with him. We called the ambulance to take him to the hospital. Then the three of us—Cotillion, Bert Larrick and myself— sat in the anteroom, waiting. When the ambulance men came Hieronymus was dead."

"And Cotillion couldn't tell what killed him?"

"No. At least he refused to give an opinion until he had made a further examination at the morgue. He's there now and I've left word at the hospital for Doctor Angelo to consult with him as soon as possible."

"I don't know anything about medical matters, but I'd say a young whippersnapper like Angelo wouldn't be likely to tell Cotillion anything."

"As county physician, Angelo will have to determine the cause of death, pending an autopsy."

"We made a mistake putting him in that place instead of Hugh Ainsworth. I hear the county commissioners are going to rectify it tomorrow. But that's beside the point now. Couldn't Hieronymus tell how he got the poison?"

"No."

"But, according to you, it must have been before six?"

"I fail to see how it could have been given him between then and seven forty-five. But there's no use in you and me speculating about poison, Norcott. All I know about it is what I've read in stories, so I'm going to wait for Doctor Cotillion's report. Let's talk about the actions of Hieronymus before six. Beginning at the time we first hear of him: at five minutes till nine last night. I traced your call."

"So Christopher said Larrick told him. To the airport, I understand."

"Yes, and we can prove Hieronymus was there at that time, at least. I'm surprised *you* didn't think of tracing the call. If you had, you could have got in touch with Hand, since you knew he was there, and the sheriff's office could have got to work on the case several hours sooner."

"I never thought of it." Norcott took the cigar from his mouth, sucked in his lower lip and dribbled smoke down over his chin. "I hear you found some girl to identify Hieronymus," he said with his eyes on Bounty's face.

"Yes."

"Who is she?"

"Summers, I believe her name is. And the next we hear of Hieronymus is at nine forty-five, when he appears here at the hotel and starts upstairs."

"What's that?" Cigar ash snowed over Norcott's coat as he stared at Bounty. "You're telling me the truth?" he demanded with apparently genuine incredulousness. "Hieronymus was in the hotel last night?"

"He stepped into an elevator, stepped out again half an hour later and left the hotel. He disappears until six this evening, when he promptly dies of poison. Suppose you were called on to prove that he didn't visit you?"

"You haven't got it in your head that he did, have you?"

"Let's quit sparring, Norcott. I'm not accusing you of anything. But you must see that it's up to you to give an account of yourself for last night."

"Yes," Norcott admitted, "I can see that. The best I could do would be to prove that if Hieronymus came here it was for a very few minutes. It was about nine forty-five when Christopher came back from the airport. He was with me till about ten-ten. He was gone then for not more than ten minutes, when he went to get Doctor Cotillion. Cotillion was here about half an hour. Then I went to bed."

"And Christopher Hand?"

"We have separate rooms. I presume he went to bed too. Listen, Sheriff, just what was your purpose in coming here? If it was to get a detailed account of my movements and Christopher's, we'll make them out on paper and give them to you tomorrow. If you had another reason, let's have it. You've caught me at a busy time."

"Did you have any communication with Hieronymus today?"

"None," Norcott answered, frowning.

"I hear you had a party tonight."

"Hardly a party. Christopher thought I ought to extend some courtesy to Doctor Cotillion. He and Doctor Lack and Angelo were together at the hospital this afternoon, so I invited all three to dinner. I hoped Angelo wouldn't accept, since he knows I have no use for him. Instead it was Lack who had another engagement. I'm not much at that sort of entertaining, so I asked Hugh Ainsworth to come and help me out. And the more I see of these big-time doctors the more convinced I am that we have a man we don't appreciate in Ainsworth."

"I agree with you there. Your table was sort of broken up, I judge."

"Yes. It wasn't long after you called Doctor Cotillion that Angelo was wanted at the hospital. Hugh Ainsworth left soon after that."

"But at seven forty-five the three doctors, you and Christopher Hand were here?"

"Yes. Bounty, I hate to be inhospitable . . ."

Bounty spat out a sliver of wood and eyed the match as if selecting a new point of attack. "Norcott," he said softly, "my purpose in coming here was to find out who stands to gain by your nephew's death."

The gray eyes were clear and penetrating and steady for fully half a minute. Then they wavered and took on a feverish brightness while a muscle at one side of Norcott's mouth began to twitch. "Bounty," he spoke huskily, "be frank with me, please. Have you any evidence that someone is trying to keep my nephew from receiving a transfusion?"

"The murder of Hieronymus is pretty good evidence."

"Why couldn't he have been murdered for some personal reason?"

"That's asking a lot of coincidence, but it's possible. My advice to you, though, is to look on his death as a blow at your nephew. And to give me your confidence. I promise that so far as I can I'll respect as private any information you give me about your affairs."

"There's nothing about my affairs needs covering up. I'd show you if I could be sure you have the right to question me. Look here, Bounty. This is the first time you and I have been thrown together. But each of us knows the stuff the other's made of. The Valley that bred us was a different place from what these young sprouts know. We had to do things it wouldn't be fair to judge by today's standards. You've killed men—"

"I haven't any patience with that kind of talk, Norcott. We were country boys, not pioneer heroes. I never killed a man."

"Well, I did. A cattle rustler. It's never been on my conscience, though naturally I don't talk about it. My nephew, for instance, would always shrink from me, if he knew it. But you look at it in the same light as I do."

The first time Bounty remembered hearing the Norcott name was in connection with that cattle rustler story. It was a standing joke in that community, he had found. "People shoot burglars today sometimes," he said. "What is it you're getting at?"

Norcott scowled. "This. We're alone here and what's said will never get outside this room. I'm indebted to you for taking an interest in this case, don't forget that. I'm ready to share responsibility for anything that happened. If you know who's to blame for the death of this donor—who had a part in it, probably an innocent one—and are trying to protect him by throwing up a smoke screen—"

"Oh, I get the point, Norcott. And I'm beginning to think there is a distinct smell of smoke in the air. Once and for all, the sheriff's office isn't responsible for the man's death. I lost a night's sleep and I've worked all day trying to find out if he needed protection and to give it to him if he did. By failing on the last, I succeeded in the first. That means your nephew needs protection. I can take my time about finding out from whom or I can keep on working before it's too late. It's up to you."

Norcott rose and went to the window, where he stood for several moments with his back to Bounty. He turned and asked: "Sheriff, Bert Larrick's place on your force is only a temporary one, isn't it?"

Bounty looked sleepy. "It's permanent so far as I'm concerned," he said. "Are you going to tell me who would gain by your nephew's death?"

Norcott returned to his chair. "No one," he answered.

They sat in poker-faced silence, chewing on match and cigar.

Norcott capitulated. "Broadly speaking, that's true," he said. "My father, James Norcott, left the estate integrally to my brother Remington and myself. He couldn't have conceived of any division of Norcott land, and Remington and I would have carried out his wishes even if we hadn't worked hand and hand together as we did. Remington married, as you know, while I didn't. His wife died soon after but left a Norcott heir. That's how we've always thought of Jimmy. Remington passed away when Jimmy was ten. He willed everything to the boy, with myself as guardian until he came of age. At that time Jimmy takes over his half of the estate. At my death he takes over mine. If he should die before he's twenty-one the entire property would be in my hands. To an outsider who thinks in terms of Mine and Thine, I suppose I'd gain by Jimmy's death. How I'd be one whit better off, I defy anyone to say."

"Are there bequests of any kind contingent on his death?"

"Not a solitary one. Remington's will is on file. You can look at it. You can look at mine. I dare say you never saw simpler ones."

"What about Mrs. Remington Norcott's family?"

"They don't enter in at all. I don't even know any of them. She was a New England girl Remington met in New York."

"Do you mind telling me what kind of a will you'd make in case of your nephew's death?"

Norcott shot Bounty a quick glance, frowned and said stiffly: "I'm sure I can't say. I've never given the matter much thought. I've been counting on Jimmy pulling through."

Bounty let it go at that. "I know your nephew only by sight," he said. "It's a sign of old age that I keep thinking of him as a child. He's not. Is there any lead to all this in his own life?"

"I'm sure there's not. As a matter of fact, Jimmy is almost a stranger in this county. He's been away the last five winters. I admit I was panic-stricken when I realized I had all the responsibility for a ten-year-old. I didn't want to let him run wild on our ranches, yet I didn't want him to lose touch with the land that was to be his someday. Finally I sent him off to school in Nashville. During vacations I've kept him by me and close to the earth. I don't know whether I've acted wisely or not. Maybe I've made the contrast between the two kinds of life too great. Maybe his mother's blood is stronger in him than the Norcotts'. She was an artistic woman, used to a culture that we don't have here. Or didn't then. But in answer to your question—except with myself and my men Jimmy has had almost no associations here."

"It's hearsay that Christopher Hand has been acting as his body-guard this summer."

"Christopher is not a bodyguard!" Norcott contradicted tartly. "It's true the danger of kidnapping has always been in my mind, this near the border. But that's not the primary reason I've encouraged a friendship between Christopher and Jimmy. Christopher is the model I've wanted Jimmy to follow."

Bounty guessed that his host was seeking to change the subject, so he put out another feeler. He hadn't got what he wanted in this interview and he wasn't sure he was going to get it. "Christopher is a companion, then, rather than a bodyguard?"

"That and more." Norcott spoke aggressively, watching Bounty's face. "I know what you're driving at, Sheriff, and I'm going to be frank with you. I'm old and set in my ways. I've seen Jimmy growing away from me. That was to be expected, I suppose. But I didn't realize just what it might mean until the end of last summer, when I saw how anxious he was to return to school. He'd been bored. The ranch was a place to get away from. One by one all the roots that held him to his birthplace were going. I had to do something. Yet I knew that to take him from school and force him to stay with me would only defeat my object. Christopher was the answer. You don't know Christopher well, do you, Bounty?"

"I'm not sure I know him at all."

"Not many people do. He's the son of one of my tenants, a good enough man but utterly lacking in ambition. I've had my eye on Christopher ever since he was a little shaver. I saw to it that he got an education and that more and more opportunities were opened up to him with the Norcott interests. I watched him closely and he never disappointed me. He's a hard worker, he has a good business head, he's popular with the men. Last fall I took him on a trip, sounded him out and finally laid the whole situation before him. We reached a perfect understanding. When we got back Christopher came to make his home with me. So when Jimmy arrived for Christmas vacation, instead of having to put up with a dull old uncle whose horizon was bounded by fences and whose bedtime was nine o'clock, he found himself palling with a live young man who was all a boy that age looks up to. He enjoyed it and was eager to come home this spring. I gave Christopher an absolutely free hand. He and Jimmy have done a lot of running around but at the same time the boy has had to toe the mark more and more. For the first time, I think, he has got a grasp of what's ahead of him. What a mighty thing land is. What a responsibility it is, with a life of its own and human and animal life dependent on it. All that Jimmy has had from Christopher, not from me."

Norcott's face had lost its leathery, dour look, his voice the little circumspect pauses with which he had punctuated his speech, and Bounty wondered if he realized how much of his emotional bias he was letting transpire.

"You've been so interested in Christopher's exact status, Bounty. I've found, since I've been in town, how many other people are. Call him my business manager, my confidential secretary, if you like. He's been relieving me of all sorts of strain and worry. I've been giving him the feel of the reins so he in turn can teach Jimmy. If anything should happen to me he can grab them and hold on till Jimmy's ready to handle them."

"And when Jimmy is ready?"

"I retire and he and Christopher carry on just as my brother and I did." Norcott cleared his throat raspingly. "Let's get this settled once and for all. If Christopher's father hadn't been alive I'd have adopted him long ago. Nothing has ever been said but I'm sure he knows that. Jacob Hand's in poor health, the mother's gone. I'm going to mark time till Jimmy comes of age. Then, if the way's clear, I'm going to put it up to Jimmy. If he's willing—and I have every reason to believe he will be—I adopt Christopher, give him the Norcott name and turn over my share of the property to him. But that's all in the future. As things stand now, Christopher has no expectations from the Norcotts but a good and steady salary. And this: I've told him that when he decides to marry I give him a certain sum as a wedding present. I did that because I thought maybe he was hesitating on account of finances."

"I understand he goes with Doctor Ainsworth's daughter."

"Yes. Carrie and Christopher have always been friends, and I've often thought they'd make a good match. I can't tell how Christopher feels and I don't like to pry into his affairs. It's an awkward and rather distressing situation all the way round." Norcott said "Uh" a couple of times and then, in a tone of finality: "Now that's the whole story, Bounty. Christopher's future is bound up with the Norcotts. If you strain your imagination you can find a reason why he should wish Jimmy out of the way. You can do the same with me. But you'd never make anyone in Hesperides believe—"

He broke off and got hastily to his feet as the telephone rang in the room whose door Hand had left ajar. "Pardon me. We have only the one phone connected here and that's in Christopher's room. When this business is over I never want to hear another one ring as long as I live."

He closed the door. Bounty eyed it but decided that eavesdropping wouldn't be expedient.

"Doctor Lack's man," Norcott vouchsafed on his return. "They've had news of the death of Hieronymus out there and the fellow was calling for the doctor to find out if I'd heard from any more donors."

"Have you?"

"No," Norcott answered, squinting at Bounty through smoke.

"There's this man on the Aleutian Islands."

"How'd you know of him?"

"Doctor Cotillion told me."

"I'm not counting on the man getting here in time. But I'm certainly grateful to Cotillion for going to the trouble of locating him. He did it through a private inquiry agency. And in that connection, Bounty, I'd like to know of a detective hereabouts."

Bounty glanced at him quizzically. "Did you say a detective?"

"Yes. If there *is* a plot against Jimmy I've got to get to the bottom of it quick. You and the Las Palmas police have sense enough to know your own limitations, I hope. This is a job for an experienced investigator. Of course, I want one whose charges aren't too high."

Bounty shook his head. "I wouldn't know where to start looking if I wanted a detective."

"How about that fellow in Brownsville who solved a case for you once?"

"Hugh Rennert? He's way down in Juchitan or some such place in southern Mexico. He's out of the picture."

"I should think you'd get him back to help you out."

"Oh, I'll worry along by myself awhile," Bounty said nonchalantly. "You were fortunate in getting Doctor Lack to take your nephew's case, Norcott."

"Very fortunate. But—"

"A case of friendship, I suppose?"

"You can't say we're friends, no. I don't understand Lack and I'm sure he doesn't understand me. He had rooms here at the Sutherland while his house was being built. I met him then. Christopher introduced us. He'd met Lack through Carrie Ainsworth, who was his assistant at the time. Christopher seemed anxious for me to get to know him, so I made it a point to see him a few times. Neither of us could think of anything to say, but when I left I invited him to spend a weekend at the ranch. He couldn't come—at least said he couldn't—and that's as far as our acquaintance would have gone probably if Jimmy hadn't got this infection."

"Doctor Ainsworth is your regular physician, isn't he?"

"Yes, whenever we have needed one. When he pronounced streptococcus I was going to take Jimmy up to San Antonio. But he suggested I call in Doctor Lack, since Lack had had a streptococcus case recently. And it's typical of Hugh Ainsworth that he stepped aside as soon as Lack took the case. Lack hesitated at first, said he was getting ready to leave Las Palmas. Then he told me he couldn't make a drive out into the country, but if I'd bring Jimmy in to the hospital he'd do all he could. Do you know Doctor Lack?"

"I've met him."

"I was wondering if he'd been sick this spring."

"I believe he has."

"He seemed changed since I saw him last. So nervous and jumpy that—well, I admit I began to wish I hadn't called him. But after he'd been with Jimmy awhile he snapped out of it and got hold of himself. It's a miracle now the way that man changes when he steps into the sickroom. Jimmy simply worships him. I still can't get on to Lack, but it doesn't matter so long as he continues to be Jimmy's savior."

"Do you know his man Beck?"

"Only as Lack's shadow."

"Christopher knows him pretty well, doesn't he?"

"Oh, I don't think so. Though they may have developed an acquaintance recently. Beck was up here this morning looking for Christopher." There was a knock at the door and Norcott sprang to his feet. He checked himself at once and stood for a moment in indecision. "I expect I'll have to cut this session short here," he said to Bounty as he crossed the room.

From the way Norcott opened the door, Bounty thought that he was ready to step outside rather than invite his caller in. This proved to be Bert Larrick, however, and Norcott said in a queerly tense and eager voice: "Oh, hello, Bert. Come in."

Bounty was on his feet and going toward the table where his hat lay, since he had no desire to let Bert in for questioning on the part of anyone except himself.

"What's the news, Bert?" Norcott asked.

"There isn't any, Mr. Norcott. Doctor Cotillion's still at the morgue, waiting on Doctor Angelo. He doesn't want to commit himself about the poison until Angelo comes."

"And I expect you have a date tonight and didn't want to stay any longer."

Larrick grinned a little. "How'd you guess it?"

"Let's be going, son," Bounty said. "Good night, Norcott."

"Good night, Sheriff. Who's the girl, Bert?"

"Oh, she's from Minnesota. I think it's Minnesota. Someplace up there."

"The one Christopher met in the lobby?"

"Yes. Good night, Mr. Norcott."

"Let's go sit down, son," Bounty said as soon as the door was closed.

"Well, just a minute. Here are your keys. I left your car in the same place."

"Thanks, son." Bounty glanced at his deputy's hip as the latter sat beside him on a couch. "And thanks for not getting that gun."

"Well, I got to thinking about it and it seemed kind of silly. Besides, if I'd gone home my mother would have known what I came for and been worried. I want to get upstairs, though, as soon as I can. I called Mallory from the morgue and told her I was coming. Darn that Chris Hand! I knew I shouldn't have introduced him to Miss Winters. He must have done a lot of talking about her at dinner because Doctor Cotillion was asking me about her too. And I found out something else about Chris that's typical of him. He was with Mr. Norcott at the hospital this afternoon when Norcott invited Lack and Angelo and Doctor Cotillion to dinner. Doctor Lack declined then and there. Yet Chris told me this evening that Doctor Lack was coming. He just couldn't miss a chance to impress me, even if he had to lie. Huh!" Larrick's voice rose, then fell. "Wonder where Norcott's going in such a hurry?"

Roger Norcott had left his room and was making a beeline for the elevators. He glanced quickly about the mezzanine but failed to see Bounty and Larrick in the secluded spot which Bounty had chosen.

"What did you learn from him?" Larrick asked.

"Not who murdered Hieronymus, son," Bounty answered, watching the elevator doors close on Norcott and wishing he had men enough to tail everyone connected with this case.

"Did you ask him if he traced that call last night?"

"Yes. He denied it."

"I wonder— Tell me, Peter, do you think that means he suspected Chris of having something to do with it?"

"I shouldn't be surprised. Or rather he's been fighting his suspicion. Of course, he couldn't very well admit tracing it now. He'd have to explain why he didn't notify our office or the police at once. If I were in Hand's place, though, I wouldn't worry about my standing with Norcott. It would take a lot of evidence to convince Norcott that Chris was guilty of anything. And even then . . ." Bounty shrugged. "Son, I'm thinking of paying a call on Doctor Lack. I wanted to wait till I had some definite information on that poison but it looks as if I might as well go on. Is it my vile imagination at work or is there scandal about Miss Ainsworth and the doctor?"

"It's a lot of small-town gossip, that's all," Larrick answered heatedly. "You probably know how Doctor Ainsworth has always gone along. A large practice but it's mostly country and he never presses people on his bills. What little money he'd saved up he lost not long ago in some land investments. Carrie went to work then and everybody thought the better of her for it. When Doctor Lack came and advertised for an assistant she landed that place. She worked for him while he had a suite here and was to have continued after he moved into his home. But the town soured on Lack and pretty soon all the self-righteous old sisters were picking Carrie's reputation to pieces. Not that they had it in for her especially, but they did for Lack. And you know how tongues wag here. . . ."

"Same as everywhere, Bert."

"No, Las Palmas is worse than other places. Carrie had to give up her position. I hear Doctor Lack felt awfully bad about it and offered to get her a job in the East . . . anything. But she wouldn't accept a thing. I suppose she thought that would only add fuel to the fire. I admire Carrie for staying and braving it out. People are already forgetting about it. She'll be able to get another place soon. That is, if she doesn't marry Chris."

"How fares romance there?"

"I'd like to know. Chris goes with her more steadily than ever now, yet it does look to me as if they'd cooled toward each other."

"Aren't you a detective, son?"

"What?"

"Nothing." Bounty hid his grin. "What about another bulletin now on Beck?"

"Why are you so interested in him? Because of that trouble of his with the police?"

"Not necessarily. He just seems to keep cropping up. He came here with Doctor Lack from Boston, didn't he?"

"Yes, the only servant the doctor brought. And the only one who has stayed with him, I think. He had a big staff of local people at first. But they've either quit or he's fired 'em. I never heard of any personal complaint they had against Lack, except that he has to have things done differently from us. And he keeps that air-conditioned house of his like a refrigerator." Larrick drew breath.

"About Beck: I guess when you call him John Belton Lack's body servant you've said about all there is to say about him. If he ever has any time off he doesn't spend it in Las Palmas. He goes everywhere with the doctor. When Doctor Lack first came, you remember, he used to get around quite a bit and meet people. Beck sort of hovered in the background then. But now he's always right at the doctor's heels. As a matter of fact—speaking of bodyguards— I've heard it said that that's what Beck really is."

"Simply because he's always with Doctor Lack?"

"That's one reason. Then, if you notice Lack closely, darned if it doesn't look as if he were afraid of something. And you remember that one big splurge of his, when he had open house. Well, I went like everyone else. Chris was there, of course, getting an eyeful. He took me up to the master bedroom. There's the funniest arrangement there you ever saw. You go into a little hall, with a dressing room on one side and a bath on the other. In a closet right inside the dressing room is one of those in-a-door beds. The only place it could be let down is in that hall. And it must fill all the space between the door of the main hall and the door of the bedroom proper. If Beck sleeps there—and he must—that means he's lying across Doctor Lack's door. And, Peter, the windows in the master bedroom don't open!"

"You know this for a certainty, Bert?"

"Absolutely. I saw Chris try 'em. I suppose Doctor Lack's afraid of being kidnapped. Queer, isn't it, the way he turned out to be exactly the opposite of what everybody took him to be at first? Remember how pleasant he was? Stiff and a little embarrassed-like, of course, but he seemed to want to make friends and be part of the town. Then suddenly he froze. Whatever went wrong, he's all set to shut up or sell his house and shake the dust of Hesperides from his feet as soon as Jimmy Norcott gets well—or else doesn't. I'd heard that and Doctor Cotillion told me tonight that Angelo had had him over there this afternoon, trying to interest him in buying the place. I rather think Doctor Cotillion might do it. He said he wouldn't mind having a winter home down here. He doesn't like our summer, though. He said he'd been feeling sick and dizzy all day."

"He looked to me as if he weren't well. He thinks it's the heat, does he?"

"Yes, he's never been this far South before. He's dressed too heavy, for one thing. And he's been on the go all day. I told him he'd better get the siesta habit while he's here."

Bounty was silent for a moment, watching to see what passengers the elevator had carried on this trip. Roger Norcott wasn't among them.

"Son, since bodyguards seem to be coming into style in Hesperides, how'd you like to be Doctor Cotillion's?"

Larrick clapped a hand on Bounty's knee. "Peter, Doctor Cotillion said you'd spoken to him about that. I've been waiting for you to say something."

"I suppose I've got the wind up over nothing. But I don't like that speech that was made to him from the hall last night. And he seems to be the means of contact with the only blood donor in sight. So I've reserved suite 5A, off the mezzanine here, for you two. You won't be able to stay here at night, of course, on account of your mother—"

"Oh, that's all right. We rent a room, you know, to that new fellow in the bank. He's always there at night. Mother won't mind."

"Well, make sure she doesn't. Because it isn't necessary to make a day-and-night job out of this. To tell the truth, one thing I had in mind was to give you an opportunity to get acquainted with Doctor Cotillion. Something might come of it."

"I was thinking tonight, driving Doctor Cotillion to the morgue, what a chance this was for me," Larrick said eagerly. "The first time in my life anybody worth while ever noticed me. It's just the kind of boost I needed. I'd got to the point of thinking I might as well resign myself to sticking in this little burg and associating with—well, you know."

"I know, son. You won't have to do that much longer. You've been pretty dissatisfied?"

"Who wouldn't be—nothing but a deputy sheriff?"

Bounty cleared his throat. "Bert, what about you and me going downstairs and getting something to eat while we talk things over?"

"I've got a date upstairs. What is it you want to talk about?"

"I thought you might have something you'd like to say to me."

"Nothing special," Larrick said, looking at his watch. "Well, if there is—"

"What's the matter?"

"Roger Norcott's coming out of the elevator."

The landowner returned to his rooms more slowly than he had left them, frowning and snapping his fingers in evident impatience.

As his door closed on him Bounty said, "I think that's Jack Simmons on the left elevator. What about asking him where Norcott went?"

"O.K. Come on. So you're going over to Doctor Lack's now." Larrick halted suddenly, then went on toward the elevators. "That's funny," he murmured. "All the time you were talking about Beck I was trying to remember something. It's just come to me. Fred Winters asked me tonight if Doctor Lack had any white-haired relatives. And Beck's got the whitest hair you ever saw." Larrick punched the elevator button.

"How did Winters come to be asking about Doctor Lack?"

"We were talking about him in connection with the Norcott case. I judged that Fred had heard of the Lack family in the East. I'll ask him."

Bounty hesitated. "Bert, I'd like to go up with you and meet these Winterses."

"Oh, Peter!" Larrick was quick to protest, with a glance at an unpressed and shiny blue serge suit. "Of course," he said then, "come on up if you want to."

"Changed my mind, son. The height might make me dizzy."

The door slid open on an elevator empty save for an operator who, as far as physiognomy was concerned, didn't belie Bert's reference to him as a dumbbell.

"Hello, Jack," Larrick said, stepping into the car. "Hold on a minute. We're looking for Roger Norcott. Seen him?"

"He just got off, Bert."

"He did? Where'd he been, remember?"

"Uh—let's see. Fifth floor."

"Thanks. Well, Peter, be seeing you."

"Fifth floor again then, Jack," Bert Larrick said to the elevator boy as the door slid shut.

"What's goin' on up there, Bert?"

"What's going on? Why, nothing. Why?"

"I was just wonderin'. Red asked me about that guy the sheriff had over here. He said I said I took him to that floor last night—"

"You did, didn't you?"

"I guess so. And then Chris Hand has been goin' up there a lot this evening."

"Chris Hand? He was on the fifth floor about seven-thirty."

"He kept goin' up after that. And he was up there last night before he went to Brownsville. I thought maybe they had a blood donor hid out—"

"How do you know Chris went to Brownsville last night?"

"He told me so. That was about eleven. My bud knows Chris— or knew him before he got the big head—so I asked him if he was checkin' out of the hotel. He's been tippin' a lot since he's been here. But he said no, he was just goin' down to Brownsville for the night."

"Jack, don't say anything about this, will you not?"

"Sure not, Bert."

"Not to anyone—even the sheriff."

"All right, Bert. Watch your step there."

JOHN BELTON LACK had intended to build a home, not a house of mystery, Peter Bounty thought as he stood in the summer moonlight and surveyed the mansion on the southern outskirts of Las Palmas.

It was a rambling structure of white-painted brick veneer and clapboard, designed on the lines of the California Colonial with borrowings of graceful iron grillwork from old New Orleans. The shutters, always closed now, were green; the tiles of the roof had weathered to an unusual shade of deep salmon. Wings at the rear were said to embrace a patio, with terrace and sunken garden, swimming pool and tennis court beyond.

During its construction, when it dawned upon Las Palmas that a Croesus had come without fanfare into the community, there had been expectations of a bride to follow and of entertainment upon a princely scale. These seemed justified when simultaneously newspapers announced on their front pages the dedication of the John Belton Lack Hospital and society editors began their columns with word that on Sunday Dr. John Belton Lack would be at home, no invitations issued, in his newly completed residence.

Bounty knew that he had missed quite a circus by going sulkily to a movie that afternoon. No one had stayed away, overawed by magnificence, for by then Dr. Lack had made himself a familiar figure on the streets. He sat on park benches and leaned against drugstore fountains, for all to rub elbows with, and many of the brats who raced through his rooms and over his flower beds that

day had eaten ice cream cones with him. Society leaders were in
the crush and matrons with marriageable daughters took heart
when they were received by a bachelor who, while no Prince Charm-
ing, was unaccompanied and in his prime. Their eyes grew keener
when they found nothing but masculinity in evidence throughout
the mansion and they descended from an inspection of the master
bedroom thinking of dinner invitations that had better be extended
forthwith. Husbands proved ready allies and began sorting out
investment prospecti. Stories went the rounds of the benefactions
which Lack had in mind, of his distinguished family connections.
He had let it be known at once that he intended to devote himself
to research, not general practice; hence, with neither professional
ethics nor competition involved, his confreres could welcome him
and discourse upon his brilliance.

Then, with the town at his feet as he had seemed to wish, something had happened. Lack went into retirement. Callers were told
that he was ill, then that he was receiving no one. A few of these
rebuffs and the tide turned against him. People convinced themselves that he was a plutocrat who had sought to curry public
favor for reasons of his own, that they had seen through him and
that now he was nursing a grudge. He became an eccentric, a lib-
ertine, and there were dark speculations as to the true nature of
that laboratory which had been the one part of the establishment
where his guests hadn't had access.

The cynical smile with which Bounty had listened to echoes of
all this had never been at the expense of the man at the center of
the hurricane. He had observed Lack (as he was well aware the
doctor had observed him) without ever trying to shove a way to his
side, and he had marked many things to the newcomer's credit.
Oddly enough, from the general viewpoint, lack of ostentation was
one of them. Once, in the bank, Dr. Lack had introduced himself,
with the headlong manner of a person taking a cold plunge or, less
figuratively, of one in the extremity of embarrassment. Perhaps,
had the meeting taken place elsewhere, Bounty would not have
waited so long to go up this winding walk to an entrance porch
where black metal furniture once had stood and to lift the knocker

on a white door. But 'twas said that John Belton Lack kept that bank on its feet and Bounty had been there taking care of an over-draft occasioned by some of Bert Larrick's last-of-the month expenditures.

He was about to knock a second time when increased illumination came through the fanlight and, after a significant amount of unlocking and unbolting, the door was opened on well-oiled hinges.

"Good evening, Mr. Bounty. Please come in." The man in black and white who stepped aside so readily must have been near the age of Bounty and Dr. Lack. His dead-white hair looked like a toupee, perfect but placed by mistake over a plain tanned face. His was the voice whose clear cultured enunciation, coming over the telephone earlier that evening, had made Bounty take it for the physician's own. "Doctor Lack will be delighted to see you, I am sure. And I hope you will not think it out of the place if I anticipate my master's welcome by a very warm one of my own. I had begun to think I was never going to have this pleasure."

Goose flesh sprang out on Bounty once the door shut him in the spacious hall. "Thanks," he said as he handed over his gray felt hat with its round oily stain on the crown. "Your vote counts as much as anyone else's. And I don't mean that literally, Beck. This is Beck, isn't it?"

"Yes sir. Doctor Lack is in his study upstairs. Will you kindly be seated while I tell him that you are here. I think he will wish me to explain that most of the downstairs is closed."

"Just a moment, Beck. Maybe I came partly to see you."

"To see me, sir?" The man's dark gray eyes would have been rather handsome had they not looked so much like those of a faithful shepherd dog, anxious to understand and please.

"Yes," Bounty said. "Where's your room? We might go sit down a few minutes and compare notes on the weather."

"I have no room, sir."

"I mean—well, wherever you keep your things."

"What things, sir?"

"Oh, just things. Everybody has things."

"I am afraid I don't, sir."

Bounty's smile was slow in coming. And uncertain when it did come, for there was no brazenness in the fellow's manner. "Is that cold-shouldering me, Beck?" he asked.

"Please, sir, do not misunderstand me. I am altogether at your service. And Doctor Lack is most kind. If you express the wish, he will keep me in the room during your visit."

Bounty shook his head. He hadn't intended to make this little speech and he wondered just why he was doing so. "I meant it, Beck, when I said I wanted to talk to you. I don't know whether you know what about or not. But I'm going to have to poke into your private life, something I don't like to do with any man. While I'm at it I may bring out some little matters that aren't of any concern to me but that might be to your employer. Before I see him I'd like to put it to you straight. Would you prefer to come down to my office with me and talk things over with me alone? I've got big ears and a lot can go in one and out the other."

Beck's eyes were lowered. Bounty wished he could have looked directly into them then, for a great deal must have been mirrored there, judging by the sudden looseness about his mouth which might have been caused by the caving in of dental plates.

"May I ask one question, sir? Is Doctor David Angelo responsible for this visit?"

"Angelo?" Bounty repeated, trying to put two and two together. "No, Beck, he's not."

"Thank you, sir." Immediately the man had his composure back. "I see that your reputation for kindness and fair dealing is deserved. But do not hesitate to ask Doctor Lack what you please about me. There is nothing that he cannot and will not be glad to answer."

"Beck, when I hear a man say his life's an open book I want to make a bet with him I can find a page missing. What about it?"

"If it were my place to do so, I should accept that bet. May I leave you a moment now, sir?"

"I think I've got an old campaign card about me someplace, if you want to take that. Maybe you'd better not, though. The picture offsets the nice things it says about me."

"No card is necessary, sir."

As the man crossed to the wide staircase which rose at the left, Bounty went to a mahogany love seat. Baroque, he thought, was the name for the border design of the mahogany brown floor and of the pale gray and white walls. White doors on either side and at the rear were closed and there was no sound at all in the place.

Beck's soft-soled shoes made no sound as he went to the rear of the upper hall or as he returned and came down the stairs. "Doctor Lack is most anxious to see you, sir."

Bounty found the waxed floor hard going. "Beck," he said as he gained the stairs, "I think I've heard Christopher Hand speak of you."

"Christopher Hand, sir? That was kind of Mr. Hand."

"I forget what he said the rest of your monicker was."

"I doubt that Mr. Hand knows it, sir. It is John."

"Middle name? I collect 'em."

"Allton, sir.

"John Allton Beck," Bounty repeated in a smothered voice and reached for his handkerchief. "Been with Doctor Lack long?"

"All my life, sir," the man answered as they went down a hall which had two white double-cross doors on the left and one on the right.

Bounty gasped and loosed a succession of violent sneezes. "'Scuse me," he murmured then, stuffing the handkerchief into his pocket. "Lead on, Beck."

The latter opened the door at the end of the hall and gave a quick discreet glance across the room before he lowered his eyes and announced distinctly: "Mr. Bounty, sir."

The room imposed itself first upon the visitor: a long book-lined study, the bar of a T, of which the hall was the upright. The severity of its gray and deep green and mahogany was tempered by touches of that same salmon shade. In front of a flat-topped mahogany desk facing the door, against a background of pale gray curtains and white and salmon drapes, posed salmon-haired John Belton Lack.

The red hair which was the butt of so many jokes about town wasn't red. Salmon described it with only fair exactitude. It was peculiar, arresting hair, fluffy-looking as if it had just been sham-pooed, but after your first stare at it you found it exceptionally handsome.

Dr. Lack's hands were clasped behind a sack coat of black or midnight blue whose natural shoulders and uncompromising straight lines did nothing to fill out his fine-drawn body. This was a pose, undoubtedly, and an effective one. John Belton Lack was master of that room and by demonstrating his mastery he projected John Belton Lack and became master *in* that room.

A man who went to all that trouble was vulnerable. Bounty strode across the thick-napped rug, extended his hand and said bluffly: "Good evening, Doctor! Glad to see you again."

Lack reacted as a poised and punctilious gentleman might react to the prick of a pin at his rear. He came forward with a little lurch and gave Bounty a cold, firm-fleshed hand, but before he spoke his eyes went over the blue serge shoulder to the door. His were pale gray-blue eyes clouded now by a milky look which made it difficult to interpret that quick glance.

"I am very glad to see you again, Mr. Bounty," he said in a low and precise but nervous voice, then came out with an incisive "Beck!" that made Bounty turn to see what misconduct the other was guilty of. To his surprise, when the man stepped dutifully forward Dr. Lack laid a hand on his back and said: "Mr. Bounty, I wish you would shake hands with Mr. Beck as you have done with me."

"Bet your life, Doctor. We should have done this at the door, Mr. Beck."

Bounty wasn't sure that Lack didn't deserve a kick for this move. Fleeting as was the alteration in Beck's countenance, the sheriff caught it and stored its image in his memory. The man had flinched involuntarily, as if Lack had borne down upon a spot which in a literal sense was unbearably sore, and a tightness at the corners of his mouth had given the lower part of his tanned face a distinct resemblance to the physician's. He presented Bounty with a strong hand which suffered by comparison with Lack's fine one but he inclined his head as he did so, and when he spoke he kept his eyes lowered.

"My master's kindness in giving me this privilege makes me wish I could serve him better, Mr. Bounty. Perhaps I can by putting myself at your service."

Lack's hand had fallen. His pale sensitive face grew paler, revealing all his bleached-looking salmon freckles, and his lower lip was held between his teeth while he stared for an instant at the floor. "Let's sit down, Mr. Bounty," he said suddenly, obviously acquiescing in Beck's definition of his own status by excluding him from the invitation.

The servant moved with alacrity to a club chair of dark green leather, shifted it a fraction of an inch and stood behind it while Bounty sank self-consciously into its depths. He was behind a companion chair in time to see his master flip up his coattails before his seat touched leather. "I beg your pardon, sir." He spoke at Dr. Lack's elbow. "I am afraid the temperature of the room is too low for Mr. Bounty's comfort."

"It is? Then regulate it. At once." That edged, nagging voice, with its little rasp of sibilance, was one which would soon chafe the nerves of a listener, since it was itself the product of nervousness as much as of the vexation which the doctor plainly felt either at his servant or at himself.

"Don't bother." Bounty was careful to delay his protest until Beck was already on his way to a gadget in a corner by one of the pair of doors that flanked the desk. "I'm not exactly a hothouse plant, Doctor."

"Neither do I want you to look for snow in the air of my home, as no doubt you did."

"I'd be the last person to do that," Bounty assured him, the while he worked out an idea about voices. "I never saw snow."

Beck was at his post again, his eyes fixed on the freckle-blotched back of one of Dr. Lack's hands. "Will there be anything else, sir?"

No, Bounty thought, that wasn't Beck's own voice at all. It was Lack's, at a moment when the doctor was calm and grave but emotionless in his dominance over a patient. Easy to believe that the servant had made a recording at such a time, that he had applied himself to its study until he had mastered it in everything it had of individuality and that now he was no more than a tuning fork to remind that voice's owner how far off pitch he was. . . .

"Yes, Beck." Whether or not the voice in his ear was responsible, the physician's voice had lost some of its insistent stinging quality and he was leaning back in his chair with more signs of relaxation than he had yet shown. "See if you can't find an ash tray for Mr. Bounty. And, Beck, we have some whisky for this occasion."

"I am sorry to say, sir, that we do not."

"Thanks just the same," Bounty spoke up. "But I don't smoke or drink."

He doubted that Lack knew what he said, so intent was the doctor on Beck's face. "Surely, Beck, we have. I had you get a bottle, you remember, with Mr. Bounty in mind."

"That was some time ago, sir. Doctor Angelo took that bottle away with him."

"Oh." Lack's eyes fell. "Quite all right. That will be all, Beck."

Bounty stared after a back which, save for that white cap of hair, might have been that of John Belton Lack with some much-needed meat on his bones. He stared for a moment at the closed door, then, realizing that he had had a match in his mouth and had spat a sliver of wood to the floor, he turned his head and spoke hastily, to cover up his lapse: "John Allton Beck. Not unlike John Belton Lack, Doctor."

"It is a rearrangement of the letters of my name, yes. Please do not form a false impression from that matter of the whisky, Mr. Bounty. Doctor Angelo will have needed it for a patient. He is an abstainer. As I am myself. I am glad to find the three of us in accord on this."

Bounty, having seen Angelo with hangovers, could only look owlish. "I'm probably not in accord with you," he said. "Alcohol and nicotine are all right. I like 'em. But they dull my other appetites. And I'd rather indulge those. When I can't—"

"Yes, yes," Lack said hastily. "That isn't the case with me. With me it's not a matter of principle, however, but of digestion. Digestion," he repeated, as if he hoped Bounty would carry on the conversation from there.

Bounty studied his face, a face which acquired no softness from the subdued glow of a lamp whose shade was of some frosty-looking material banded with salmon. Remove John Belton Lack from all this stage setting, divest him of the halo that wealth, birth and scientific achievement gave him, and what had you? Superficially, a man who thirty or more years ago was a freckled redhead like that Sutherland bellhop. Regard him more closely, however, and every feature of him became distinguished, refined by the fervor of a fire deep within him and peculiar to him. Those freckles, for instance. They made his skin look rather like a speckled eggshell, but you wouldn't notice them and think how they enhanced his appearance if there weren't illumination behind to throw them into relief. Yet, for the man's own sake and for that of others, Bounty thought that some good yellow yolk inside that shell would be safer, even if it did make for opaqueness. Yon Cassius had a lean and hungry look.

"Do you mind telling me something about Beck, Doctor?"

Lack sighed and stared at the sharp crease in one of the knees of his trousers. "After that blunder of mine I owe you an explanation, Mr. Bounty. I have reason to know how anxious Beck has been for you to come here. During our first days in Las Palmas I had him make a survey of the community, in order that he might assist me in certain projects which—which came to naught. I wanted a social study but I have wondered at times if he didn't misunderstand the term. He has since undertaken to advise me as to the acquaintances I should seek. First and foremost of these was yourself. And I may say, Mr. Bounty, that in this case I concurred with him without reservation. If you feel that a personal compliment is out of place, pray take that as one paid to a public official." Lack's smile was a constrained one but it was a smile. "So on your first visit I acted on an impulse and gave Beck an opportunity to meet you on an equal footing. In a way, I felt, it was his right. He knew I was sincere, yet you saw what happened. All he wanted was to make a lackey out of himself for you. That's exactly what he shall do hereafter."

"Well, Doctor, precisely what is his position?"

"Beck is my valet," Lack stated emphatically. "Disregard that gesture of mine and treat him as such."

"I imagine in this instance it's particularly hard for both of you to keep your footing always in mind. You two must have grown up together."

"Scarcely that. Beck has been with me fourteen years."

"I understood him to say all his life."

"Did he say that?" Lack's manner became fluttery again. He took an ivory paper cutter from the drop-leaf table beside his chair and began to bend it back and forth. "Well, if that's the way he wants to put it, all right."

"I suppose he meant that when he came to you he shed his old skin and grew a new one."

"Something like that." Firmly Lack put down his plaything and folded his hands.

"How inquisitive would you consider me, Doctor, if I asked how much you pay Beck?"

"I don't mind telling you that Beck shares everything I have."

That rotund statement grew and grew in Bounty's mind until it became all at once exceedingly vague. "You don't pay him straight wages then?" he persisted.

"Wages? No."

"Well, suppose he wants a new suit. Not to wear on duty necessarily. Just new duds. How does he go about getting them? Does he ask you for money or has he credit at the stores?"

"Beck doesn't have to worry about clothes. We wear the same size, so I keep him supplied from my wardrobe. Well supplied. In fact, I buy many of my things with Beck in mind."

"Suppose he wants a lollipop?"

Lack stared at him blankly. "A what?"

"A lollipop," Bounty repeated innocently. "You know—something tasty, sugary, frivolous."

"Beck and I don't eat those things. Our digestion won't permit it."

On that "our digestion" Bounty had to nip off the end of a match. "I never see Beck around town, except occasionally when he's driving you," he said, pursuing his study of the workings of paternalism. "What company does he keep, do you know?"

"What company?"

"Yes, who are his friends here?"

Lack became remote. "I can't say that I have found Hesperides a very friendly place, Mr. Bounty. Doctor Angelo is the only visitor who ever comes here. And our friendship dates back to other days."

"If you don't mind, Doctor, I was talking about Beck. Hasn't he made any friends of his own? Christopher Hand, for instance."

"Hand?" The name went up Lack's nasal passages. "I don't know what you can be thinking of, Mr. Bounty."

"Beck knows Hand, doesn't he?"

"May I ask if Hand is a friend of yours?"

"Not at all, Doctor. Let's have the dirt."

Lack frowned. "There isn't any dirt. I was merely going to answer your question in the only way it can be answered. Beck knows Hand as an individual to whom I am not at home."

"What have you got against Hand, Doctor?"

"Oh, nothing, nothing!" Lack said ill-humoredly. "As a matter of fact, I feel sorry for him. But that is no reason I should let myself be worn out by his visits. After my—my open house he took to calling almost every day. I know I have hurt his feelings but I saw I had to hold him at arm's length. He calls me Doc. Is that enough?"

"Plenty. His father is a patient of yours, isn't he?"

"I have examined Jacob Hand. At Mr. Norcott's request. That is a professional relationship, not a social one. I wish someone would explain the distinction to young Hand."

"Suppose Beck happened to like Hand, Doctor?"

"I don't dislike him, Mr. Bounty, please understand that. If he would ever quit slapping me on the back I might even find a means of helping him make some adjustments. He is groping after immaterial things and he can't take his eyes off the material."

"I'm still talking about Beck, though. He and Hand—well, I'll put it this way: both sort of gravitate about wealth. What if they found each other congenial and wanted to go out and make mud pies together?"

"I'm not sure I grasp your meaning. Beck is a free agent, of course. But he must be fifteen years older than Hand. His background is different. It's ridiculous to think of any congeniality between them."

"But just supposin' that there were. What attitude would you take?"

Lack held his right hand in front of him and stared at it as he rubbed together the tips of the sensitive fingers. "I should have to ask Beck to put an end to it," he said, "as promptly and painlessly as possible."

That's what Bounty thought. "Where does Beck spend his time when he's off duty?" he inquired casually.

"Why"—the tiny diamond on the little finger flashed as Lack subjected his, left hand to the same scrutiny—"he is always with me."

"Surely not always, Doctor. You must give him an afternoon or evening off now and then."

"I took him with me to see a revival of *The Life of Louis Pasteur* not long ago."

Bounty sighed. "Doesn't he ever spend a week end down at the beaches? He looks more tanned than when I saw him last."

"You must be mistaken. I hadn't noticed it. But Beck wouldn't have to go to the beach if he wanted to swim. I have a fine pool at the rear of my house. It's dry, because I don't swim. But if he were to take it into his head that he needed that form of exercise, he could fill it whenever he wished."

"It strikes me Beck's a very lucky man," Bounty said, priming the other for more pointed questions.

A tiny smirk at one side of Lack's mouth told how pleased he was. "Beck doesn't have a care in the world," he said. "Except myself. And he seems to bear up under that, don't you think?"

"Oh, admirably. But still, Doctor, I'd like to seize on that statement that he's with you all the time. Just how literally do you mean that? Take these last two days for example."

"The last two days? All right." Lack accepted it as a challenge apparently. "Saturday and Sunday. Beck has been out of sight or sound of me only twice. And then for no more than half an hour at a time."

"I was thinking that someone had mentioned seeing him at the airport last night."

"He was there, but for only a few moments. I sent him with my car to meet Doctor Cotillion. I had him return when I learned the plane was late. Oh, I see what gave you the idea that Beck and Christopher Hand were friends. When Beck called me about the plane he told me Hand was there with a car. I thought there was no need of both of them staying."

"There seems to have been a misunderstanding about who was going to take charge of Doctor Cotillion."

"Yes." Lack's manner grew hesitant, then he plunged ahead. "I expect you're wondering why he is not a guest here. With Beck my only servant, I didn't feel that I had the facilities. And there *was* a bit of awkwardness about the matter. I was taking it for granted that Mr. Norcott would see to his entertainment. But when I talked with him yesterday I saw that he thought it was up to me. So I made reservations for him at the Sutherland."

Lack had side-stepped something here, Bounty thought, but he decided to leave that for further examination. "And when was the other time that Beck was separated from you, Doctor?"

"This morning. My paper wasn't delivered and he went to get me one."

"What about the time you spend in the hospital?"

"He never leaves my side. He is more than my assistant. He's my right hand."

"He assists you in the research you do here in your home?"

"I have done no research here," Lack said bitterly. "My life in Hesperides has been a futile pottering, one round of caring for my animal needs."

"Do you keep any poisons in your house, Doctor?"

"Poisons! No, I keep no poisons." The milky suffusion was back in Lack's eyes. "Is that what brought you here? To link my home with the death of that blood donor tonight?"

"How did you hear the news, Doctor?"

"Doctor Cotillion called to cancel the engagement we had at nine-thirty. He had volunteered to collaborate with me on tests of the man's blood, to determine whether he still had immunity to streptococcus. He said you wanted as little publicity as possible. So I have been waiting for you to broach the subject. I didn't think you would go at it in this way."

"Don't be too hard on me, Doctor. I'm no detective, as I was given to understand tonight. Did Cotillion say anything about the cause of death?"

"No, he had just arrived at the morgue. He promised to call me later."

"Had you had any experience with this J. J. Hieronymus?"

"Experience? Why no."

"He never visited you or communicated with you?"

"No." Lack twisted the ring about his little finger. "Tell me, Sheriff—I suppose I had better address you as Sheriff now—do you actually put any credence in this talk of a plot to intimidate our blood donors?"

"What do you think, Doctor?"

"How should I know? Mr. Norcott spoke to me about it at the hospital this afternoon. It all seemed so vague, so fantastic, that I was inclined to dismiss it lightly."

"And what did you think when Doctor Cotillion called?"

"Of my patient. This may be his death warrant. But you evaded my question."

"I'll answer it this way: I hear something crawling about on the floor and I can't find it. It may be a conspiracy. It may be some perfectly harmless critter. But a man was bitten tonight with fatal results and it's up to me to do some exploring. I came to get you to help me."

"I'll help you. Certainly I'll help you." Lack got to his feet and slipped his hands into his pockets. "But when you come and ask these questions about Beck—" He caught his breath. He turned on his heel, strode around the desk and stood looking at Bounty across the expanse of polished mahogany. "So that's it, is it?" The rasp in his voice was a vicious one. "You came to trump up another charge against my man. While you pretended this was a friendly visit. I offered you my friendship once, Bounty, in all humbleness. You rejected it. Yet I was ready to give you another chance tonight. I see now you're like everyone else in this Godforsaken country. You're envious of me. You're hitting at me where you can hurt me the most. But if you think I'm helpless, you're mistaken. You don't realize the legal forces I can bring against you." He sat down. "Say what you have to say now. And be quick about it."

Bounty lolled in his chair, telling himself that he had been right about this man. There were potentialities for cruelty in the set of that finely chiseled mouth and in the gleam of those mother-of-pearl eyes. At a memory he felt like crossing himself. Someone had quoted someone else as saying that anger brought out a resemblance between John Belton Lack and Peter B. Bounty. . . .

"Lack, my friend," he said easily, "let's you and I take a drive out into the desert one of these days. Where we can't see anything but each other and space. Each of us has rancor to get out of his system. I have, I know. When you introduced yourself to me I wasn't at ease. I didn't want to fawn on you like everybody else, so I suppose I acted churlish. I'm envious of you, if you wish. Because of some of those immaterial things you have. But tonight, when I found I had an excuse to come here, I jumped at the chance. I thought I could show my friendship by clearing your man right at the outset of this business. Before any more suspicion is turned on him and before things get out of my hands. Now—"

Both looked at the door as a light knock sounded. "Come in," Lack called.

Beck entered, glancing quickly at Bounty before he looked at Lack, and said: "Doctor Angelo is downstairs, sir."

"Bring him up."

Beck seemed to have lost the power of movement and stood staring at Lack's hands, which were folded on the desk.

"Bring Doctor Angelo up at once, Beck." The flick in that voice sent the man posthaste out the door.

Lack frowned after him for several moments, then looked at Bounty and said evenly: "Mr. Bounty, I let myself be carried away just now. That happens so often that I have ceased asking people to forgive me. I am afraid you must accept my temper if you accept me. But I am always ready to acknowledge when I have been unfair. I was to you. You are doing your duty exactly as you should. I don't like it, but then I dare say you don't either."

"Bygones are bygones, Doctor."

Beck returned. "I am sorry to say, sir, that Doctor Angelo had left by the time I got downstairs."

Lack crooked his neck and looked up at him from under sharply circumflex eyebrows. "What's this, Beck?" he snapped.

"I thought I heard a car drive away as I was going down, sir. When I failed to find Doctor Angelo in the hall I looked outside. His car was neither in front nor in the drive."

"He left no message?"

"No sir."

"This sounds very odd, Beck. Get Doctor Angelo on the phone at the earliest possible moment."

Heedless of decorum, Bounty slung a leg over the arm of his chair. He was becoming extremely curious about Angelo's off-stage activities. "Wait a minute, Beck," he drawled. "Did you tell Doctor Angelo I was here?"

"No sir."

"My car's out front. Did he ask if Doctor Lack had company?"

"No sir."

"Can you hear the knocker from here, Beck?"

"Yes sir."

"Well, then . . ." Bounty turned to Lack. "Angelo hasn't had time to get any place yet. I'd like to take this chance to ask Beck some questions."

Lack stiffened. "Must we go over that again?"

"Trouble is, we haven't been over it at all, Doctor."

"Please, sir," Beck interposed, going to the desk. "May I remind you that Mr. Bounty has been most considerate this evening? It is part of his duty to question me. By doing so before you he shows his respect for you and he gives me the benefit of your counsel. Please do not fail me, sir."

Beck was smart, Bounty decided. Also, he was willing enough to admit, Beck seemed straightforward, although that tan gave the lie to some of the doctor's statements about him.

Lack cleared his throat several times, loudly. "I hadn't looked at things in just that light, Beck." He spoke in a mollified tone. "But your interests are mine, of course. I shall always make them so. I must say, this is very fine, Beck. Very fine. I am really very happy to be of service to you." A lump seemed to form in his throat and he reached for his handkerchief. "Sit down, won't you?"

Beck stared for an instant at the salmon hair. "Thank you, sir," he said with an effort. He brought a straight chair from against the wall and placed it at a corner of the desk. Bounty, watching closely, saw little white arcs appear at the tightly held corners of his mouth as he sat down and gripped his knees.

Something perverse had left the room. It was as if an electrical discharge had cleared the air or an unfelt breeze had cleaned it of particles of irritating dust. Bounty knew that the change emanated from Lack, who had crossed his legs and was leaning back and staring at the ceiling, like a contented man about to blow a smoke ring.

Bounty wondered if he were tossing up a handful of pepper as he said: "What I want, Beck, is a little history of yourself. Beginning last night about eight, say, and continuing up to the time you opened the door for me tonight. Feel equal to it?"

Lack lifted a hand. "Beck"—he spoke in a judicious tone—"I believe Mr. Bounty is justified in making that request. It is hard, I know, to have one's privacy invaded but we mustn't think of that. Give him an account of your actions, holding back nothing but making it as concise as possible. Are you comfortable there, Beck? We might move to other chairs."

"Thank you, sir. I am very comfortable." Beck folded his arms and looked directly at Bounty. Odd, the latter thought, how he seemed increasingly to assume faint reflections of Lack's facial expressions. Their mouths were dissimilar but when Beck's fuller, grosser lips met in that prim way you recognized Lack's primness. Fourteen years of this close association and one man, the dominant one, without a doubt would have left more than outward stamps of his personality on the other.

"At eight o'clock last night I served Doctor Lack his dinner as usual," Beck stated. "At eight forty-five he excused me and I drove his car to the airport to meet the nine o'clock plane. Since the plane was late, I returned, arriving here at about nine-fifteen."

"Let's have the particulars of your stop at the airport," Bounty said.

"I arrived at exactly nine, sir. Mr. Christopher Hand was waiting in his car. He got out as I did, greeted me and we entered the waiting room together. I looked at the bulletin board, saw that the Chicago plane was late and went to the telephone booth. I called Doctor Lack and received his order to return. I did so at once."

"Hand was waiting on you?"

"He was waiting on the plane, sir, but I believe that he had been sitting in his car until I arrived."

"He knew you were coming, then."

"Yes sir."

"How'd he know it?"

"Doctor Lack had told him and Mr. Norcott that afternoon that he was sending me."

"And did you know Hand was going to be there?"

"Yes sir. During the discussion at the hospital it was arranged that Mr. Hand should drive Doctor Cotillion to the hotel, since he was already staying there. I was to be at the airport merely to pay Doctor Lack's respect to Doctor Cotillion."

Lack stirred in his chair. "Mr. Bounty, I can't say I like these tactics. It sounds as if you were trying to trip us up on some statement. It can't be of the slightest importance—"

"I don't really think this is of importance either, Doctor. But if I find many more statements that don't jibe, I'll begin to think it is. You said you had Beck come back from the airport because he told you over the phone that Christopher Hand was there with a car. Yet you knew Hand was going to be there."

"All right," Lack said sulkily. "I wanted Beck here, that's all there is to it."

"Fair enough. And, Beck, since we're at dagger's points, I wish you'd tell me why you thought it necessary to call Doctor Lack."

Beck was silent for a time, too long a time, gazing at the opposite wall. "I hadn't had my own dinner yet," he said suddenly. "I hoped that Doctor Lack would give me permission to return and eat it."

"Of course!" Lack clapped a hand on the arm of the chair. "I won't have Beck go hungry just for the sake of a courteous gesture. I must say, Sheriff—"

"Score one for you, Beck." Bounty had had to grin but there was no amusement in his eyes as he looked back at the valet. "How many calls did you put in at that telephone booth?"

"The one, sir."

"Any idea who had used that booth just before you?"

"No sir."

"All right. Let's hear just what passed between you and Hand."

Beck hesitated and his breathing was uneven. "Nothing of any consequence, sir," he said at last.

Lack frowned and his eyes moved slowly in that direction. "Mr. Bounty seems to think it is, Beck. Better tell him."

"Very well, sir. Mr. Hand—"

"You need not call him Mister."

"Yes sir. Hand said: 'Hello, Beck. I was beginning to think you weren't going to get here. How's Doctor Lack?' I replied that Doctor Lack was very well. As we went into the waiting room he said: 'I expect Doctor Cotillion will want to see Doctor Lack this evening. If he does, I'll bring him over. That is, if Doctor Lack will be at home. He never seems to be any more.' I told him that I was unable to say as to my master's plans but I suggested that he call first. I went to the telephone then. I returned, told Hand of my orders and left him."

"Open book, Beck," Bounty said softly.

"I beg your pardon, sir? Oh." The man's face stiffened. "I forgot to mention," he said deliberately, "that when I went to the booth I found I had no money. I had to go back and borrow a nickel from Hand."

"What's that?" Lack turned on him. "Why, Beck!"

"I knew you would wish me to call, sir, and I saw no other way to do it. Hand had no smaller change than a quarter. He told me to go to the vending machine across the room, get him a package of cigarettes and keep the nickel. I did so. When I left, I thanked him again and told him I would repay the loan as soon as possible. He said to forget it and reminded me of something he has asked for several times. Labels from Doctor Lack's suits. That was all. I returned and reported to Doctor Lack. Then I cleared away his dinner things and prepared my meal. He was kind enough to come to the kitchen and keep me company while I ate. Doctor Angelo arrived as I was finishing. I let him in, then returned to the kitchen. Afterwards I went to Doctor Lack's dressing room and was busy there until Doctor Angelo left about eleven. I assisted Doctor Lack to retire, then read to him."

"Hand didn't bring Doctor Cotillion over, then?"

"No," Lack answered. "Doctor Cotillion called me, as I told you. Hand seemed to have him in tow and was taking him to meet Mr. Norcott. So I made an appointment with him for eleven-thirty this morning. And, in case you want to know, Mr. Bounty, Beck read to me most of the night. I am troubled by insomnia and he reads me to sleep regularly. I lost track of the time but he told me this morning it was about four when I finally dropped off. Four, you said, didn't you, Beck?"

"Yes sir. I hope, Mr. Bounty, you will not think this a task for me. I enjoy reading and Doctor Lack is kind enough to consult my tastes. If I have your leave to continue, I retired then and arose at my usual time, seven. I bathed, shaved, dressed and had my breakfast. I was putting the study to rights when Doctor Lack rang about eight-thirty. I served him his breakfast in his bedroom. I had discovered that the morning paper had not been delivered and I received his permission to go after one. I was absent for not more than half an hour."

"Where'd you go for a paper?"

"To the newsstand in the lobby of the Sutherland."

"You passed at least one newsstand on the way."

"No doubt I did, sir. I am none too familiar with the town and thought only of the hotel. While I was there I decided it might be well to repay Hand's nickel. I went to his room but Mr. Norcott informed me he had not returned from Brownsville." Beck paused. "You had a question, sir?"

"No," Bounty said. "Go on."

"I left the money and a note of thanks with Mr. Norcott. I came back and gave Doctor Lack the paper. While he was reading it I called the hospital and got a report on how young Mr. Norcott had passed the night. Doctor Lack transmitted some orders through me. He arose about nine-thirty. Until shortly before eleven-thirty I was assisting him to dress."

"Two hours to dress, Doctor?" Bounty said maliciously.

"What's that?" Lack had been inattentive, slumped down in his chair. "Oh, not always that long. This was the morning for a shampoo and Beck likes to take his time at that. Also, I'm inclined to dawdle. But perhaps you had better continue, Beck."

"Yes sir. I drove Doctor Lack to the Sutherland, went in and called for Doctor Cotillion at eleven-thirty. Then I drove them to the hospital, was with them for an hour or so, returned Doctor Cotillion to the hotel and Doctor Lack here. I served Doctor Lack his lunch at one. Afterwards"—Beck hesitated—"he came to the kitchen and sat with me while I ate. We remained there for some time, talking. At three-thirty I drove him to the hospital again, where he met Doctor Cotillion, who was with Mr. Norcott and Christopher Hand. We were there until about five, when I drove Doctor Lack back here. Shortly after our return Doctor Angelo brought Doctor Cotillion and I showed them over the house and grounds. From six-thirty until seven-thirty I was with Doctor Lack in his dressing room. At eight I served him his dinner. He finished at nine. When you knocked, Mr. Bounty, he was sitting with me in the kitchen."

"Then, Doctor, you didn't have another dinner engagement, as you told Mr. Norcott," Bounty said.

"No. That was one of the little lies we have to tell in order to live in a society and have a modicum of privacy. I'm under a strict diet. I can eat few of the things other men do. I prefer not to go and be a skeleton at the feast."

"If there are no more questions, sir," Beck said to Bounty, "have I your permission to retire?"

Bounty stared cross-eyed at the end of a match. "You've had your say, Beck?"

"Yes sir."

"Guess that's all then." Bounty suppressed a yawn. "Pardon. By the bye, Beck," he said as the valet rose and carried his chair to its place against the wall, "I haven't had time to look at my funnies today. What was the paper you got this morning?"

"The Hesperides *Sun*, sir."

"Good. It has Flash Gordon and Jungle Jim. Wonder if I might have your copy. It'll be my bedtime reading."

"I am afraid I have disposed of the paper, sir."

Lack had been staring moodily at the desk. He looked up now, with interest, and said: "If it's the comic section you want, Mr. Bounty, I can supply you. Call Doctor Angelo, Beck, then bring it to him. I forget which of the bathrooms I left it in."

"Yes sir." Beck went mechanically to the door.

There was silence when he had gone. Had Lack met Bounty's eyes, he must certainly have read disgust there. Bounty felt as if he had taken John Belton Lack's immaculate patrician hand only to discover that those weren't freckles on his skin but malignant discolorations.

"So you're a devotee of the comic strips, too, Doctor?"

"As a matter of fact—well, yes, I am. Beck has learned not to destroy that section on Sunday but to leave it where I can pore over it at my odd moments during the day. Somehow, Mr. Bounty, I didn't imagine you needed that escape into a world of fantasy and derring-do."

"Everybody needs it at times. The kingdom of Mongo and the Java Seas are healthier places to escape to than some I can think of. Do you let Beck look at your colored pictures, too, Doctor?"

"Excuse me a moment, Mr. Bounty," Lack murmured, opening the center drawer of his desk and busying himself with its contents. "I just remembered a very important memorandum I must look up." He raised his head to call, "Come in," at Beck's knock.

Folded under his arm Beck had the brightly colored outer section of the Sunday newspaper. "Doctor Angelo is on the line, sir. I found him at his apartment," he said to Lack, then turned and handed Bounty the paper without meeting the latter's eyes.

"I'll talk to him here," Lack said. He drummed on the mahogany and didn't look at Bounty while Beck produced a telephone from a compartment at his side, plugged in the wire, set the instrument in front of him and placed the receiver in his hand.

"David?" His voice strained at eagerness but his eyes rested in a milky brooding stare on the back of the man who was moving soundlessly to the door. "What do you mean by going off that way? I wanted to see you."

Bounty rose, went into the hall after Beck and closed the door.

Beck stood waiting, his face impassive, his eyes lowered.

Bounty unfolded the paper, glanced along the top, folded it again and stuck it into a pocket. "I didn't know the Sutherland had quit stamping the name of the hotel on every paper they sell," he said quietly and turned back to the study. "Sorry, Beck. I gave you your chance."

10

"Wʜᴀᴛ ʜᴀᴠᴇ ʏᴏᴜ got all these windows and blinds down for?" Bert Larrick demanded, tugging at his collar as he strode back and forth across the hotel room, between the bed where Fred Winters lay flat on his back, disgorging smoke, and the chair in which Mallory sat with half-closed eyes. "You'd think we were expecting a Mexican air squadron to fly over and bomb the town. I tell you there's nothing to be afraid of. There's no crazy killer running wild. What if somebody did knock at your door? Why couldn't it have been somebody to see you on business, Fred?"

"Quit pacing," Fred said. "Call the morgue again and try to find out what Hieronymus died of."

"No use. Doctor Cotillion won't have talked to Doctor Angelo yet. Mallory, you've got to have some fresh air. You look as if you were about to faint. Come on, let's go up to the roof garden."

Mallory lowered her hand, with the wadded handkerchief into whose corner her teeth had been sunk. "I'm feeling better now. It was the smell of that flower, whatever it is. It was so strong when we came in I had to close the windows."

"Oh, that. That's snake cactus. There's a lot of it on trellises down in the court. Say!" He put a hand on the arm of her chair, rocking her a little. "You'll live in Hesperides a long, long time before you have a combination like tonight's. Each of those plants blooms one night a year. They're full at midnight and when daylight comes the petals all wilt and drop off. And most of them have chosen tonight, when there's a full moon. I tell you, it's an omen

113

or something. Let's go down and watch one and when it's in full bloom you can pick it. It won't last but it wouldn't last anyhow. And you can always say you picked cereus in Hesperides. I'll show you how to do it without getting hurt. Because you have to be careful with plants and flowers down here. The more beautiful they are, the more likely they are to have sharp spines—"

She gripped his wrist. There was that knock again. Not the thump they had heard the first two times but a smart rap like the last.

Fred was off the bed and padding toward the closet in the north wall. No tray was handy, so he dropped his cigarette stub into a milk bottle, where Mallory heard it sizzle.

"*Boo!*" Larrick formed the word with his lips and grinned from ear to ear as he tiptoed to the bath on the south side of the room.

His grin as they planned what they should do if their caller returned had all but succeeded in making Mallory feel that they were acting childishly. Looking at Larrick, she had a little of that feeling even now. Then she turned and saw Fred going into the closet and so clear-cut was a memory that she wondered if she would be laughing, out of sheer terror, when she opened that door. She couldn't have told how old Fred was, that summer when he had come on a visit to her home, but she remembered the tight knee-length pants he had on the night her parents left them to play with the boy from next door. Hide-and-seek was their game, and she knew she had giggled then at the sight of Fred's fat little backsides as he scooted into a closet, behind one of those old-fashioned double-cross doors which their nurse said no evil could pass.

It wasn't a double-cross door which Mallory opened, but neither was there anything evil-looking about the man who stood in the hall. A spare man who was almost completely bald, she saw when he removed his hat. The sun had been at work on his long face for sixty or seventy years probably, so that the only expression she could observe was in his narrowed steel-gray eyes. She felt that in a glance they had taken in every detail of her appearance.

"Miss Winters?" His was a twangy voice that would be more accustomed to addressing men than women.

"Yes."

"I'm looking for Mr. Fred Winters."

"Who is this, please?" Fred had told her to ask that.

"Roger Norcott."

Fred came out of the closet. He took a step or two toward the door, looking Norcott over. "I'm Winters," he said. "Anybody with you?"

"No."

Fred turned his head toward the bath. "Oh, Deputy!" he sang out.

Larrick emerged, his face blank with surprise. He stared at the man on the threshold and said: "Why, hello, Mr. Norcott."

"Hello, Bert." Norcott smiled a little. "Thanks for taking care of my man."

"We'll be in the hall, Deputy." Fred looked at Norcott rather than at Larrick as he spoke. "I just wanted you to know—in case I was gone too long. Lead the way, Norcott. I'll follow you."

He stepped into the hall and Mallory automatically closed the door and turned.

Larrick's eyes were fixed on her, harder than she would have thought possible. His voice was deeper, too, and his drawl had vanished. "What did Norcott want with Fred?"

"Bert, open a window."

11

"JAIL BIRD? OH, JAY BIRD," Dr. Lack said into the telephone as Bounty returned to the study, sat down and got out his funny paper. "Why, I wouldn't know."

The physician listened for several moments, with deepening frown and compressed lips. "I'm sorry, David." His words were scored by the tapping of a penholder on the desk. "That's all I can say. To you. Beck told me nothing of this. Bring that coat back here at once. He shall spend the rest of the night, if necessary, repairing it to your satisfaction. You'll come? Good." The penholder was abandoned. Four fingers of Lack's left hand were flat upon the desk while the thumb pressed a button. "I'll want to hear more of that trouble at the hospital. Yes, I'll back you in any action you see fit to take. Good-by, David."

Lack replaced the receiver and glanced at Bounty, who chose that moment to put away his paper and look solemn-faced and receptive.

"Do you know anything about jay birds, Mr. Bounty?"

"I ought to."

"What sort of—of devilment are they connected with in local superstition?"

"Why, you never see 'em on Friday because they've gone to fill a date with the devil."

"I'm afraid that's not it. It seems to be what they do to other birds and their young."

"No superstition about that, Doctor. They destroy the nests of other birds and kill their young."

Lack stared at him in a startled, half-incredulous way. "That must be it," he said and turned his stare on Beck as the latter came into the room. He let the valet stand for some time across the desk from him before he spoke. "Beck"—his voice was astringent—"is it asking too much of you to treat my friends with courtesy when they call?"

"I always do so to the best of my ability, sir."

"Doctor Angelo made a request of you tonight."

Beck stiffened. "I beg your pardon, sir. Doctor Angelo made no request except to see you."

"He asked you to sew a button on his coat."

"You have been misinformed, sir."

"Your manner was so insulting that he left the house."

"You have been misinformed, sir."

"I haven't!" Lack banged a fist upon the desk. "I'm sick and tired of this, Beck. I won't have my friends driven from my house because you think you're too good for them. Remember how much you owe to Doctor Angelo. He is coming back. You will meet him at the door and apologize."

"I owe him nothing, sir. I have no reason to apologize."

"You have chosen a poor time to try my patience, Beck." Lack's voice sounded as if his throat were parched. "When I am realizing the full extent of your obligation to me. I clothe you and I feed you. Now I stand between you and—"

"Please, sir. You are tired and worried, I know. But remember that you have a guest who is trying to keep some of his respect for you. Make him your friend. Explain the situation to him and be guided by his advice. His head is clear."

Beck inclined his head, turned and walked from the room, giving Bounty a long sideways glance that made the latter jump up and follow him out again. "Oh, say, Beck," he said for Lack's benefit, "I want you to put in a call for me."

"Will you come into the guest room, sir?" Beck whispered in the hall and escorted Bounty through the first door on the left.

This was unmistakably a man's room, with a beige carpet and modern furniture that hinted at the severity of a monastic cell. A moment in it, however, and the color of salmon began to come out at you.

Beck stood with his back to the door. This time his head was up so that Bounty, seeing the hysteric gleam in his eyes, wondered if it might not have been there all the time. It was a gleam which wouldn't have been so disturbing if it came and went like the one in Lack's eyes. But this was steady. That was why it might have escaped notice.

"May I ask, sir, if you have anything further to say to me regarding my actions?"

"Not now, Beck. My invitation still holds good. Anytime, day or night, that you feel like talking, don't hesitate to rout me out."

"Thank you, sir. I shall try to explain when I have the opportunity. But please take my word for it that I am the one at fault in this house. A nobler and more generous man than Doctor Lack never lived. I have been so anxious that you and he become friends. I have racked my brains to devise a means of bringing you together. He needs you so badly." A hysteric intensity was coming into Beck's voice. "There is little reason why you should trust me, sir. But I am asking you to do it. And to help me. Not for my sake but for Doctor Lack's. I do not know what Doctor Angelo means by this move of his tonight. But I have learned to distrust him."

"What's it all about, Beck?"

"David Angelo is the worst of the flies that have been drawn to Doctor Lack's money, sir. I have done my best to stand in his way for years. At present he is trying to persuade Doctor Lack to move to Mexico City, where he would handle his investments for him. I cannot go there on account of—a difficulty about a passport. That is why Doctor Angelo wants to poison my master's mind against me. You see how he has succeeded. He brought no coat over here tonight and said nothing about one. No money was ever stolen from his apartment. But every time he comes he manages to put me in the wrong and to humiliate me. And tonight he has some special purpose. I knew it as soon as I saw him. I am afraid, sir. May I ask if anything was said over the telephone about his moving into the house or staying for the night?"

"Not that I could tell, Beck."

"That is what he has been working toward. He dropped a hint this afternoon—about how hot his apartment was. He knows that once he is in this house, he is in for good. Because Doctor Lack could never bring himself to do such an ungentlemanly thing as throw him out."

"And you want me to do the strong-arm stuff?"

"No sir. But the door to the right of Doctor Lack's desk leads to his examining room. The lock was picked at the time of his open house and the catch does not work well. Unless one slams the door, it comes open an inch or two. I shall try to give notice of Doctor Angelo's arrival. Could you make an excuse to go into the examining room? And could you—conscientiously—eavesdrop, sir?"

"Sure."

"Thank you, sir," Beck said fervently and knelt. "With your permission. Your shoestring—"

"For Pete's sake, get up from there!" Bounty cried in consternation, dashing to the door. "Don't ever do that again. You embarrass me." When he was safe on the threshold he turned back and grinned. "Know who first said, 'Thou shalt not listen at keyholes,' Beck? A deaf man."

Dr. Lack's anger seemed to have subsided when Bounty returned to the study, to sit down and tie his own shoestring.

"I suppose I ought to ask your advice," the physician said grudgingly, busying himself with the desk set. "You're used to Mexicans and I'm not. Although I like what I've seen of them here. So much so, in fact, that but for one obstacle I should probably have moved before this to Mexico City, where I could have the mountains around me. And David, the only Mexican I have known at all well, has been a loyal friend. But we had the same difficulty in Boston that we're having here. However, it has become so acute recently that I'm at my wit's ends to know what to do."

"I'm not sure I get the drift, Doctor. What Mexican David are you talking about?"

"Why, David Angelo. His Mexican blood is a point of honor with him. That is as it should be, although I admit he seems a bit too prickly sometimes. He knows Beck doesn't like him and may read more into his manner than is there. Tonight now, he lost a button from his coat at the hospital. Since he was coming to see me anyway, he wore the coat over and asked Beck to sew it on for him. No doubt Beck didn't want to do it. But I think he would with what grace he could, since he knows my wishes. But something in his words or manner cut David to the quick."

"Then you're taking his word against Beck's."

Lack shrugged. "One of the two is lying and there's no earthly reason why Doctor Angelo should."

"You say Beck doesn't like Angelo. Why?"

"I think the truth of the matter is that he's jealous of David. But it's Beck's own fault if he is left out in the cold when David's with me. David has done all in his power to make for good feeling. He worked as hard as I to protect Beck from persecution."

"Persecution?"

"That trouble about the theft in Doctor Angelo's apartment was persecution pure and simple."

"I never knew the particulars of that, Doctor."

"Well, Doctor Angelo is a bachelor, as you know. He keeps no servant and is too much occupied with affairs at the hospital to give much thought to housekeeping. We made the arrangement that one or two evenings a week he should stay here with me while Beck went to tidy up for him and attend to his clothes. One day he missed some money from a drawer and reported the loss to the police. Beck's visits there came out during their inquiry and naturally he was chosen as my whipping boy. David came while the police were here. He was indignant, of course, and put a stop to the proceedings by announcing that he had found the money."

"But he hadn't?"

"No, and he made no further effort to discover the culprit. Pilfering such as that goes on in every large apartment house. If David hadn't dissuaded me, I should have brought suit against the police

department. Beck, poor inexperienced fellow, got the issues confused. The police were trying to vent their spite at me on him."

"So Beck can't even have a persecution of his own."

"What?"

"I say, how did Beck get the issues confused?"

"Oh, he went so far as to say that Doctor Angelo had attempted
to frame him. Or something of the sort. But what I wanted to ask
you was this: is there anything particular about the way a servant
greets a guest that may offend a Mexican? Some little convention
that has no special significance for us but that lends itself to mis-
interpretation on Angelo's part? Beck must be making some error
of commission or omission."

"You've got to catch your Mexican first."

"What? You mumble away there, Bounty, and I can't understand you."

"Hell," Bounty had to say, "Angelo's no more a Mexican than
I'm a Frenchman because in one of her less lucid moments my
mamma plastered me with a bunch of French names."

"Oh, but he is," Lack corrected peremptorily. "And I have ad-
mired him for the way he has faced the prejudice of you people
here. I have suffered from it myself, simply because I came from
another part of the country. So I have a faint idea of what David has
had to go up against. That has made for a closer bond between us."

Since persecution seemed a favorite theme here, Bounty wondered if Angelo hadn't chimed in for a purpose. The latter was
county physician and head of the John Belton Lack Hospital by
the grace of the man whose money had built that institution. And
whose money, it had been hoped, would continue to flow over
Hesperides. Now that Lack was no longer lord of the ascendant
and it seemed certain that no more was to be looked for from his
munificence, his protégé was in a precarious position and doubtless realized it.

"I wouldn't distress myself about Angelo," Bounty said dryly.
"This isn't like the rest of Texas, where everyone goes around remembering the Alamo all the time. Most of the Valley population

comes from other parts of the country too. I can name you a dozen families from Massachusetts. If anyone but you ever thought of Angelo as being a Mexican, it wouldn't make any difference."

"Evidently you have had your head in the ground," Lack said curtly. "Racial prejudice is behind this move to oust Doctor Angelo from the hospital."

"So he has convinced you of that, has he? Use your head, Lack. You're letting yourself be bamboozled. Listen to Beck. I imagine he sees through Angelo all right. That's why Angelo is trying to pry him loose from you, unless I miss my guess. I'll give you a few reasons why people want Angelo out of that hospital. Inefficiency. Neglect of duty. Drunkenness—"

"I won't have this slander!" Lack banged at the desk again. "You heard Beck say Doctor Angelo had taken that bottle of whisky. Now you make him out a drunkard. I suppose you'll go and broadcast that now. You're prejudiced against him yourself. I should never have confided in you."

"Not if you wanted to be yes-yessed. Angelo was at his apartment?"

"Yes."

"Had he been to the morgue yet?"

"He is going there before he comes here."

"What's this about trouble at the hospital?"

Lack stared at the desk for a time. "There was a little difficulty with Christopher Hand's father," he said cautiously.

"Let's have it, Doctor."

Lack was grave. "It's a situation that it's easy to misinterpret unless you know old man Hand. As for his physical condition: to put it simply, he has a weak heart. If he will take care of himself, he may live to fill out his four score years and ten. That doesn't mean spending the rest of his life in bed, but he must give up all work about the farm. Simply sit on his front porch. And even then take care not to rock too hard. I've done all I can for him. I've told him just what is before him. His son asked me about his staying on at the hospital. If the father were satisfied there, that might be the best course. But he's not. He wants to go home. He's suspicious of everyone. Especially of Mr. Norcott. He has babbled to the nurses and to everybody who would listen about his son being weaned away from him. He has heard echoes of the streptococcus case and of the need for transfusions. He doesn't understand and I think what's in the bottom of his mind is that we're taking blood from Christopher and giving it to James Norcott."

"Is his room near Jimmy Norcott's?"

"No, he's on the first floor and the wing Mr. Norcott has reserved is on the top. But several times he has started to go up there and been stopped. Beck and I stopped him once, when I'm sure all he wanted was someone to visit with. Tonight he seems to have set his mind on going up to see if Christopher were there. He's afraid to enter an elevator and so was climbing the stairs when they found him. He's strong as an ox but a little exertion like that and he's done for. I judge everyone at the hospital is more or less afraid of him. Unnecessarily, I'm sure, because to me he's just an overgrown child who will obey if you speak firmly enough. But there is danger in the situation. Danger for him if he persists in climbing those stairs. Danger for young Norcott if Hand ever gets to the top and creates a disturbance. And if anyone tries to restrain him by force, I'm afraid that would anger him and precipitate a fight—in which his heart would blink right out."

"How did they handle him tonight?"

"One of the nurses had the presence of mind to call Miss Ainsworth, who induced him to go back to his room. I understand she is a friend of his son." Lack played delicately with the desk set. "Doctor Angelo had Christopher called and told him he would have to remove his father in the morning. Really I think that's the only thing to do. I don't know how Christopher has taken it but I can imagine. I'll try to see him tomorrow and explain how much better off his father will be at home. I can't undertake to go out into the country to see him but I could accomplish nothing if I did. It's merely a question of the old man resigning himself to life in an armchair."

"Did Angelo take measures to see that there would be no more trouble tonight?"

"Christopher will stay with his father until he goes to sleep. I'm not worried about that. But I can't help feeling disheartened about the case. Because, between you and me, when Hand returns to that farm he'll go right on living as he always has done. And that will be the end. Sometimes I think that's what he wants. If so, it will be quick and painless. And after all . . ." Lack shrugged and stared straight ahead of him.

"You're convinced, then, that Hand doesn't intend any harm to Jimmy Norcott?"

"I'm convinced of it. Oh, I know how it looks. With someone dealing out death to Norcott's donors. But if there's anyone in Hesperides I'd say was incapable of intentionally harming James Norcott, it's Jacob Hand."

"By the way, how well guarded is Jimmy Norcott?"

"Guarded? Why, he's the only occupant of that wing. No one is allowed there except nurses and doctors and the regular hospital attendants. He has a nurse with him all the time."

"He receives no visitors, I suppose?"

"Only his uncle and Christopher Hand."

"From the beginning of his illness, have you had the slightest reason to suspect that anyone—anyone at all—has tried to prevent his recovery?"

Lack shook his head decidedly. "Reporters have been hanging about and any number of people have come for one reason or another connected with the case. But none have got past the office. I asked particularly this afternoon when I had talked with Mr. Norcott. All precautions are being taken against an attack on the young man, you can depend on that."

"Leaving it up to me to protect his blood donors."

"I would like to think we shared that responsibility, Mr. Bounty. And that reminds me. Beck has the guest room ready for you. I want you to stay here tonight."

Bounty stared at him. "This is rather sudden, Doctor."

"I know. But I have my reasons." Lack beat a tattoo on the desk. "You're a good man, Bounty, who's being wasted. In fact I think you had better be planning to remain with me. You fit into things very nicely here."

"Doctor, I couldn't possibly stay here all night."

"I'd like to know why not?"

"I can't be away from my own home overnight, that's all there is to it."

"You're not married. You live alone. You will be much more comfortable and happy here."

"I have someone at home," Bounty said gently.

Lack's face quivered, then became ascetic as he got it under control. "Am I to understand that you—that it's a—a female?"

"Very female. Name's Carmen. I want you to meet her sometime, Doctor. You'll love her when she cuddles up to you and tickles you under the chin."

"Bounty, stop this!" Lack choked and mopped his face with a handkerchief. "You're disgusting. I am forced to revise my entire opinion of you."

"Let's talk about blood donors then. See if I have this straight. Hunting for them is like tracing a family tree. You locate one person of the right blood group who has recovered from streptococcus. Then you can get from him the names of the people who gave him transfusions. Each of these in turn will supply you with further donors. It's not as simple as that, though, is it?"

"No." Lack was the cold and cautious physician again. A little wary, Bounty thought. "In the first place, transfusion isn't always necessary for recovery. In the second, immunity is lost within a few months. This man who died tonight now, it's not certain that he was still immune to streptococcus. That's why I told you over the phone late this afternoon that I wanted to test his blood tonight."

"Well, how many B-blood donors, supposedly still immune, do you have wind of?"

"Sheriff, news of them has been pouring in for days. Yet every one I have tested, or had tested by competent men in other cities, has proved a disappointment."

"How many donors besides Hieronymus were there in this Chicago case?"

"One other. So many names have gone through my head the last few days that I can't say for sure right now which was his. We have learned nothing at all as to his whereabouts."

"How many people here have known the names of either or both these men?"

"Mr. Norcott and Christopher Hand. David Angelo, Beck and myself."

"What about Doctor Ainsworth?"

"Ainsworth? Why, I don't think so. Although Mr. Norcott may have told him. I scarcely know Doctor Ainsworth. He has kept himself so in the background in this case that I'm only just finding out what a very able man he is. I must get better acquainted with him."

"How did you five come to know the names of the Chicago donors?"

Lack answered as if he were on the witness stand.

"I"—he emphasized that of course—"was the one who knew of Doctor Cotillion's case. As soon as I saw I was going to need donors, I wired him for information regarding his. When I failed to receive an immediate reply I remembered—rather, Beck remembered—that this was his vacation time. So I wired the hospital in which he had given the transfusions. They replied that they had misplaced the records of the donors and that Doctor Cotillion was not within reach. He was on"—Lack's face became a delicate pink— "on the Great Lakes somewhere. But the superintendent dug up newspaper files and sent me what data he could. This consisted merely of the names—with Chicago and St Louis, I believe, the only addresses. I gave this information to Mr. Norcott, of course, and that meant to Christopher Hand. As head of the hospital, Doctor Angelo was in conference with us. And Beck attends to my correspondence. Mr. Norcott and I started inquiries but until today had heard nothing whatsoever of either man. Yesterday I had a reply from Doctor Cotillion, to whom my message had been forwarded. He said he couldn't recall the names of the donors on the spur of the moment. And anyway he would be unable to tell me where they could be found. But he volunteered to leave his—to fly down, I mean, and assist me."

Bounty regarded him curiously. "Why the delicacy about where Doctor Cotillion was?"

Lack brushed at a sleeve which bore no speck of dust. "Doctor Cotillion was on his wedding journey," he answered primly.

"Oh, his honeymoon." Bounty hadn't been mistaken, then, in thinking that sap still ran strong in the middle-aged pedagogue. "He tells me he has located yet another donor."

Lack's face was freezing, his eyes were becoming charged with milk, and Bounty knew he was hot on the trail of something or other. "Yes," Lack said, "a man by the name of Miles."

"What do you know about him?"

"He is—or was this spring—a graduate student in anthropology at the University of Washington. At present he's on an expedition to the Aleutian Islands. I dropped him from consideration when I learned that. The distance is so great. Besides, I was pinning my hopes on these Chicago donors."

"You found out that much about Miles yourself?"

"Yes. But Doctor Cotillion was more optimistic than I. He called me last night and I told him the situation. He got in touch with some private inquiry agency and employed them to find Miles. He told me this afternoon that they had established contact with him. There should be more news tomorrow. In the meantime there is nothing to do but sit and hold my hands. It's that feeling of helplessness which is about to drive me frantic."

"How did you come to hear of Miles in the first place, Doctor?"

"Through sources in Boston."

"Is that where he was ill with streptococcus?"

"No, he was in a Seattle hospital. That was some time ago. Although he probably still has immunity, his donors will have lost it."

"Has Miles ever given a transfusion?"

"I'm not sure." Bounty was positive that the ringing of the telephone, still connected on the desk, was a welcome interruption for Lack.

The doctor snatched up the receiver, then hesitated, with mouth half open, and Bounty wondered how long it had been since he had answered a telephone for himself. "Hello," he said. "Doctor Lack. John Belton Lack. Oh yes, Mr. Norcott." He listened a moment, then a quick smile sprang to his lips and he leaned forward. "Thank heaven!" he exclaimed. "In the nick of time. Yes, I'll be here the rest of the night." The smile faded. "Oh, don't let that worry you, Mr. Norcott. You may count on me. For any amount. Certainly. We can arrange that tomorrow. No, please don't say that, Mr. Norcott. There's little enough that I can do. No, of course not. Good-by."

Either he had difficulty in getting the receiver back into place or he pretended to have in order to delay meeting Bounty's eyes. For Bounty was looking at him steadily.

"Mr. Norcott gave you word of another donor," Bounty stated.

Lack nodded and was silent for a moment. "Mr. Norcott asked me to keep it a secret," he said in sudden decision. "But I don't think that applies to you. The second man whom Doctor Cotillion used this spring has arrived in town. He is registered at the Sutherland Hotel. Mr. Norcott has seen him and is sending him to me to make arrangements for a transfusion."

"What's his name?" Bounty was on his feet and going toward the desk.

"The name." Lack stared at the telephone. "Mr. Norcott didn't mention him by name. It's on the tip of my tongue. Beck will know." He put a hand under the edge of the desk and pressed a button.

Bounty restrained his impatience and asked: "What else did Norcott say about him?"

Lack hesitated. "I don't know that I should—"

"I couldn't help but hear. Money is involved."

Lack looked up at him with milky eyes. "Nothing matters, Sheriff, but that we have this man's blood. Understand that."

"Even if you have to pay through the nose for it. Is that it?"

"Yes. The man demands twenty-five thousand dollars for the risk of giving the transfusion. He knows of the death of the other donor and naturally is frightened."

"And Norcott agreed to pay?"

"He had to temporize, since he didn't have that sum available in cash. I don't know what my attitude would be if this were another man's patient. But I make no bones about the fact that I am going to help Mr. Norcott pay." Lack looked at the door as Beck entered, looked back at Bounty and said firmly: "In case you are thinking of extortion charges, Sheriff, there are going to be none. Is that understood?"

"That's up to you and Norcott, Doctor."

"Very well." Bounty would have sworn that Lack was enjoying this. "Beck," he asked deliberately, "what was the name of that other Chicago blood donor?"

Beck stood with his eyes fixed on the top of Lack's head. He might have been engrossed in a philosopher's thoughts. He might have been deliberating on the choice of a tonic to apply to the clean scalp which shone through the salmon hair.

"Does Mr. Bounty know there were three donors, sir?"

Lack's face went pale. "You understood what I meant," he flicked out. "There were only two who gave transfusions. What were their names?"

"John Joseph Hieronymus and Fred Winters, sir."

Bounty ripped out one of his cow-hand oaths. "Sorry, Doctor. Sorry, Beck. That was at my own thickheadedness. Where's another telephone connected, Beck?"

"In the master bedroom, sir."

12

Bert Larrick stood at the telephone in the fifth-floor hall of the Sutherland Hotel. "O.K., Peter," he said. "No one will hear me here. Though I might as well have talked in Fred Winters' room. Because I think I know what you're going to tell me. He's a blood donor."

"How'd you find it out, son?"

"Roger Norcott came to his room a while ago. He and Fred went out in the hall to talk and Mallory told me."

"Sort of long in telling you, wasn't she, son?"

"That's what I thought at first. But when Fred came back he explained everything. He flew down from New York to give Jimmy Norcott a transfusion. But after he got here he began to hear rumors of a plot against the Norcott blood donors and thought he'd lie low and see what was what."

"When did he hear these rumors?"

"Oh, I don't know. Last night or this morning, around the hotel, I suppose. Then I came over this evening and wanted Mallory to identify Hieronymus and he thought for her sake he wouldn't tell me until after that was over with. But when he saw Hieronymus fall down—well, I guess he was pretty scared and couldn't make up his mind what to do. And when somebody started knocking at his door he got the jitters sure enough. I gave him away, of course, by introducing Chris Hand to him and Mallory in the lobby. Chris must not be as dumb as he used to be. He connected the name Winters with the name of the donor they were looking for. He found out Fred's room number and came and knocked a couple of times. Later

Mr. Norcott came. That's where he'd been when we saw him go through the mezzanine. Looks sort of funny he didn't ask us about Winters, doesn't it?"

"He probably wondered what we had up our sleeve. The Winters room is on the fifth floor, is it?"

"Yes."

"What did Norcott and Winters have to say to each other?"

"Oh, they just talked about the transfusion. Mr. Norcott wants Fred to go see Doctor Lack and make arrangements. So you wait there. Here's what we're going to do. I'll take Mallory out home to stay all night with my mother—"

"I wouldn't do that, son."

"Well, I certainly am. She wouldn't be able to get any sleep here in the hotel. And I want Mother to meet her anyway. Fred and I will drive her out there and then go on to Doctor Lack's. I expect I'll stay with Fred, either here or at the hospital if he decides to spend the night there. Don't you think, Peter, that he'd better have a gun now?"

"Orders, son. No guns. Keep an eye on him and find out all you can about him: what he's been doing since he came to Las Palmas and what people he's seen."

"He's stayed in his room and hasn't seen anyone. Peter, you sound—"

"Winters saw Hieronymus at the airport last night, didn't he?"

"Yes, Hieronymus happened to be the man he asked about hotels. But it was dark and Fred says he didn't recognize him. He'd never seen him but once before, you remember. I told Fred about Hieronymus being up here on the fifth floor last night but he says he didn't come to his room."

"Well, son, keep your thinking cap on. Maybe I can tell you something when I see you that'll help you fit everything together."

13

"DOCTOR COTILLION, PLEASE."

"The guy makin' passes at a stiff?"

"Yes," Peter Bounty told the morgue attendant in deep disgust.

Bounty lay stretched out on a chaise longue whose cover was garlanded in green and salmon. His head was sunk into a white silk pillow until the salmon braid at the corners stuck out like donkey's ears beyond his own. The lamp on the telephone stand had another of those frosty shades banded by salmon.

He shivered and shivered again. Not only because the master bedroom was cold. He was thinking of Bert Larrick and wondering if he were acting wisely in withholding from his deputy information and suspicions about Fred Winters. But Bert wasn't good at dissembling. Besides, the boy was hardheaded and if he had fallen for that blonde, who was probably Mrs. Winters—or its equivalent—all the time.

"Doctor Cotillion? Sheriff Bounty speaking. Can you tell me the cause of Hieronymus' death yet?"

Cotillion made a throaty sound. "I'm still reserving my answer till after I've talked with Doctor Angelo."

"And he hasn't appeared?"

"No."

"Well, Doctor, I hate to pester. But it isn't curare, is it? Or a deadly Mexican scorpion? If so, I'm giving up."

Cotillion's chuckle was too throaty for good humor. "No, Sheriff, you can stay on the job. Where are you?"

"At Doctor Lack's. Are you where you can answer a question or two on another feature of the case?"

"Yes."

"There's some information I want about your previous streptococcus case. First I'd like to verify the names of the donors."

"They're correct as Doctor Lack has them."

Was this fencing or wasn't it? "J. J. Hieronymus and Fred Winters," Bounty said.

"That's right."

"Who dealt with these donors in Chicago—you or the patient's family?"

There was a long silence. The band on the lamp tinted Bounty's left hand with salmon. Knowing of the Midas touch, he scrutinized that hand—palm, back and finger tips—wondering if he were experiencing the salmon touch of John Belton Lack.

"I presume you have a reason for broaching this subject, Sheriff," Dr. Cotillion said with asperity. "Hasn't Doctor Lack told you of the case?"

Bounty partially crossed his fingers. "Naturally he thinks it better that I get the particulars from you."

"Well, since the patient was my wife, I was the one who had the dealings with the donors."

Bounty jogged up and down with satisfaction on Dr. Lack's soft chaise longue. He wanted substantiation of his theory and he wanted it at once. "Were these donors acquainted with each other?" he asked.

"Yes, they were acquainted."

"Did either or both of them take advantage of your need to extort money from you?" Bounty must have waited for half a minute. "If so," he said then, "I have no interest in following it up, Doctor."

"Then why are you asking?"

Bounty hesitated. "Because I've got a hunch that what happened then may throw light on what happened tonight."

"How? Let's quit sparring, Sheriff. I know that you know Winters is in town."

"Want to tell me how you knew it?"

"I'm not at liberty to. Let's have an answer to my question."

Cotillion held high cards here, so Bounty said: "In confidence, Doctor, I think a game of that sort was played once. It worked and an attempt was made to play it again. For higher stakes maybe. Whether there was collusion or not, I don't know. But I'm considering the theory that one man increased the market value of his blood tonight."

"I see. Winters. What proof do you have, Sheriff?"

"None as yet. I'm handicapped by not knowing what Hieronymus died of."

"I see," Cotillion said again. "My answer will be off the record, will it?"

"Yes."

"Very well. Naturally I should be most unwilling to have the business raked out in public. Hieronymus and Winters did come to me after I had typed their blood. They stated their case plainly and, I must say, politely enough. Fifty dollars was our standard fee for donors. They were in a position to ask more, they said. They set their price at five thousand a transfusion. I had to agree. They drew straws, I think, for their turns. I took blood from Winters and then from Hieronymus. The death of Mrs. Cotillion made it unnecessary to call on Doctor Lack's nephew when he arrived. Let me make it clear, Sheriff, that he had no part in the racket."

One of Bounty's feet slipped to the floor. He swung it back up and collected himself enough to say: "Oh no, I'm sure he didn't. But he must have known Hieronymus and Winters?"

"I'm under the impression that he met them. Perhaps not."

"Did you have dealings with these donors afterwards?"

"None. I had no desire to see them again. I wanted to forget the whole miserable business."

"I expect so. Well, Doctor, I won't keep you any longer. Is there any use in my asking why you won't commit yourself now about this poison?"

"I'm afraid to," Dr. Cotillion said and hung up.

Bounty hung up and lay for a time, whistling *The Eyes of Texas* low and dolefully.

The master bedroom, using furniture which advertisements had taught him to recognize as early nineteenth-century, occupied the east end of the main part of the house. Windows at front and rear were so small and so masked with drapes and curtains that these seemed almost like tapestries hung on blank walls. He went to examine them. Bert was right. They didn't open. Upper and lower sashes were set solidly in their frames.

Partitioned off at the corners on the east, with a bed between, were a dressing room that might have served a squad of men and a bath in the colors of black onyx and ivory. The same arrangement had been followed at the end by which Bounty had entered. Dressing room and bath here were identical with the others, save that doors opened into them both from the bedroom and from the foyer. In a closet just inside the dressing room he found the bed of which Larrick had spoken. It was turned up vertically on its rollers but when pushed out into the enclosed hall it would come down and, as Bert had said, barricade the occupant of the bedroom from the rest of the house.

Bounty clucked his tongue. Everything did point to a Nemesis in the life of John Belton Lack, there was no doubt of it. He brought from his reading a select company of sinister figures, one-eyed sailors from the sea and dark ex-convicts out of an Australian or Andaman past, yet he couldn't hit on one that would not look absurd skulking in the sunlight of the Magic Valley. . . .

Beck was in the hall, by the railing at the head of the stairs.

"Which dressing room and bath are yours, Beck?"

"Those at this end, sir."

"I judge Doctor Lack doesn't mind which bathroom, at least, he uses."

"One is exactly like the other, sir."

"Where do you sleep?"

"I let down a bed into the entrance hall of the master bedroom, sir. Doctor Lack is troubled by insomnia and in that way I am near if he wishes anything during the night."

Bounty studied this face with its even, recently acquired tan as minutely as he had studied a freckled face which had no tan at all. "Is Doctor Lack going to tell me about his nephew?" he asked quietly.

"Yes sir. You must not let him change his mind. I was not sure you knew of Mr. Malcolm. I was going to tell you of him if my master did not." Beck's head came up with a jerk that must have caused his stiff collar to cut into the flesh at the back of his neck. "Mr. Malcolm is coming!" he exclaimed, staring at Bounty. "I should have thought of it sooner."

"Where's he coming from?"

"We do not know, sir."

"Well, what did you get then—a telepathic message?"

"No sir. But Doctor Angelo knows Mr. Malcolm is coming and that he must work fast."

"There's no love lost between them?"

"Mr. Malcolm despises Doctor Angelo where I must fear him. Every decision is a battle for my master and Mr. Malcolm fights them for him. With Mr. Malcolm here, Doctor Lack is safe. Without him . . ." There was that effect of dental plates caving in. "This conspiracy against the blood donors, sir." Beck steadied his voice with an effort. "I was with Doctor Lack this afternoon when he talked with Mr. Norcott. Mr. Norcott made the statement that no one stood to gain by the death of his nephew. Therefore the conspiracy was the invention of an extortioner. But the supposed extortioner is dead. That leaves the question of motive in doubt. I hesitate to ask you if the facts bear me out in this, Mr. Bounty."

"There's a hell of a lot of doubt about the motive, I'll say that."

"Then I ask you to consider this, sir. If another prospective donor dies—or even another and yet another—there will be no doubt in the mind of anyone that the purpose of the murderer is to bring about the death of young Mr. Norcott. And if one of those killed happens to be named Lack, no one will suspect that he died, not because his blood was of a certain type, but because it was the same blood that flows in the veins of John Belton Lack. The millionaire."

It was Bounty's turn to stare. "Beck," he said, "in the words of Shakespeare, maybe you've got something there. Let's come out with it. Your idea is that Angelo murdered Hieronymus to throw us off the scent when he murdered Doctor Lack's nephew and heir. Or is his nephew his heir?"

"Yes sir."

"Do you have any grounds for this suspicion that I don't know about?"

"None, sir, that I can call to mind at the moment. But I know Doctor Angelo and what he is capable of. And I know that Mr. Malcolm will come with seven-league boots the moment he hears he is needed. And, wherever he is, he must be within reach of the radio."

"He'd surely send a message ahead, wouldn't he?"

"Yes sir. That has been worrying me."

"You're sure Doctor Lack has received none from him?"

"I am positive, sir."

"You told me Angelo was here this afternoon."

"Yes sir. With Doctor Cotillion. He has been trying to interest some buyer, in order to cut Doctor Lack loose from Hesperides."

"Could he have intercepted a message then?"

"I do not think so, sir. I was with them most of the time."

Bounty plucked at his lower lip. "This has got me sidetracked, Beck. But I'm glad you told me. I'd better get in the study while Doctor Lack's mind is made up."

"May I ask you, sir, not to mention to him that I have been responsible for casting any suspicion on Doctor Angelo? I feel that I have been loyal rather than disloyal in doing so. But it is characteristic of my master that he will rise to the defense of anyone whom he feels to be unjustly accused. And Doctor Angelo has been working on his sympathies already."

"O.K., Beck. If I spring that theory on Doctor Lack I'll spring it as my own."

Bounty had a grin on his lips as he entered the study. Instead of seeking his chair again he went to the desk behind which Lack sat, his face still so pale that Bounty could have counted his freckles. With guile, but with more good will than guile, Bounty put a hand on Lack's shoulder and was concerned to feel what meagerness of flesh was under that plain fine cloth. He patted John Belton Lack as he would have patted a high-strung horse, thoroughbred or not, and his voice was the gentle bantering voice that hadn't changed much since the days when horses heard it. "What's the matter, old man? Water so muddy you can't see bottom?"

Lack put his hands over his face. "That's it, Bounty. I can't make up my mind. Everywhere I turn, I feel there are enemies. And my head's so tired tonight . . ."

It was a mighty desk, the stronghold of a millionaire and man of affairs who could bring underlings scurrying to him by pressing those bell buttons under the edge. Bounty's eyes were sharp as he looked from the shallow center drawer to the tier of drawers on the left and to the single drawer above the telephone compartment on the right. On each he discovered the same scars in the dark wood, where a chisel or some such instrument had been at work.

"Try putting your feet up."

Lack lowered his hands. "What?"

"Let me show you. Slide your hind end back in that chair now and just let yourself go. Upsy-daisy!" Bounty caught Lack's heels and deposited his feet on the desk, one atop the other. Grinning, he surveyed the red-faced doctor and shook his head. "You haven't got the knack of it yet but it'll come," he said, seating himself on the desk and getting out a match. He bit off a sliver, removed it from the tip of his tongue with a fingernail and stared at it as he asked: "Have a burglary here?"

Lack glanced down at the tier of drawers. "My guests' way of making themselves at home," he said weakly.

"Oh, at your open house?"

"Yes, they read every letter of mine, Bounty. They pawed over my clothes. They took what they wanted and dirtied what they didn't want."

"I heard souvenir hunters had been busy that day but I didn't know it had gone as far as this." Bounty glanced at the two doors in the rear wall but decided to angle for the information he wanted. "Did you lose much of value?"

"Not in dollars and cents."

"Faith in human nature, I expect."

"Can you blame me? And can you blame me for not wanting to talk about it?" Lack linked his hands behind his head and stared at his polished shoes. "I want you with me when I see this donor, Bounty. Meeting strangers is an ordeal for me."

"You couldn't run me off right now, Doctor. Did this man Miles give a transfusion to the streptococcus patient you had in Boston?"

"Yes."

"And your patient was . . ." Bounty waited a moment and said: "Your nephew?"

Lack stared at him, his face frozen. "How did you know about my nephew? Did Beck tell you?"

"No. Doctor Cotillion mentioned him. I judge he took it for granted that you and I were working hand in glove, as we should, and that you had told me."

"I would have eventually. I'm no fool. I told Beck I'd tell you the moment I had word from him. Bounty, my nephew is the only close relative I have in the world. Nothing must happen to him! That's why I want you to drop everything else and solve this case at once. Tonight. Hire men and set them to work on it, if necessary. At my expense. I'm making you my agent, giving you full powers—"

"Wait, wait, Doctor. I'm sheriff, remember. Public servant and all that. I'm working hard as I can. What's your nephew's name?"

"John Malcolm Lack. He is named after me."

"And where is he?"

Lack's chin went down until it touched his chest. "I don't know," he said simply.

"Well—tell me about him."

Lack's chin rose. "He is the most brilliant young man—well, I'm sure he is one of the most brilliant young men in America. He's twenty-seven, with a fine future ahead of him in any field he chooses. He makes a host of friends wherever he goes. One of those lighthearted fellows whom everyone likes. He looks just like me, Bounty. Save for his hair; it's somewhat lighter than mine. Quite a bit lighter, in fact. But really, people often take him for my son. He might as well be. His parents are dead and he looks up to me as a father. What Uncle John says—"

Bounty fought back a smile. "I'm sure I'd like him. He would do as a donor for Jimmy Norcott?"

"Oh yes. His blood belongs to group B and I feel sure he still has immunity to *Streptococcus viridans*. He has always been in excellent health, I have seen to that."

"Well, does he know that you need him here?"

Down went Lack's chin again. "I don't know whether he does or not. My lawyers in Boston are moving heaven and earth to find him. But so far they haven't succeeded. I haven't wanted publicity about him because—because it is most embarrassing to me to have to admit that I don't know where he is."

"When was the last time you heard from him?"

"Six weeks ago. He wrote me from San Francisco that he thought he would take a boat south, through the Panama Canal or maybe around South America, and join me here. I have a room waiting on him across the hall from mine. All his things are there. But whether he is near or far from me tonight I don't know."

"Can't you get information about him from shipping offices or places like that?"

"This is why I have tried to avoid publicity," Lack said miserably. "Malcolm—for some reason he prefers his second name to his first—is a bit unsettled. The wanderlust, I suppose it is. He does things I can't understand. Instead of staying by my side as he should he takes odd jobs—smelly, poorly paid jobs—in this place and that. He has even worked his way to and from Europe. Once with animals. Cattle or something. I worried myself sick about him then. And he didn't let me hear from him all the time he was gone."

"I started to do that when I was about that age. I lost my nerve. I've regretted it ever since."

"Oh, but Malcolm doesn't have to do things like that. He has an adequate income from his father's estate. And, of course, everything I have is his."

"As it happened," Bounty said, "I wouldn't have had to work my way across either. That's not the point. But let it go. Publicity or no publicity, your lawyers have tried to pick up your nephew's trail in Frisco?"

"Yes. They report that if he sailed it must have been on some tramp vessel. Or under another name. He has done that. John Black is a name he has used. John Elton Black."

Bounty looked at him quizzically. "He seems to have taken a cue from Beck."

"Possibly. And I must say I am afraid this is a case where Malcolm had his tongue in his cheek. Beck is partly to blame. He is inclined to sympathize with the young man and to encourage him. But there's going to be a stop put to such nonsense. I have always dealt too lightly with Malcolm. This time I'm going to put my foot down. He's going to take his place as my nephew and heir. I want you to have a talk with him, Bounty, and show him he owes it to me. I don't know, you might even be a good influence on him."

"Better call the local scoutmaster, Doctor. I'm trying to be a good influence on one youth and the strain's about to get me down. It was on your nephew's account you wanted me to stay in your home?"

"That was the immediate reason. Beck insists we are going to hear from Malcolm at any moment. And he seems to have a sort of sixth sense about Malcolm's visits."

"How many people in Las Palmas know of your nephew as a blood donor?"

"Doctor Angelo knew him in Boston. I have told Mr. Norcott of him, with the request that he keep the knowledge to himself. Christopher Hand, of course, was present when I did so. Hand wants to be told the moment he arrives. I suppose he sees himself presenting Malcolm to Las Palmas society."

"And Doctor Cotillion knew him in Chicago."

"Yes, that's why Doctor Cotillion was so ready to aid me in this emergency. I sent Malcolm to him in his hour of need. Malcolm arrived too late to give a transfusion but the will was there."

"Doctor Cotillion didn't waste any time getting married again, did he?" Bounty said suddenly. "The first Mrs. Cotillion must have died about—two months ago, wasn't it?"

"Yes," Lack answered, taking his feet down. "And I must say I don't approve of such haste. He should have waited—"

"Oh well, he waited till school was out." Like the major general in *The Pirates of Penzance*, Bounty thought he heard a noise downstairs. "Those doors lead to your laboratory and examining room, don't they?" he said, sliding off the desk.

"What were to have been my laboratory and examining room. They have never been in use."

"They were broken into during your open house?"

"Yes. Those were the only two doors I had locked. I thought that was sufficient. I didn't know it was necessary to post armed guards in order to have one's privacy respected in Hesperides."

"I'm afraid you got Hesperides mixed up with Utopia, as some of the rest of us did. I'd like to take a look in there, if you don't mind."

"Go ahead. Everybody else has." Suddenly Lack turned his chair about, rose and said with an air of resolve: "I'll go with you. Though I swore I would never set foot in there or in my laboratory again. I won't in my laboratory. That was the worst blow. It was to have been my holy of holies. They profaned it."

"Don't go in on my account, Doctor," Bounty protested with his hand on the glass doorknob.

"Yes," Lack said firmly, taking the knob from Bounty's grasp and turning it. "I have found it hard to stay out of here lately. I feel as if I had left part of myself here." He pressed the light button and walked forward ahead of Bounty. "Why, Beck must have been in this place!" he exclaimed at once. "I see he has set it to rights. And cleaned the drawings from the walls. He should have left them. They were so appropriate. Anatomical studies."

It was a long white room which had studio windows on two sides and which must form the upper east wall of the patio, corresponding with the laboratory on the west. When he could, Bounty shunned such places, but even to his eyes this was—or had been—a paragon of modern well-equipped examining rooms. One object drew his attention at once. By the examining table in the center stood an instrument the like of which he had never seen before but which he guessed, from the adjustable glass eye, to be some newfangled X-ray machine.

"What's this, Doctor?"

Lack was ranging about, fingering things, patting them, as agog with excitement as a child permitted at last to come downstairs on Christmas morning. Poor fellow, Bounty thought, forgetting the qualities which offended him in the physician.

"That?" Lack said. "Oh, that's a sun lamp."

"A sun lamp!" Bounty's tone was a dumfounded one. "Isn't that bringing coals to Newcastle, Doctor?"

"Well, yes. But I like to be out in the open as little as possible. Beck talked me into buying that thing. He thought sun baths might do me good. I tried it once and told him to put it in here out of sight."

"I bet Beck uses it." Bounty was looking sheepish, now that he saw how a tanned and an untanned man could have remained inseparable.

"No," Lack said, "of course he doesn't. I told him what I thought of it."

Bounty was silent for a moment. "Why don't you like to be out in the open?" he asked then, quietly.

He got no answer. Lack had passed through a door at the rear and switched on the light of a small white-tiled bath. He stood for an instant, looking about, then went into action. He yanked towels from a rack and slapped them back. He opened the glass door of the medicine cabinet over the washbowl and poked among the toilet articles inside.

Bounty's attention was on a far different kind of cabinet, a white metal one which stood in a corner. He scrutinized its locks and swung open the double doors. The wide shelves within were empty.

Lack came out of the bath, carrying a shaving brush and feeling the bristles. He strode across the room to the desk beside the door and, after a bit of fumbling, found a bell button and pressed it.

When he turned, Bounty was sitting on the examining table, chewing at a match. "Doctor," Bounty said with a nod at the cabinet, "you told me you didn't keep any drugs now. Did you at the time of your open house?"

Lack came toward him and braced his thighs against the corner of the table. "Yes," he answered sibilantly, "I had some."

"Much of a supply?"

"Yes, I laid in a considerable stock while my home was being decorated. So I could begin work at once. Most of it I bought in the East, since so many things are hard to get here. And I didn't want to run short in the middle of an experiment. It was all stolen."

Cold crawled up Bounty's backbone. "Poisons included?" he asked.

Lack nodded. His eyes were milky and his fingers twisted frantically at the damp-looking bristles.

"Any idea where the stuff went to?"

"None. The house was full from two until dark. It wasn't until the next day that we discovered these doors had been forced. Something was taken from every room. Mostly by irresponsible children, I have tried to believe. But this must have been the work of drug addicts. In the scramble they scooped up everything. Beck kept a list."

"He did? Did you make an effort to recover any of it?"

"No. I was ill for a fortnight afterwards. With the hangover from my experience. All I wanted was to shut the world out. If I had reported this I should have had the police here, turning me and my house inside out. I couldn't bear the thought. Oh, I know it was criminal carelessness on my part. But, if you want the truth, I hated the world and the people of Hesperides for what they had done to me."

"I sympathize with you. But you see how this may have boomeranged back at you. Whatever poison killed this blood donor tonight may have come from here."

"But mine was taken a month ago. And anyone who wants poison can get it."

"Not as easily in Hesperides as you think. When we start tracing the poison responsible for the death of Hieronymus, we'll have an arrow before us all the time pointing to this cabinet of yours."

"You're an alarmist, Bounty. Why, if the contents of that cabinet caused his death . . ."

"Somebody," Bounty finished for him deliberately, "probably has enough nontraceable weapons in his possession to wipe out every damned donor you get here. And that somebody may be any resident of Hesperides."

Beck stood in the doorway of the study. He was looking at neither Bounty nor Lack but was staring dull-eyed at the open door of the bath.

Lack made for that door. "Come with me, Beck," he ordered with a snap of the lingers. "I want an explanation of this." By the washbowl he stopped and waved the shaving brush about dramatically. "Have you been using this bath?"

Beck came to attention with his back to Bounty. "Yes sir," he said, "I have used it at times."

"And why, may I ask, do you come back to this dinky little place when you have your own bath, with every luxury you could possibly want?"

"In order not to disturb you, sir."

"Oh. Well." Lack cleared his throat. "There's no danger of disturbing me. And you'll be having Mr. Bounty think I'm a sorehead. Take all this stuff back up where it belongs." He set down the brush and snatched a partially rolled-up tube from the lower shelf of the medicine cabinet. "And this old toothpaste. We're using that new brand now."

"I know, sir. I thought there was no need to waste what was left of the other."

"You and I don't have to go in for that kind of economics, Beck. Here." Lack thrust the tube at him. "Throw this away. You have plenty of the other in your medicine cabinet. I was wondering this morning why you didn't use it up more rapidly."

Bounty, flat on his back on the examining table, watched Beck carry the tube to a refuse container in the examining room, press his foot upon the pedal and, when the lid flew open, drop the tube inside. "That's the brand of toothpaste I use," he observed. "I'd sure hate to change."

"You'll find the other is much better," Lack told him, pausing to examine the lock as he came out of the bath. "Hurry, Beck. Because Doctor Angelo will be here shortly. Lock this door and give me the key." He shoved his hands into his hip pockets and stood teetering on the balls of his feet while his eyes roved about the room—without meeting Bounty's, however.

"That's right," Bounty said. "Just keep ignoring that drug cabinet and it'll go away."

"Beck," Lack called over his shoulder, "give the sheriff a list of the drugs that were stolen from this cabinet." His eyes lighted on the glass eye which was staring down on Bounty, whereupon the latter, knowing what was coming, cursed himself seven times over.

Lack whirled and craned his head forward to scrutinize the face of the valet, who was impassively clearing the medicine cabinet. "Beck, Mr. Bounty mentioned your tan. You are tanned. You have been using this sun lamp."

"Yes sir."

"When?"

"The only time I could, sir: after you have gone to sleep."

There was panic in Lack's voice: "And you have let me sleep there—exposed . . ."

"Yes sir." Beck left the bath, carrying his toilet articles wrapped in a towel. He locked the door and presented the key to Dr. Lack with the words: "It might be better to put your trust in locks here- after, sir." He went to the desk by the door, opened a drawer and came back with a typewritten sheet of paper, which he gave to Bounty. "You will find this list complete, sir," he said and turned to Lack. "There is the knocker, sir. You may wish a moment to com- pose yourself."

The doctor started mechanically to the door. "You're coming in, Mr. Bounty?"

"Not just yet. I've got some reading to do."

Beck held open the door for his master. He closed it then but an instant later a crack appeared.

"Aconite," Bounty read and after a few moments his eyes be- gan to skip lines. It was a long, long list, all the more terrible be- cause many of the names were unknown to him or only vaguely comprehended. . . .

"David!" Lack's voice strained now at heartiness. "You have no idea how good it is to see you coming in that door. How are you this evening?"

Bounty folded the paper, put it in his pocket and swung his feet to the floor.

"How are *you*, sir? That's more important. If you don't mind my saying so, you looked very tired this afternoon. I have been worrying about you ever since." Bounty, tiptoeing to a position where he could see into the study, thought of the words as oozing from Angelo's fat throat.

Angelo stood at Lack's left side, so that his rear was to Bounty. He had his fingertips on the desk and was leaning forward with some of the deference of a bow. His dark coat pinched him at the back and was short for him, making Bounty long for a paddle as he viewed those prize well- larded hams.

"I'm feeling fairly well, thank you, David. Do sit down." Lack sounded like a benignant graybeard and looked rather like a purring cat and Bounty thought: So that's the approach to his nibs! Angelo was the favored worshipful disciple in the presence of the master.

"Your pulse first, sir." It seemed to Bounty that there was a barely controlled intensity in Angelo's voice which made him overdo the unctuousness.

But Lack was lapping it up. "David, I won't be coddled," he said, extending his hand nevertheless. "Is Beck fixing your coat?"

"I think so, sir. I gave it to him. Although it went against the grain with me to do so."

"Just what happened downstairs when you first came?"

"Oh, nothing, sir. Please forget it. I shouldn't have been so sensitive."

"No, tell me. Some things have come up tonight that make me think you may have been right about Beck all the time."

"I thought he couldn't succeed in pulling the wool over your eyes forever, sir. But don't let me be the cause of any trouble, please. Perhaps Beck does have difficulty understanding me, with my accent."

"Your accent? Why, David, you haven't a trace of Mexican accent. And I never noticed that Beck failed to understand you."

"He doesn't when you are present, sir. When he meets me at the door it's another matter." Angelo freed Lack's wrist and carefully lowered his coat sleeve. "But let me ask if Beck has been keeping your chart regularly? I want to look at it while I'm here."

"What chart?" Lack demanded aggressively.

"Why, I suggested that Beck have you step on the bathroom scales every morning and make a record of your weight. I can see that he forgot it. I'm sorry, because I don't like the rate at which you have been falling off lately." Angelo stood with his hands on the swelling curves of his hips and spoke with affected sternness: "And I'm going to make it my business to see that something is done about it, sir. I have just about decided that it's my duty to move into your house and attend to some of these things myself. What would you say to that, sir?"

"Why, David"—Lack was fluttery—"I couldn't have you make that sacrifice. You know the way I live."

"A sacrifice to be near you, sir! That's a good one. And I know exactly how you live. Your wardrobe is in perfect order but you yourself aren't. All Beck is interested in is seeing that your morning bath and shave put you in good humor. That's his job, of course, and he knows it pays him to do it well. You are so kind and lenient that he twists you around his finger. But you know how I feel. He has a morbid influence on you. He's a constant reminder of death—"

"Don't say that, David."

"Very well, sir. Pardon me. But I do think it more important that a chart of your weight be kept than that you be so perfectly groomed." Angelo laughed softly. "Maybe it wouldn't be wise for me to take you in charge, though. I'd soon have you so plump that you'd be forced to get a new wardrobe. As I'm going to have to do. Just think of that, sir! You having to watch your waistline."

"Why, David, I don't know what to say. I would like to have someone with me I was sure I could trust—"

"That's all I want to know!" Angelo said quickly, slapping a palm on the desk. "It's settled. I'll tell you what. I was planning on sleeping at the hospital tonight. My bag's in my car, already packed. But it's not necessary that I go there. I'll make this my first night under your roof. Which means, sir, that you can go to bed as soon as your callers leave and sleep soundly. Think how good it will be to go to sleep knowing you have nothing to fear. Shall I ring for Beck?" He reached over the corner of the desk and held his finger on a button as he asked: "That donor hasn't appeared?"

"Not yet. What callers do you mean, David?"

"I took Doctor Cotillion from the morgue to the hotel and left him with Mr. Norcott while I came to see you. I think they'll be over for a council of war. That is, if they can get through the lines of the law. I don't know what to say about this poisoning case. Before we show our hands—" Angelo straightened, turned toward a chair and his eyes fell on the crack in the door. "Is someone in there, sir?" he asked Lack in a quick aside.

"It's the devil," Bounty said, stepping into the study. "You were about to mention him, weren't you, Angelo?"

Little lights seemed to be scintillating on Angelo's black pupils. They were dimmed for an instant as he raised a plump white hand, its back darkened by lank hairs, and passed a palm over the black lacquered hair on his head. "Good evening, Sheriff. So that was your car out front. I saw your undersheriff sitting there and decided he was relieving you when Beck—" He turned to Lack and forgot to be deferential. "Did you know Bounty was in that room?"

Lack's face wore a dazed look. He nodded.

"Do you know that Beck told me he had gone?"

"No," Lack said and his eyes went to the door and narrowed as Beck came in.

"If I were you, sir, I'd find out why he did."

"I shall. Beck, did you inform Doctor Angelo that Mr. Bounty had gone?"

Beck seemed to have perked up and to have more of the soldier than of the servant in his bearing as he came to a stop directly in front of Lack. "Yes sir," he said steadily. "I thought it did not matter what I told him since he twists all my words to suit his purpose anyway."

Lack stared at him speechlessly. Bounty, resting a hip on a corner of the desk, could have counted the physician's freckles, so clear-cut were they on his white skin. (Bounty was puzzling over the presence of the undersheriff outside. When Mrs. Broddus said Gus was to stay home at night, Gus usually stayed.)

Angelo had gone to a chair and with the manicured nail of his little finger was stroking his mustache where it rose to a point that partially concealed the mole nestling below his right nostril. "So the man admits at last to a lie," he said, his eyes flickering from Lack to Beck. "Let me ask him a question, sir. Beck, it seems odd to think of you helping an officer of the law. But you may be saving your own skin. Did you lie to me this time at the sheriffs instigation?"

"Lay off, Angelo," Bounty drawled. "He did what I told him to. Seems I can't be too particular about the means I use to get information. That's all, Beck. Thanks."

"Wait there," Angelo said and turned to Lack. "With your permission, sir, I should like to ask him to do something for me." At Lack's nod he looked back at the valet, reached into a pocket and brought out a key container. "Drive my car into the garage, Beck. Bring my bag in and put it in the guest room. Your master probably has other work for you, so I won't ask you to unpack."

"Unpack for Doctor Angelo," Lack ordered, "and see that everything is done to make him comfortable."

Beck kept his eyes steadfastly on Lack's face. "May I remind you, sir, that the guest room is ready for Mr. Bounty?"

"He declined it," Lack said shortly, looking down.

Bounty swung a leg back and forth. "Doctor, after you spoke of your limited facilities I thought I'd be imposing on you. But I would like to know I had the use of that room. I live some distance away and you never know when you might need a sheriff in your home."

Angelo caressed his mole with his left hand and Bounty saw that there was another of the things, very hairy, at the base of that thumb. "The front room, then, Beck," he said smoothly.

Lack brought down a hand. "That's Malcolm's room, David," he said firmly. "Every object in it I have arranged just so. I'm sorry, but he must find it that way when he comes."

Angelo's eyes rested for an instant on a day bed below the east window. They returned to Beck and he said: "Bring my bag in here, Beck. It doesn't matter where I stay so long as I'm where I can watch over Doctor Lack's health."

Bounty thought it was his turn again. "It strikes me, Angelo, that with an autopsy on your hands you'd better park your bag at the morgue for a spell."

Angelo studied him, as one studies a new antagonist who has stepped into the arena. "This is becoming very embarrassing to me, sir," he said, turning to Lack. "In Mexico when we say, 'My house is yours,' we mean it. You have told me so often to make myself at home here that I was taking you literally. I would rather think the mistake was mine than that you are not master in your own house."

"We shall see about that." Lack spoke brusquely. "Beck, take Doctor Angelo's bag into the west dressing room. Make closet and drawer space for him and put his things away. He is going to have the use of that room while he is here."

Beck didn't budge. "There will be confusion, sir, and you will be the first one to be annoyed by it."

"Very well, Beck. Doctor Angelo is taking your place in my rooms. You are going to the servants' quarters."

"That's where I have wanted to be all the time, sir. But think of Mr. Malcolm, please. Is this going to make his home-coming more pleasant?"

"There's one more step, Beck. And I'm prepared to take it." Lack sat forward, his gleaming mother-of-pearl eyes fixed on the other. "You lied to me this morning. My paper was delivered. You hid it so that I would send you after another—"

"Oh, cut it, Lack!" Bounty said. "You're only showing yourself up."

"Stay out of this, Bounty! I gave you a dime, Beck, to buy that paper. You deliberately stole that, as I have always thought you stole from Doctor Angelo. You say you paid Christopher Hand a nickel. That means you had five cents left. All the money you want is yours for the asking, Beck. But I won't have you stealing from me." Lack put out a hand. "Give me that nickel back."

Beck's head went down. He slid his palms up over his face and ran his fingers through his neat cap of dead-white hair. He straightened and his face was white beneath its tan. Deliberately he thrust a hand into a pocket of his trousers and brought out a nickel. He held it on his palm a moment, staring at it. "Yes sir," he said and flung the coin at Lack's face.

"Good for you, Beck!" Bounty cheered, then almost swallowed his tongue, for the nickel had struck Lack's right eye and brought a cry of pain from him.

The doctor staggered to his feet and reeled backwards, both hands clapped over that eye.

Angelo was beside him in an instant. He put an arm about Lack's waist and drew him toward the door, saying solicitously: "Come to the bedroom and lie down, sir. I must look at that eye at once." He glanced over Lack's shoulder at Beck and then at Bounty. There was concern on his face, undoubtedly, but also triumph. "I don't know what you came here for, Sheriff," he said. "But you've found something to do. Put that man under arrest and take him away. He's shown his hand at last."

Bounty shook his head. "I don't have any handcuffs with me."

Angelo's eyes narrowed. "We'll see about that," he said and helped Lack out the door.

Bounty didn't look at Beck for a time. When he did the man hadn't moved but stood with bowed head in front of the desk. His silence began to work on Bounty's nerves. Perhaps not the silence itself so much as the thought that something had died in Beck. The latter was a mechanism whose motive force was either gone or too weak to make itself felt.

"Aw hell, Beck!" Bounty said gruffly. "Don't take it so hard. You didn't hurt him. And if ever a man was asking for it—"

"Please don't, sir." Beck spoke as if from pain. "I will go with you. You won't need handcuffs."

"I'm not going to arrest you."

The valet looked at him with lackluster eyes and then down. "Doctor Angelo will try to force you to, sir. I would rather go than cause you any trouble."

"There won't be any trouble," Bounty said with more confidence than he felt. "Anyway, I owe it to you to stick by you. I've blundered in here tonight and ruined every playhouse you had—"

"Please don't, sir," Beck begged again. "Will you take his place? For a while. That is the only way you can help me."

Bounty stared at the end of a match until his eyes hurt. "Get a smile on your face and show me to the front door!" he barked out, then grinned. "Is that what you want?"

"Yes sir. Thank you." Beck held open the door into the hall. "You are not deserting him, sir?" he asked in an undertone.

"No," Bounty said. "And you aren't either."

The man made no reply but fixed his eyes on the door of the master bedroom. He kept them there until he was at the head of the stairs.

"Here." Bounty thrust the funny paper under his arm. "I'm going to step outside a few minutes. While I'm gone, sit down and read that."

"Thank you, sir."

Bounty watched him unlock and unbolt the door. "I'm giving you orders now, am I, Beck? Then tell me the truth. What is Doctor Lack afraid of?"

Beck opened the door and stepped back. "That, sir," he answered, looking out into the moonlight which silvered the white porch, the lawn, the street and the familiar dusty coupé on whose running board sat Undersheriff Gus Broddus, bareheaded and in his shirt sleeves.

14

HONEYSUCKLE HUNG HEAVY on the trellis in front of the veranda of the Larrick home, a white cottage, in need of paint, on the northern outskirts of Las Palmas. Honeysuckle, the familiar sight and smell of it, made this a sanctuary in an Ultima Thule where narcotic flowers bloomed at midnight and were dangerous to touch.

Only between the steps and the front door did the moonlight have a clear pathway, reaching almost to the feet of Mallory Winters and Bert Larrick, where they stood just inside the dimly lighted living room. Fred, behind one of the pillars, was in shadow but he had made a peephole in the vines through which he could see into the street.

"Bert"—it was a whisper—"don't go."

"Don't go? Why, Mallory, I've got to. I can't leave Fred in the lurch. Don't worry—"

"Call the sheriff. Have him come and take Fred to that doctor's house."

"I can't do that. It would look like I was afraid."

"It wouldn't. And Fred hasn't any right to ask you to go with him. He hasn't told you—"

"Say there, Bert!" Fred called softly. "How about breaking that up and coming on? It's getting late."

"Just a minute." There was no one in the doorway of the living room. "What's the real reason you don't want me to go, Mallory? Tell me. Is it because . . . ?"

15

THE MOON WAS the full-faced moon that stood over the valley of the lotus-eaters. Its light plated Gus Broddus' big blond head and the close-fitting white shirt which was a product of his helpmate's sewing machine.

The breeze was one which had been nippy when it left the Gulf of Mexico but now was languishing. Peter Bounty went down John Belton Lack's walk slowly, filling his lungs.

"No night for a married man to be on the prowl," he told his undersheriff.

Gus rose as he approached and stuffed down his shirttail. His shirttails were always giving him trouble, for it was there that Mrs. Broddus economized most on cloth. Bounty often thought of Gus as a horrible example of what he might have looked like had he married a domineering woman a score of years ago and then let himself slide. Not that Mrs. Broddus could be held accountable for her husband's bunions and lumbago, of course, but these last were only contributory causes of his sagging appearance.

Before Gus spoke Bounty knew that he was chock full of emotion. "Howdy, chief. I just thought I'd take a little walk while the womenfolks were gettin' ready for bed. Happened to go by the hotel and saw Bert. He told me where you were. I didn't feel like goin' in, not bein' dressed, so I thought I'd wait awhile and maybe you'd come out. Doc Angelo tell you I was here?"

"Yes. What was Bert doing?"

"He had some blonde on the string. Or she had him on the string. She was checkin' out of the hotel. Bert was showin' off as usual." Gus didn't altogether share Bounty's enthusiasm for Larrick, who was given to punning on his name.

"Were they alone?" Bounty asked.

"Some fellow was with 'em. Looked like a city slicker to me."

"I think he is, Gus. But he's also a blood donor."

"Another one, chief! And you're lettin' Bert take care of him. No wonder the guy was scared."

"You really think he was scared, Gus?"

"Something was wrong with him. I thought at first Bert had him under arrest. Where were they goin'?"

"They're coming out here." Bounty took a holster with a revolver from the running board. He hefted it but made no comment.

"That's for you, chief. I knew you wouldn't have one."

Bounty laid the holster down. "Thanks, pardner," he drawled, "but it gives me prickly heat to wear a gun. Better take that home and put it away among your keepsakes."

"Hold still, chief. Unless you want a tussle." Broddus caught up the holster, slipped it on Bounty's belt and buckled it. "Fourteen years I've had to follow you around and do this."

"Has it been that long, Gus?"

"Almost. Maybe in fourteen more years you'll get some sense. There!" The undersheriff punched his superior's hip. "I feel better now. I've been sort of worried about you, chief."

Bounty sat on the running board and stared at John Belton Lack's white and salmon house, thinking how much one man can take out of another during fourteen years. Talk about blood transfusions . . .

"Mighty fine house, ain't it, chief?" Broddus rocked the car as he sank down beside Bounty. "Don't suppose you went and showed your ignorance in it like I did. I started in soon as I got inside the front door. They said there was a powder room off the hall. I thought it was where Doc Lack kept his gunpowder."

"That's right, you were at the famous open house."

"The missus made me come. I've had to shave twice a day ever since."

"Know where the study is? Second floor rear. Were you back there?"

"Sure. That's where Carrie Ainsworth was showin' folks about. The missus asked Carrie if the drapes and things were supposed to match the doctor's hair. Carrie said no, they were coral."

"Coral? Oh, I mean Carrie was Doctor Lack's assistant then, wasn't she?"

"Yeah. And Chris Hand was there, actin' like he owned the place. With Bert Larrick not far behind him."

"Did you get to see the laboratory and examining room?"

"No, Carrie explained they were locked."

"What time in the afternoon were you here?"

"Early, soon as I got the dinner dishes washed."

There was an interval of silence and Bounty said: "You're wanting to know what's going on, Gus. Well, so'm I. Four or five men have the jump on me. Hieronymus was poisoned somehow. How did you hear about it?"

"Oh, the neighbors started callin' the missus to ask what she knew. Talk, talk, talk was all there was. I got disgusted. I knew Bert would be off courtin' somewhere and not helpin' you, so—well, I thought maybe you might need me."

"Not tonight, Gus. Better get your beauty sleep. Did you walk all this way?"

"The missus had the keys to the car." Broddus pulled up his socks. "Chief, you're in trouble."

Bounty looked up at the moon. "Am I? What are people saying?"

"Oh, lots of things. That you gave this guy the third degree. That you doped him so he'd talk. The whole town's stirred up. It's mostly B. Matthew Rone's doin'. He was spoutin' oil when I was at the hotel. I had to get out or I'd have socked him. You know the county commissioners are meetin' tomorrow at ten."

"So they are. And E. Matthew is making political hay while the moon shines."

"He thinks they'll suspend you and appoint him. Good thing you got the chairman of the commissioners on your side."

"Yes, Rolf Jester always stood behind us in Cameron County. He'll stand behind us now. Let's not worry. I feel I slipped up on something. I know I did. But I didn't have anything to do with the death of this man, Gus. Do I need to tell you that?"

"Hell, chief, I wouldn't believe you if you said you did."

"Thanks, Gus. Just where was Hieronymus when you took him in custody at the hotel?"

"He'd just come in the front door. I was sittin' there and spotted him right away. He bought a paper at the newsstand and was lookin' around for a chair when I ups and pounces on him."

"Did he seem at all sick? Dopey?"

"No, I couldn't say as he did. He acted sort of scared-like when I told him I wanted him to go with me. He said there must be some mistake, he hadn't done anything wrong. I told him that's what they all say. One thing, chief, I thought of this evening. E. Matthew Rone was headin' for him when I went up to him."

"How near did Rone get to Hieronymus?"

"Not closer'n forty feet. I think the desk clerk had called Rone and told him to shoo the guy out."

"Did Hieronymus see Rone coming?"

"I don't think so. But it was hard to tell which way his eyes were turned, behind those big specs."

"Did Hieronymus have anything to eat or drink while you were bringing him to the office?"

"Not a thing, chief. Isn't that Roger Norcott's car turnin' the corner?"

"Yes." Bounty rose. "Thanks for coming, Gus. But if I were you I'd go home and make peace with the wife. Take my car and save your feet."

"To hell with you, chief. I'm not Bert Larrick. I'd walk a mile to spare you— Oh well. Anyway, I'll sit here and bay at the moon awhile. I might as well stay out now till they're asleep at home. I've got the couch in the living room while the mother-in-law's there."

Bounty unlocked the door of his car as Norcott's long limousine slid up to the curb behind. "In that case get in and be comfortable."

"I brought a pair of handcuffs, chief. Some I've been lettin' the neighbor kids play with. Want 'em?"

"Not now." Bounty watched Christopher Hand climb from behind the wheel of the other car, Roger Norcott and Dr. Cotillion from the back seat. "Save 'em for the next visitor."

"Tell me, chief."

"The young man you sized up as a city slicker," Bounty said and cut across the grass to intercept the trio that had started for the walk.

Norcott halted first, sent his cigar stub sailing over the grass and stood patting his lips with a handkerchief. "Right on the job, I see, Sheriff," he said as Bounty came up. "Do you mind enjoying the moonlight a while longer? We want a conference with Doctor Lack before we make it a round table."

"Gentlemen!" Bounty spoke as if they were meeting for the first time that night and as if he hadn't heard Norcott's words. "Do you mind enjoying the moonlight a moment or two? I want a little conference before I start listening to all the things you have to tell me."

He left them standing on the walk, crossed the porch and knocked. Beck didn't open the door at once. When he did he was breathing hard and a glance at his face told Bounty that he had steeled himself to do so.

Bounty stepped inside and motioned to him to close the door. "What's the word, Beck?" he asked then with a glance at the upper hall.

"Nothing, sir."

"Well, I'm going up. As soon as I'm inside take these men to the study. Tell 'em I'll join 'em there."

"Yes sir." Bounty had started up the stairs when Beck called to him. "Please, sir," Beck said with a hand on the newel post, "I notice you are wearing a gun. May I suggest that you leave it with me? It pulls your clothes out of shape so."

Four treads were between them but Bounty could hear the man's breathing in the stillness.

"I'm afraid my clothes are hopeless now, Beck." He went slowly up the stairs, wondering if the power were within him to cope with this situation. He was dog-tired, empty of stomach, befuddled of brain. He tightened his belt, when he had knocked at the bedroom door, and wished he could tighten something about his head to hold it steady.

The door was locked, he found when his rap brought no immediate response. He tried again, the door was opened and Angelo stepped out, locking the door behind him.

"I'll take that key, Angelo."

The physician looked at him for a moment with narrowed, thoughtful eyes, then laughed and handed over the key. "I'll trust you with it awhile, Sheriff. Let's go in the study."

"Let's go to my room," Bounty said, leading the way to the rear.

"*Your* room?" Angelo's laugh was soft.

"Want me to say it in Mexican?" In the guest room Bounty stood with his back to the door, as Beck had stood earlier, and demanded: "How's Doctor Lack?"

Angelo resumed his contemplative study of him, his full lips seemingly ready to twitch into a smile. "I can't figure you out, Sheriff." He spoke in a confidential tone. "I wish you'd tell me what your game is."

"Pinochle," Bounty said. "Like to go over and play it in the county jail? How's Doctor Lack?"

In his shrug, at least, Angelo was altogether Mexican. "The injury to Doctor Lack's eye may be very serious." There was some professional gravity in his voice. "The pain is intense. And if you knew him at all you would know what a shock this attack was to his nervous system. I have given him a sedative and am taking him to the hospital for observation." He paused, plainly inviting a protest from Bounty.

The latter was listening to sounds in the hall. "Doctor Cotillion is here," he said. "I'm going to ask him to take a look at Doctor Lack first."

Angelo hesitated an instant, then nodded. "I'm glad to know how much confidence you have in me, Sheriff. Doctor Cotillion may examine Doctor Lack, if you insist. Now let's settle something else. I say I have authority to see that this house is closed and everyone out of it when I leave with its owner. What do you say?"

"That you're sailing pretty darned close to the wind here, Angelo. Be careful. I'm staying in this house tonight. You aren't."

As Angelo gazed at Bounty the glow in his eyes was like something phosphorescent coming to the surface of dark water. "Have you put Beck under arrest?" he asked, stroking his mustache.

"No."

"Are you going to?"

"I'm no Don Quixote, Angelo. But I told you once to lay off Beck. I never said anything I meant more."

"You have me down as the villain of this piece, don't you, Sheriff? And Beck as the faithful persecuted servant. Yet all you have to go on is what you've seen and heard tonight. What do you know about Beck? Nothing. He committed suicide once. You didn't know that, did you? Doctor Lack injected adrenalin into his heart and wouldn't let him die. Or brought him back to life, however you choose to put it. He has hated Doctor Lack ever since. And been getting his revenge ever since. Doctor Lack suffers from agoraphobia. Do you know what that is?"

"Yes. Fear of space, the out of doors."

"Doctor Lack is a psychasthenic."

"I'll have to pass on that."

"The psychasthenic is under constant tension and is unable to make decisions. His state arises from lack of security in childhood. Now Beck has played on those fears of Doctor Lack's and has kept his friends from helping him overcome them. Oh, it has been a sweet and long revenge. And the man has been sly as the devil about it. But he has had something else to work for." Angelo paused and moistened his lips.

"Talk fast, Angelo, if you're going to talk."

"You have probably heard of Malcolm Lack," the doctor said with a very faint wheezing sound.

Bounty nodded.

"What have you heard?"

"You're doing the talking."

"Whatever impression you have of Malcolm Lack has been formed by listening to his uncle and to Beck, that I'm sure of. Ask anyone else and you'll be told that Malcolm is the black sheep of the family. He stays away from his uncle so Doctor Lack won't catch on to him. He knows Doctor Lack's five millions are his someday. And it's Beck's job to hurry that day. Then they'll split. With no risk at all. Because Doctor Lack's death, if their plans work out, will be a suicide. For fourteen years Beck has kept him reminded that there is an easy escape. And Doctor Lack is nearer now to taking that way out than he ever has been. I'm going to stop him, Sheriff, if I can. By any means I can. Beck assaulted Doctor Lack tonight. You can't deny that. I'm going to see that charges are filed and pressed against him, if not through your office, then through the police. Which shall it be?"

Bounty said, "I'll arrest him."

Angelo gave him a little bow. "Thanks, Sheriff. Now you to your murder and I to my patient." He started toward the door, from which Bounty hadn't moved, but stopped, his face in its sudden absorption reminding Bounty of one of those Billiken dolls that people used to keep on mantels. Something sinister and Japanesque lurked behind its roly-poly exterior. "There's a thought there, Sheriff, that you might work on. Young Norcott's death would be a greater shock to Doctor Lack than a blow in the eye. Beck knows that. And perverted as he is . . ."

"I'm listening only to facts that can be proved now, Angelo."

"I've given you enough to make you lock the man up before that blood donor gets here."

"Speaking of locking up . . ." Bounty slipped the key from the lock behind him. Quickly he opened the door, stepped into the hall, closed the door and locked Angelo in.

Beck was standing at the door of the master bedroom and Bounty thought that his hand had just fallen from the knob.

"Our callers are in the study, Beck?"

"Yes sir."

Bounty's eyes were keen as Beck came toward him but he scarcely looked at the man's face. "Ask Doctor Cotillion to step out here a moment, please."

"Say, Beck," Bounty heard Christopher Hand call as the valet opened the study door. "Where's Doc Lack? We came to see him."

"Doctor Cotillion—" Beck seemed unable to continue.

In the moonlight Cotillion's face had been a dark and forbidding mask. Seeing it by the light of electricity, Bounty's immediate thought was that the Chicago physician had been taken ill. His skin was the color of tarnished lead, dank-looking, and his mouth was a powerful trap whose spring is loose. Bounty didn't like the look in his bleary eyes. If it wasn't downright fear which they showed, it was something akin to that.

"Come in and I'll talk to you before Mr. Norcott, Sheriff," he said as Beck was closing the door at his back.

"I want you to look at Doctor Lack first," Bounty told him, going toward the front of the hall.

"What's wrong with Lack?"

"A June bug flew into his eye. Tell him that's what I said and see if he doesn't agree." Bounty unlocked the bedroom door and stood aside, his face unconcerned.

Cotillion gave him a stare as he passed. "A June bug?" he said.

"Maybe it was a lightning bug." Bounty closed the door and turned to Beck. "Raise your hands, Beck," he ordered quietly.

"I beg your pardon, sir?"

"I said raise your hands."

Beck's eyes went shut but there was no expression at all on his face as he obeyed. His body quivered as Bounty's hands touched it, then stiffened. "The inside coat pocket, sir," he said. "If you're another man who must play God."

Bounty didn't speak for several moments. He was too empty and cold and sick at sight of the knife which he held in his hand. It was a surgical knife, he knew, from the case in the examining room. Small. Probably used for lancing. . . .

He narrowly escaped cutting himself as he got it into one of his own pockets. "Come with me, Beck."

"Yes sir," Beck said, opening his eyes. "I am sorry to add to your worries, sir."

They went down the stairs in silence and out the front door, leaving it unlocked. Even in the breeze words didn't come to Bounty but as they passed into the moonlight his hand was gripping Beck's arm tightly.

Gus Broddus got out of the car at their approach and his mouth fell agape.

Without a doubt he had never heard Peter Bounty's voice so harsh. "Handcuff this man," Bounty said. "He is under arrest. Keep him in the car until I can talk to him."

Bounty turned, went hastily into the house and up to the study, where he stood in the doorway, looking at Roger Norcott and Christopher Hand.

Norcott, sleepy-eyed, was leaning back in a chair. That night had added at least a dozen years to his appearance. It seemed to have given Hand maturity too. He sat behind the desk, his hands with their rings clasped in front of him, his eyes fixed on the mahogany, and the odd thought came to Bounty that he looked more in place there than had John Belton Lack. That desk was made for big and solid men.

"Well, gentlemen," Bounty said, "let's start clearing the deck. I want to be told all that you two know about this blood donor, Fred Winters."

"And we want to be told what you know about him, Sheriff," Norcott countered, sitting up and getting out a cigar.

"Fair enough. Your turn first."

Norcott looked about for an ash tray and, seeing none, put the unlighted cigar in his mouth. "Christopher was the first one in our connection to get wind of him. Tell the sheriff what happened, Christopher."

Hand raised his eyes and looked at the wall midway between the two men. "I was in the hotel lobby before dinner," he said with plainer articulation than Bounty had ever heard from him. "I ran onto Bert Larrick by the elevators. He told me about the checking up you were doing on Hieronymus. And about you bringing him over for some girl to identify who'd seen him at the airport. Just then a girl and a man stepped out of the elevator and Bert introduced me. Miss Winters and Mr. Winters was all he said. But as they were walking off it struck me that was the last name of the Chicago donor we were looking for. I didn't know what to think. I was on my way to take Doctor Cotillion to dinner. So I went on and asked him if he'd had any word about a new donor. He hadn't. He said it must not be the right man because he'd been over here till about six-thirty and Doc Lack hadn't spoken of him. But when I got to our suite I called the desk and found out Winters' first name. Sure enough, it was Fred, the name of the man we wanted. Doctor Ainsworth and Angelo were there then and the five of us talked it over. I went downstairs to see what I could find out."

"What time was that?" Bounty asked.

"I'm not sure exactly. But when I got to the lobby I ran into big excitement and heard that the man you'd brought over had had a stroke of some kind. I looked through the crowd for Winters but couldn't find him. That's what I was doing when you saw me on the mezzanine."

"How many times had you been to knock on Winters' door?"

"Twice. Nobody answered. I went there rather than phoning because I wanted to see who was in the room with Winters."

"Yet you didn't see fit to tell me about Winters."

"I'll explain that," Norcott said. "After Christopher knocked the first time at Winters' door he came down and talked to me. By then you'd called Cotillion to attend Hieronymus. Here's what I figured: if you and your deputy knew Winters was our donor you must have a reason for keeping him under cover. I wasn't going to tip off our hand till I knew what that reason was. If you didn't know—well"— Norcott shrugged—"it seemed to me the fellow would be just as safe if you weren't told. Or safer. You'd had one donor in your charge and let him be killed. I told Christopher, Doctor Ainsworth and Angelo that mum would be the word for a while."

"How did you and Winters finally get together?"

"I suppose you were here when I called and Doctor Lack repeated our conversation. I didn't make any mention to him of the donor when he called while you were there because I was afraid you might overhear."

"Thanks. Doctor Lack has been the only one of all of you who seemed to remember that it's a citizen's duty to give information to a law-enforcement officer."

"That's what Doctor Ainsworth said." Hand spoke up.

Norcott nodded. "Hugh took little part in our discussion but he did express that opinion. As to Doctor Lack, he might not have been so generous with his information if he'd known . . ."

"What?" Bounty demanded when Norcott paused.

"How much mystery there is to the part your office has played in all this," Norcott replied with considerable heat. "Listen carefully now, Sheriff. As soon as you left me at the Sutherland, I went to Winters' room myself. I got no answer but went back after a time. The girl—his sister or cousin or whoever she is—opened the door. I asked for Fred Winters and told who I was. Immediately out popped Winters from one door and your deputy from another. Winters had Larrick identify me. Then he came out into the hall with me while Larrick stayed with the girl."

"And Winters told you his price for a transfusion was twenty-five thousand bucks."

"Yes, and I stalled. First because I simply don't have that much cash on hand and he said he had to have it when the banks open in the morning. If the money wasn't forthcoming then he was catching the plane back to New York. Second, I saw he was scared and I felt pretty sure he could be brought down to reasonable terms. But he was a little smarter than I thought for. He came back with the suggestion that I get Doctor Lack to chip in."

"How did he come to make that suggestion, do you know?"

"I couldn't say, Sheriff. But he seemed to know as much about Doctor Lack and his finances as I did. And my guess would be that he got his dope from one Bert Larrick. Do you begin to get the point, Bounty? The first time any of us saw Winters, Larrick was with him. Larrick seems to have been with him most of the time since. I told Winters I'd bring him over here to discuss the money and the transfusion with Doctor Lack. He refused to ride with me and said Larrick would drive him. Where is Winters now, Sheriff? A straight answer."

Bounty had got a match sliver stuck in his throat. "Winters is with Larrick," he managed to say.

"Where?"

"On their way over here."

"How long have they known each other?"

"Since about seven o'clock this evening."

"And the girl—how long has Larrick known her?"

"He met her this evening too."

"The three of them became pretty thick, didn't they, never to have known one another before? Winters trusts Larrick when he doesn't anyone else—"

"Oh, Mr. Norcott!" Hand broke in, as if unable to contain himself longer. "I can tell you the secret. Bert's fallen for the girl. That's all. He falls for a different one every week or so, doesn't he, Mr. Bounty?"

"Sometimes twice a week," Bounty affirmed.

"She looked like a nice girl," Hand went on. "But I wouldn't say either she or her cousin wasn't using Bert. When Bert has a crush on he hasn't a lick of sense, has he, Mr. Bounty?"

"Not a lick."

"Well," Hand said, looking anxiously at Norcott, "that's all there is to it. Bert's in love again."

Norcott smiled sourly. "I seem to be in the minority here. When did you and Larrick become such bosom friends, Christopher?"

"We're not friends. We don't like each other at all. But I know Bert's no crook. He doesn't know anything about Winters' racket, does he, Mr. Bounty?"

"Not a thing."

"I might remind you, Christopher," Norcott said, "that Larrick isn't a high-school kid any longer. If he hasn't tumbled to Winters he needs a guardian himself. And I might remind the sheriff that I've known Larrick all his life, not just a few months. But I'm not bent on making him out a rascal. What I'm trying to do, Bounty, is to bring it home to you that you're in no position to blame us for not rushing to you with every bit of information as it came our way."

"I'll grant that—so far as the story has gone," Bounty said reluctantly. "Now, Chris, you and I seem to be on the same side. So don't you think you'd better tell me about spending last night in Brownsville?"

Hand looked down quickly. "It hasn't anything to do with this business."

"Little Saturday night party?"

"Yes."

"Where'd you stay?"

"With some people in a trailer in a tourist camp. They've gone now."

"People named Smith, I suppose. When did you get back to Las Palmas?"

"About noon."

"Oh, see here, Sheriff!" Norcott protested. "You're carrying this too far. I knew Christopher spent the night down there but I didn't think it necessary to tell you when you asked. I don't know where he stayed and I don't care. That's his own business. If every young man in Las Palmas— Do you know where Bert Larrick was last night?"

"No, but I do know that Hieronymus stayed overnight in Brownsville—at a tourist camp. Want to change your mind, Chris, and say you registered at a hotel as John Doe in order to get away from it all?"

Norcott tore the wrapper from the cigar as he jerked it from his mouth. "Where's that knocking?" he demanded, trying to look past Bounty into the hall.

"Darn it!" Bounty said with a snap of the fingers. "I bet somebody was in that room I locked up." He went to the guest-room door and turned the key. "Why, Doctor Angelo!" he exclaimed as the county physician came out. "What in the world were you doing in there?"

There was a fixed smile on Angelo's lips but his eyes stood out black and hard against his white face. "Wasn't this a bit silly, Sheriff?" he asked softly. "I didn't want to raise a rumpus but there's a limit to what I'm going to take from you." His eyes flickered to the study door and to that of the master bedroom. "Is Doctor Cotillion with my patient?"

"Yes. Go on in the study and sit down and I'll see what Doctor Cotillion has to say."

"Evidently I haven't made it clear to you that I'm Doctor Lack's physician."

"I think there's something in your contract with the county, Angelo, about you engaging in private practice. I'll look it up. In the meantime, better go in and sit down and get out of the road."

Angelo shrugged and sauntered toward the study. "I wonder," he murmured, almost dreamily, "if Mr. Norcott wouldn't be interested in hearing about this situation."

Bounty hastened to the door of the master bedroom, knocked lightly and stepped into the foyer.

Doctor Cotillion came out of the further room and the grave, aged look on his face made Bounty's heart sink. "Doctor Lack is asleep," he said slowly. "It seems to have been a very strong sedative that he took. But I don't think there's anything to worry about."

"Did you look at his eye?"

"As well as I could. He was sleepy and didn't want me to. I'm no oculist but he says the eyeball isn't damaged and I'm inclined to agree with him. I'd have a good man look at it tomorrow, however."

"Do you think Doctor Lack should go to the hospital?"

"Not tonight at least, if he has someone here to look after him. To me, Sheriff, Doctor Lack is a man who suddenly has reached the point of exhaustion—physical, mental and emotional. When I met him this morning I thought I saw this coming. Doctor Angelo knows more of his general condition than I, of course. But I'd say a long and complete rest is imperative for him. As far as tonight is concerned, I advise you to let him sleep. I'm telling you that because you seem to be in charge here."

"Am I?" Bounty said with satisfaction. "What did he say about the June bug?"

Tired and dull as were Cotillion's eyes, a little shrewd humor came into them as he looked at Bounty. "I'd give a penny to know what happened here tonight, Sheriff. Doctor Lack answered that if you said it was a June bug, it must have been a June bug. He wanted me to tell you he hoped you'd be comfortable tonight. He said to tell Beck—"

"What?"

Cotillion shook his head. "He was dropping off to sleep and I didn't catch it."

Bounty opened the door into the hall. "Thanks, Doctor. Let's go back to the study. I hope you're prepared to tell me what killed Hieronymus."

"Yes, Sheriff, I'm prepared to tell you."

Angelo had been holding forth to some effect, Bounty knew the instant he stepped into the study. Norcott and Hand looked like men suddenly galvanized out of a lethargy and still bewildered by their state.

"What's this about an attack on Doctor Lack, Sheriff?" Norcott demanded at once.

"An attack?" Bounty repeated blandly. "You embarrass me no end by asking that. Doctor Lack sprang up from that desk there and put a hand to his eye. Beck happened to be standing across from him and Doctor Angelo, who was sitting where he couldn't see any of it, jumped to the conclusion that Beck had struck him. He insisted that I arrest Beck and I did. Now it turns out that it was a June bug got in Doctor Lack's eye." He turned to Angelo, leaning so far back in a chair that his face was obscured. "Only a June bug, Doctor Angelo. We have the testimony of the man who was hit."

"The whole thing sounds fishy, Sheriff," Norcott said. "But what I want to know is about Doctor Lack's condition."

"Doctor Cotillion, will you tell these gentlemen what you told me about Doctor Lack's condition?"

Cotillion did so, slowly and abstractedly, looking at none of them and seemingly at nothing.

Norcott listened, his cigar held between two fingers. With his teeth ready to clamp again upon its end, he looked as if he were snarling. "That's all very well," he said brusquely. "But what about my nephew? Is Doctor Lack going to be able to continue taking care of him?"

There was a long dumfounded sort of silence, during which Cotillion sat motionless, breathing with half-open mouth. "I hadn't thought of that," he said at last in that same faraway manner.

That silence had been a dumfounded one on Bounty's part, at least, because neither had he thought of this aspect of the affair. Vague suspicions began to form in his mind as he remembered the words spoken outside Dr. Cotillion's room the night before. He wondered what Angelo's move was going to be here. . . .

"Oh, you probably think I'm selfish." Norcott spoke impatiently. "But that was the first thing in my mind."

Angelo made a pyramid of his fingers and said from the obscurity of his chair: "It might be to your advantage, Mr. Norcott, to get to the bottom of this. This man Beck is a vicious character. I gave the sheriff a theory about him—"

"Let's not go into theories now," Norcott interrupted. "Doctor Cotillion, what's your answer?"

Bounty thought that the physician was never going to speak. "I don't know that I'm the one to say, Mr. Norcott," he said finally. "It's not the actual care of your nephew which has helped wear Doctor Lack down, but all this suspense and worry about donors. He's not at death's door, however, by any means. I have an idea that tomorrow he'll have something to say about this himself."

"But if he has to take a rest, you can carry on, can't you? You've examined Jimmy. Doctor Lack has told you about him. There's no reason why a change of doctors should affect Jimmy's case, is there?"

"No, no." Cotillion stirred in his chair. "With due respect to Doctor Lack's ability, I can take charge of him if need be. But until you talk with Lack I wish you'd continue to think of him as your nephew's physician."

He would have said more, but Bounty interrupted: "Gentlemen, all this talk can wait. But I have a question that I'm going to have answered right now. Doctor Cotillion, what caused the death of Hieronymus?"

A sound that was half sigh and half grunt escaped from Cotillion. "Aconite," he said.

Bounty stared at him blankly for a moment, thinking of aconite only as the name which had headed the list of the contents of Doctor Lack's drug cabinet. Then his eyes suddenly narrowed. "Isn't aconite swift death, Doctor?" he asked in a voice which had some of the sibilance of Dr. Lack's.

"Yes." With release of his information Cotillion began to manifest the excitability which he must have been keeping curbed. His voice grew oratorical and filled the room. "Do you see now, Sheriff, why I wouldn't give you an answer at the hotel, although I could have? Do you see why I wanted to talk to your county physician before I did to you? Why I wanted the support of Mr. Norcott and Doctor Lack? I was with Hieronymus ten or fifteen minutes. I don't know what was the matter with him. Nothing, perhaps, except fear. But when I left him he most certainly had not been poisoned by aconite. You have no one's word for that, however, save my own. And between then and the time the orderlies found him dead—who entered that room? Your deputy, I know. Perhaps yourself. I can see only one solution, Sheriff. One of the three of us administered that poison."

Quicksand sucked at Bounty again. Yet all evening it had been in the back of his mind that sooner or later he was going to find himself facing this dilemma.

Ash tray or no ash tray, Roger Norcott had lighted his cigar. "There's some way out of this," he said. "We stopped by Mr. Palladay's office, Sheriff, but found that you had it locked. I've never been in there, but Doctor Cotillion tells me there's no entrance except through the anteroom. Is that correct?"

"Correct," Bounty told him, wishing now that he had sat by himself in that damned black leather and chromium office until he thought this out.

"And no one else went into that office?"

"No one else." Bounty wasn't going to say that Larrick had gone in—to telephone—but that he himself hadn't. He was remembering what he should have remembered long ago about the conversation following Bert's exit from the office.

"I thought of suicide, of course," Norcott persisted. "Doctor Cotillion pointed out that there would have to be a container. There was none on the body, he said. I was going to look on the floor."

"There was no container," Bounty said. "I made a routine examination of the office before I left it." He hesitated, debating the advisability of trying to talk to Cotillion alone. But there was Norcott, vigilant as a lawyer. "Can you tell me how the poison was taken, Doctor?"

"I think so. In whisky. Less than a spoonful would have been fatal. The taste isn't particularly unpleasant. In whisky it might well pass unnoticed."

"Did Hieronymus have the smell of whisky about him when you examined him—alive?"

"I think not."

"But he did when you examined him—dead?"

"I didn't notice it until after I got him to the morgue. I couldn't think at first how it had escaped me in the manager's office. But I believe I know now. You remember how strong was the odor of night-blooming cereus those orderlies let in. The man might have been drenched with whisky and I wouldn't have smelled it."

Norcott cleared his throat. "Sheriff—" he began, then stopped as the clangor of the knocker echoed up through the hall.

Bounty dashed out and almost took a header on the stairs. What Norcott had been going to ask he knew full well. Had sheriff or deputy had whisky in his possession?

Larrick must have been leaning against the front door, for Bounty's opening of it precipitated him into the hall. He grabbed Bounty's arm and shook it while he gulped and said: "Is Doctor Lack here? Doctor Cotillion? Anybody. Get 'em, Peter. It's Fred Winters. And Beck. They're out in front. And I think—they're both dead."

"Steady, son, steady." Bounty glanced up at the procession coming down the stairs: Norcott and Dr. Cotillion, Christopher Hand

and, at the rear, Dr. Angelo. "Let's go out." As they crossed the porch he added in an undertone, working his tongue on the consonants in the Mexican manner: "Don't do too much talking, son."

He looked upon a moonlit tableau which the artistry of a designer of scenery had saved from the results of a dramatist's lack of restraint. Gus Broddus stood between corpses, with the moonlight glinting on glass in his right hand. Fred Winters lay at his feet, stretched out upon the grass between curb and sidewalk. The door of Bounty's coupé was open and the moonlight struck one of Beck's polished shoes. In the interior Beck's hair was a burnished white helmet that rested on the back of the seat and didn't move.

"Chief," Gus Broddus said, as if he were going to cry, and moved awkwardly aside.

Larrick sat cross-legged on the grass and put his hands over his face. Norcott, Angelo and Christopher Hand stopped on the sidewalk but after a moment Hand went to Larrick's side and sat down.

Dr. Cotillion knelt beside Winters. The moonlight was too bright and Bounty turned away from the ugliness of a death which from the appearance of that face might have come from asphyxiation. Hieronymus had had that look on his face. Beck, too, must have it, and Beck's countenance was one which Bounty resolved not to see until it was at peace.

"God in heaven, Bounty! Is that Malcolm Lack?"

Bounty whirled. Dr. Cotillion had risen and started toward the coupé but had stopped like a man who checks himself before setting foot on a slippery street. He was staring at Beck's face. "Oh no," he said after an instant. "I see. It's Doctor Lack's man."

Bounty watched him thoughtfully as he went around the car to open the opposite door. The sheriff turned his head then and saw that the exclamation had brought Dr. Angelo forward. Angelo went to the side of the car, walking as if there were dew on the grass, struck a match and peered inside. His face looked white and pasty. "Yes, Doctor Cotillion," he said with a soft laugh. "That's only Beck."

Gus Broddus had come up and put a bottle in Bounty's hand. Bounty looked at its label and froze like a dog at point. It was a pint bottle, less than half full, and the brand of its whisky was the brand of the whisky which Bounty had carried from the sheriff's office to the Sutherland Hotel.

Dr. Cotillion returned and leaned against a fender, his wide shoulders slumped. "Both dead," he said. "Aconite again."

"And this, Doctor?" Bounty handed him the bottle.

The physician uncorked it and sniffed at it. He poured a little of the liquor into the palm of his hand and sniffed again. "Aconite," he pronounced and returned the bottle.

Roger Norcott advanced, his cigar glowing redly. "Well?" he said from his throat. "What happened here? Why doesn't somebody explain? Larrick."

The deputy lowered his hands and stared straight ahead of him. "I had the whisky." He spoke in a high-pitched unnatural voice, and Bounty wasn't sure he could have stopped him had he been determined to. "I had it at the hotel. I borrowed Peter's car there to drive to the morgue and I put the bottle in one of the door pockets. When I got back to the hotel I forgot about the stuff. When I remembered, Peter had already come out here in the car. I took Fred Winters home with me. Then we drove here. Fred had been wanting a drink. The whisky had been for him in the first place. And there was Peter's car, with Gus and that fellow sitting in it. We went up and I got the bottle out of the pocket. I gave it to Fred and he took a long drink and handed it back to me. Then I passed it to Gus. He asked Beck if he didn't want a snort and gave it to him. Just then Fred fell down and called to me to do something for him. He twisted a little and then—and then he was just dead. I started to run to the house when Gus yelled to hurry—that he thought Beck was dying too. It all happened so quick—"

"Where did you get the whisky, Bert?" Norcott asked in a calmer, almost paternal tone.

Bounty sat down, too, and looked at the moon. "This is no time or place for an inquest," he said. "But we might as well thresh some of this out now as later. That seems to be the same liquor I've had at the office since last March—"

The undersheriff gasped and put a hand to his stomach. "Chief, you remember—I—"

"Yes, Gus. You broke the seal on it and took a drink—a little over a week ago, wasn't it?"

"Week ago last night, chief."

"Did you feel any ill effects?"

"No."

"Very well. So far as I know, no one else touched that bottle until tonight. Bert called me from the hotel and asked me to leave it at the desk for Fred Winters when I made my trip there with Hieronymus. I wrapped it up and wrote Winters' name on it. What about that paper, Bert?"

"It's there—on the floor of the car."

"I laid the package on the counter at the hotel," Bounty went on evenly. "There followed the scene with Hieronymus and I didn't give it another thought."

"Did you give Hieronymus a drink at the office?" Norcott asked.

"No. But if I see what's coming, this is important. He saw me take the whisky out of my desk and wrap it up. Bert, do you want to carry on the story?"

"Well," Larrick said, "I never thought of the whisky either until after we had Hieronymus in the manager's office. Then, when I went out to meet Doctor Cotillion, I saw it lying on the desk. I knew Fred had gone upstairs so I picked it up and put it in my pocket."

"But it had been lying on that counter in the lobby all that time, had it?" Cotillion asked. "With the name of Fred Winters on it."

"Yes sir, I suppose so. Then I went in with you, Doctor Cotillion, when you saw Hieronymus. I laid the bottle, still wrapped up, on Mr. Palladay's desk. You remember I told you what it was in case you needed a stimulant for Hieronymus."

Cotillion nodded. "And Hieronymus heard. I think I know what's in the sheriff's mind."

"When I went back in the office to phone for the ambulance," Larrick continued, "I stuck the bottle in my coat pocket again. It was there when we went out to Mr. Bounty's car to go to the morgue. It's such a close fit for me behind the wheel that I took the bottle out and slipped it in a pocket of the door."

"So Hieronymus must have been dead when you were telephoning."

"I guess so. I know he didn't move but—but I didn't go near him."

"Did you notice, Bert—or could you tell—whether that bottle had been unwrapped when you took it from Palladay's desk?" Bounty asked.

"I don't know, Peter."

"Doctor Cotillion, could Hieronymus have taken a drink from the bottle after you left him, then wrapped it up again and got to the couch before he died?"

The physician was silent for a moment, pulling at his lower lip. "Sheriff," he said with an uneasy laugh, "for my own sake and for your deputy's I'd like to give you an unqualified yes in answer to that. The man would probably have moved quickly, for fear one of you would come in and discover him filching the whisky. But the orderlies told us they found him stretched out full length on that davenport, didn't they? And isn't there a water cooler at the head of the davenport?"

"Yes."

"And I suppose there are paper cups or something?"

"Yeah." Christopher Hand spoke up. "Paper cups. I was in there talking to Mr. Palladay once and took a drink of water."

"Well then," Cotillion said, "my guess would be that Hieronymus poured himself out a drink, then wrapped up the bottle and carried the cup to the davenport. He sat down, drank and tossed the cup into the receptacle. Then he lay down and the poison struck him. In his weakened condition he'd go out"—the doctor snapped his fingers—"like that. It's not surprising he couldn't give a cry that we would hear through that partition."

"That would make the time right, would it?" Bounty inquired.

"To a second, I'd say."

"So that's the truth of the matter, is it?" Norcott said. "These two donors—and Beck—drank poisoned whisky that wasn't intended for them at all."

Bounty rose sneezing, for the ground, baked by the sun all day, now had the nighttime chill of the desert. "I'll answer yes, Norcott," he said grimly, "so as to make you sleep better. I'll think no in order to get some sleep myself. Gentlemen, this meeting stands adjourned. Bert, will you run in and call the morgue?"

"I'll go with you, Bert, and show you where a downstairs phone is," Christopher Hand said as he rose with Larrick. "I want to get our hats."

"Be sure and bring Doctor Angelo's hat," Bounty called. "He's leaving too." He looked at Angelo as he spoke but the latter made no rejoinder. Bounty rather wished that he had. Angelo had become too suddenly a wooden figure in the background.

"Let me talk to you a moment, Sheriff." Norcott drew Bounty a little distance away. "I'll see you in the morning," he said. "Don't think I'm leaving you in the lurch now that I know . . ." He paused. "Bounty, where did you get that whisky?"

"Jack Cosgro, the Cameron County sheriff, gave it to me for my birthday. A joke of sorts attached to it, Norcott." Bounty's voice took on a drawl. "I don't drink and everybody knows I don't drink."

Norcott was hurrying on: "Well, Broddus' testimony shows it was all right when you got it. Somebody slipped into your office and poisoned it. That could be done, couldn't it, easy enough?"

"Oh, easy enough. People are in and out of that office of ours all day. It's the best loafing place in the courthouse because we don't have enough work to do to keep us busy."

"Was the desk where you kept the whisky locked?"

"No, nothing in it worth locking up."

"Well, you must have enemies."

Bounty smiled. "You're wanting your doubts dispelled, aren't you, Norcott?"

"Oh, I don't mean personal enemies. I honestly believe you're the best-liked man in this part of Texas. I know how people always turn to you when they're in trouble. Whether they'll stand behind you when you're in trouble is another proposition. But what about the political setup? We haven't any machines functioning in Hesperides yet but they're sure being built for the next election. And you know as well as I that a few dollars slipped into the right palm would take care of a bit of poisoning."

"There's nothing at stake but the sheriff's office. That's not worth murdering me for."

"Don't be too sure." Norcott lowered his voice. "We both know one man who wants the office—wants it bad. He ran against you once and I know for a certainty that he plans to file again."

"I can't see E. Matthew Rone as a conspirator, can you? He couldn't keep his voice down enough."

"Rone's from Hidalgo, remember, and I know him better than you do. Because he blows a lot, people think he's harmless. He's not. He's got no more compunction in him than a wild bull."

"Wild bulls don't use poison."

"He may have learned some things since he's been at the hotel. And, Bounty, remember, that whisky lay on the counter where he could get at it."

"But it had the name of Fred Winters on it."

"Did he see you put it there, though?"

"I'm sure he did."

"Well then, he may have taken that chance to get you in dutch. Unless you can clear up that matter of the whisky to everybody's satisfaction, you're done for politically in this county. Forever. This case is going to stink to high heaven." Norcott paused for breath. "Haven't you made enemies through arrests, Bounty?" he asked in desperation.

"You know our record in Hesperides: a nice big jail and not a soul has stayed in it overnight."

"Well—women. I hope you take this in the right way. But you have the reputation—"

"You flatter the old man, Norcott." Bounty watched Larrick and Christopher Hand come down the walk. They weren't talking but each had an arm across the other's shoulders.

"Well, maybe the poison wasn't meant for you," Norcott said. "Maybe it was meant—for Larrick."

"Bert would be less likely to take a drink—now—than I. Everyone knows that."

"Broddus then. Bounty, you talk about me wanting my doubts dispelled. That's what you want."

"Maybe I do, at that. Let's call it a night."

"Well, Chris," Larrick was saying, "I'll see you in the morning. I'm driving Doctor Cotillion to the hotel."

The two young men had been distributing hats. Dr. Angelo put his on his head, turned without a word to anyone and walked with his little swaying of the hips toward the driveway where his roadster was parked.

Bounty gazed at his back, speculatively, until he heard Norcott say with a catch in his voice: "Christopher, there's only one man who can save Jimmy's life now. Get him for me." Norcott had been standing with a foot on the running board of his car and looking up at the moon. His movements were those of an old man as he got into the front seat beside Hand. He kept his head up until Hand started the car. Then it sank and his handkerchief was a streak of white going to his eyes.

Bounty turned to Larrick, who stood at Dr. Cotillion's side. "Son"—his eyes fell briefly to Winters—"is this going to make any difference in your plans?"

"No. I've got my suitcase in the car. And I'd rather wait till morning to break the news to Mallory. It's not going to be so hard telling her about Fred's death—it's not as if he'd been her brother— as about the rest." Larrick swallowed. "Chris told me how Fred was going to sell his blood to Mr. Norcott. That's true, is it?"

"That's true, son."

"What a damn fool I was!"

"No more than I, son. Listen. Here's the key of Palladay's office. When you go to the hotel I wish you'd confiscate all the used paper cups about the water cooler—without ruining any fingerprints, of course—and have Doctor Cotillion see if there's been aconite in one. You can phone me at home if you do it right away. If not, here. I'm staying with Doctor Lack tonight."

Cotillion put a hand on Larrick's arm. "You still mean to entrust me to this young man, Sheriff? Or him to me?"

"Yes, Doctor. And I want to ask you a question. What made you mistake that man in my car for Doctor Lack's nephew?"

"The white hair, I suppose. I knew Doctor Lack was expecting his nephew. I assumed you would take measures to guard him. And for an instant, seeing that corpse—"

Bounty's voice was curiously flat: "I understood that Malcolm Lack had hair the color of his uncle's. Although lighter."

Cotillion stared at him. "Why, I met the chap only once. But he's a towhead if I ever saw one."

"Does he look like Doctor Lack?"

"No, except perhaps for the eyes."

"Are you sure about this, Doctor?"

"As far as physical characteristics go, yes. Malcolm Lack doesn't have his uncle's fine features or his freckles. He is as pale as Doctor Lack, however, and of somewhat the same build. When I met Doctor Lack I could see no resemblance at all, except occasionally in the eyes. But after I'd been with him awhile I got to feeling that he and his nephew showed their blood relationship in some way I wasn't able to put my finger on. Both are volatile. Maybe that's it."

"Does Malcolm Lack look anything like Beck?"

"Much more like Beck than like Doctor Lack. You seem bothered, Sheriff."

"I am."

Larrick had been waiting for a chance to break in. "Peter," he said, back at his old familiarity of address, "you remember I told you Fred Winters had wanted to know if Doctor Lack had any white-haired relatives. Well, I asked him about that. He was vague, said he thought he'd met somebody named Lack once, with white hair, and wondered if he was a member of that rich Boston family. If Doctor Lack has a nephew—"

"Winters must have met Malcolm Lack in Chicago, where Lack had gone to give a transfusion too. He'd be anxious to know if Lack were available for a transfusion. If he were, that would decrease the demand for Winters' blood."

"That's just the way Fred talked." Larrick spoke bitterly. "As if blood were a commodity to be bargained over."

"That's what it has become. And now"—Bounty was silent for a moment, thinking—"a person with immunity to streptococcus and with the right type of blood could demand whatever price he chose."

Hearing the ambulance, Bounty bade them good night and walked over to Gus Broddus, who stood with his hands in his hip pockets, staring at the moon.

"Get those damned handcuffs off Beck, will you, Gus? I'm going to ask you to wait here while I go home and pack some things. Then I'll send you home in a taxi."

"O.K., chief. Bringin' Carmen over?"

"I wish I could. She hasn't been feeling well lately and I'm worried about her."

"Something she et probably." Broddus cleared his throat. "Chief, here's something I thought I ought to tell you in private. About that fellow Beck. After you went back in he wouldn't talk but just sat there lookin' at the house. I kinda got to likin' him, though. So when Bert and Winters came up and got out that liquor I passed the bottle over to Beck and told him he'd better have a drink. I thought it'd cheer him up. Well—Bert didn't see this—but I still had the bottle in my hand when Winters fell. I'm not sure but I don't think Beck was goin' to take it. I'm not sure either that he saw what had happened to Winters, because I was standin' in the way. But he did pull it out of my hand just as I was turnin' around to see what was the matter. And by the time I could turn around again to stop him—it was too late. He'd already drunk. And, chief, he was smilin' as he handed the bottle back to me. He said, 'Thank you,' just as polite as could be. And he asked me if I'd tell Doctor Lack something for him."

"What, Gus?"

"He died just then and didn't get to finish."

16

In some men a homecoming to the small one-storied cottage south
of the courthouse (a cottage not yet paid for, incidentally) would
have aroused invidious comparisons between their lot and that of
John Belton Lack. Not so Peter Bounty. He was too busy thinking
of the stir that the sound of his car was causing inside that house.
The place was dark, yet he tooted his horn as he turned into the
drive. On his way to the front door he whistled *The Eyes of Texas*
and pounded on the whitewashed bricks of the wall and on the
window screen. He unlocked the door but waited a moment, tan-
talizingly, before he opened it.

From close to the floor of the hall great greenish-yellow eyes
glowed up at him. He switched on the light, grasped his knees and
got ready to run forward. But Carmen crouched motionless, stared
at him and after an instant mewed.

Bounty told people that Carmen was part Persian but in his
heart of hearts he knew that she wasn't. True, her hair was rather
long and by dint of much stroking had become smooth and almost
silky. But there was a curious brindled look about it which he had
seen on no other animal except lions. He had dug a grave for
Carmen the same day he found her lying in his front yard, bat-
tered and starved, the madness of terror in her eyes. The hole in
the flower bed had been filled in, however, and the chloroform
bottle remained as it had come from the drugstore, for Carmen
had told Peter she didn't want to die now that she knew she was

safe. No cat ever had a stronger will than Carmen. She lived and thrived and soon was putting on the airs of a grande dame.

During the day Carmen got along well enough with Maria, the elderly Mexican woman who in her slipshod fashion kept the house spick and span, although Bounty suspected that she took advantage of Maria's apprehension of her to do a bit of queening. Only on the occasion of one of his rare absences in the evening did she show that there were memories of what the world had been without Peter. Upon his return they always went through the same performance, Carmen making sport of her fears by pretending to be afraid of him, he chasing her through the house until she was ready to be caught and caressed while she assured him that it was all in fun. Tonight, however, she didn't throw up her crooked tail and scamper away. She mewed like a little kitten and looked from him to the open door.

Bounty closed the door with his foot, picked her up and rubbed his nose against hers. "You know something's wrong, don't you, baby? Don't be afraid. Nothing's going to hurt us."

He carried her into the living room, flopped down on the sofa and put her on his chest. He stroked her under the chin, where cats like to be stroked, and talked to her in Spanish as she liked to be talked to, explaining why he had to go out again that night. She clung to him, understanding, until the telephone rang.

The telephone was an object of great interest to Carmen, so Bounty took her with him as he went to the rear of the house, where adjoining the southeast bedroom was a space which the builder had evidently intended to serve as a dressing room but which Bounty used as den, library and (it must be admitted) catchall.

"Fine little cat you are!" he said, feeling Carmen's full stomach and knowing he had left too much food for her when he visited her late that afternoon. "You've gone and scandalized Doctor Lack. Won't he feel silly when he finds out about you? Hello."

At the sound of Bert Larrick's voice Carmen struggled free of Bounty's arm and jumped to the floor, scratching him just a little as she left him. Carmen shared Gus Broddus' opinion of Larrick.

He was a trial to her, bolting in as he did almost every night, imposing upon her master's good nature, usurping the attention that was rightfully hers.

"We found the cup, Peter," Larrick said. "It was right on top of the used ones. Doctor Cotillion examined it and said it had had whisky and aconite in it. So I guess that's that."

"Thanks, son. Bring it to the office tomorrow and we'll see about fingerprints."

"They're sure to be Hieronymus'."

"I know. But we've got to make the evidence binding. Son, I wonder if you know of some woman—some private nurse, maybe, not connected with the hospital—who'd go to Doctor Lack's tomorrow and perhaps stay several days."

"I know the very one, Peter. I was thinking about her while Doctor Cotillion was telling me about Doctor Lack. Carrie Ainsworth."

"Why, from what you told me, son—"

"Oh, sure. But just the same I think she's the one. She's had lots of experience and she knows her way about that house. I know pretty well how Carrie feels and I believe she'd go. If she did, it might solve some problems."

"For whom?"

"For her and Chris Hand maybe. He doesn't want her to have to work—"

Bounty wasn't listening. He was staring at Carmen, who lay on the floor, twisting a little and giving tiny cries of pain.

"I'll think it over, son," he said hastily. "Good night."

He dropped to his knees. His eyes were small and hard with alarm. "Carmen baby," he said, putting out his hands. "What's the matter with you?"

17

ON HIS WAY to the courthouse steps at eight o'clock the next morning, Peter Bounty passed E. Matthew Rone, in a new and bigger
pearl-gray Stetson, holding forth to a knot of his cronies.

"Hi, Elmer!" Bounty called. "Brown. Skinner. Brand. Lynch."
Every man jack there saw himself wearing a badge before the day
was out. "Early for Santa Claus."

Rone shifted his cigar to the other side of his mouth, spat into
a flower bed and, as soon as Bounty was on the steps, delivered
himself of some witticism that brought guffaws.

Like most cities of the Magic Valley, Las Palmas is the result
not of random accretion but of planning. In Mexican fashion it has
a park, Yznaga, as its hub. Flanking this on the east is the munici-
pal auditorium, on the west the courthouse, of uniform Monterey
architecture. The sheriff's office is in the southeast corner, on the
first floor rear, so that Bounty usually found it more convenient to
use the back entrance. This morning, however, he was on parade.
He went down the corridor in belligerent mood, snapping out greet-
ings right and left, not pausing to notice what reception they got.

Gus Broddus was at the telephone as he let himself into the
office. "Yes, yes, I'll tell him," the undersheriff said wearily and
slammed down the receiver. He looked at Bounty, his blue eyes
watered and he had to lower them. "Too many dames callin' this
office," he complained.

"Gladys?"

"Yeah. Madder 'n a wet hen. Says Bert had a date with her last night and stood her up."

"Gladys might as well fly back on the perch for a while. Bert's busy elsewhere." It was like a ritual, gone through with daily and repeated now to make this seem like any other Monday morning, and Bounty knew that both of them wanted to prolong it.

"Want to leave that door shut, chief?"

"Let's." This was the part of the business day that Bounty liked best, with everyone in high fettle from sleep and breakfast and glad to postpone for a few moments application to the old grind. His office had become a clearinghouse for news garnered and jokes heard since last quitting time, but this morning there would be only questions to which he could give no answers.

"You don't look like you got much sleep, chief."

"Not much, Gus. I lay awake planning how to deploy our forces so as to cover all the ground." Bounty tilted back in his padded swivel chair, put his feet on the desk, then promptly took them down and from force of habit looked to see if he had scuffed the varnish. He was finding it hard to live up to this impressive furniture which the Hesperides commissioners had purchased in the first flush of pride in their new charge. "I expect the sensible course is to call on the police to help us," he said.

"Fat lot of good that'd do." Broddus gave him the answer he wanted. "With Tanner and E. Matthew Rone thick as they are— and brothers-in-law. They don't want this case solved till after the county commissioners meet."

"I hate to believe that, Gus. I swear I do."

"You're too trustin', chief," Broddus admonished, sitting in Larrick's chair.

Being privileged from long association with Bounty in Cameron County, the undersheriff had his own sanctum in the room adjoining the main office. Bounty, who really hadn't intended to bring Gus with him to Hesperides, was far from being averse to the arrangement, which let him keep Bert at his side, installed at a desk exactly like his, so the boy would feel the responsibility of his position.

Bounty searched through his pockets for a match. "I stopped by the house on my way here," he said, "to see how Carmen was feeling and to give her something to eat. Rolf Jester called. The commissioners are meeting at ten, all right, and Rolf says he knows there's a move on foot to suspend me from office pending investigation of this poisoning. Rone's supporters, such as Sam Spicard, will probably point to the urgency of taking action before more donors arrive. Jester says they're in the minority and haven't a chance of accomplishing anything."

"Jester's always sayin' cheerful things like that."

"He's the original optimist, I know. But I think he knows what he's talking about here. And, aside from being chairman, he swings a lot of influence. At any rate, he said to go about our business and he'd see no action was taken this morning. There's considerable routine business to be transacted and the question of the John Belton Lack Hospital is scheduled to come up."

"That's about Angelo?"

"Yes. From what Jester says, there's no doubt he'll be removed and Doctor Ainsworth put in his place. That will take time. And after ousting the county physician the commissioners will be apt to go slow about making any more changes immediately. They'll think of the publicity. So let's not get in a stew about our jobs."

"That's an order, chief."

"And another thing, Gus. Let's be careful what we say to reporters. A man from the *Sun* caught me this morning. I made a brief statement about last night. I neglected to say, however, that Beck had been under arrest at the time of his death. That'll come out in time, I suppose, since so many know it. But let's not stick our necks out."

"That's an order, chief."

There was a brief silence. Both men stared at the drawer by Bounty's left ankle.

"Gus," Bounty said, "you heard what was said last night about Malcolm Lack, the doctor's nephew?"

"He sounded awful vague to me."

"I know, but when I got up this morning I tossed a coin. Heads we concentrated on him. Tails we didn't. Heads won. How'd you like to spend the day at Doctor Lack's?"

"Waitin' for the nephew?"

"For him or a message from him. Answer the phone and the door and sign for any telegrams. Don't let Doctor Angelo in the house."

"What's that hippopotamus up to, chief?"

"I wish I could be sure." Bounty told briefly of the physician's actions the night before. "Did he come out to my car while you were sitting on the running board?"

"Nope, he parked in the drive and went straight to the front door. He looked at me mighty close, though."

"You weren't there when he came the first time?"

"No."

"Well, from the way he acted when Doctor Cotillion mistook Beck for Malcolm Lack, I feel sure he's on the lookout for the young man. He has the advantage that he knows Lack by sight. And incidentally, Gus, there may be more truth than malice in what Angelo said about this nephew. Let me know at once if he puts in an appearance. I'm not going to try to keep this office open all day but I'll leave word with the telephone operator where I'm to be found. From what you said last night, I judge you're acquainted with Carrie Ainsworth."

"I know her fairly well. Her dad's our doctor."

"I took a long shot this morning and asked her if she'd give me some help about taking care of Doctor Lack. She's on her way here now. I hope she'll be willing to go out to his house."

"I doubt it, chief," Broddus said awkwardly. "After all the talk there's been."

"Well, we'll see. There's the key to Doctor Lack's front door. I expect you'd better mosey on out now. He was asleep when I left and I'd rather have someone in the house when he wakes up. If he should wake while you're there alone with him and want to know what's happened, just put him off and call me."

"O.K., chief," the undersheriff said, rising and stuffing down his shirttail. "Don't you think you ought to tell me one more thing about Lack? Is he nuts?"

"Nuts?" Bounty frowned quickly and shook his head. "No, Gus. I'm sorry if I gave you that idea."

"Oh, I already had it. I've heard it rumored around town for some time. I never talked to him but once—that day he came and asked for you and had me show him through the jail. But he acted darned peculiar then. Twittery. And, seein' how careful you were about him, I thought I'd better ask."

"I have another reason for wanting Doctor Lack taken care of," Bounty said; then, because there was so much about last night which he couldn't explain to Gus—so much that he himself didn't understand—he put a hand to the telephone. "Pardon me, Gus. I want to get the sheriff's office in Brownsville as soon as they open up."

Toll charges were mounting against Hesperides County when there came a knock at the door, light but not at all timid, and Bounty said: "Got to go now, Cosgro. Check up as soon as you can. I'll do as much for you someday."

On his way to the door he tried to put on an official manner but found that he couldn't. "Howdy, Miss Ainsworth," he drawled. "Come right in."

"Hello, Mr. Bounty." Carrie Ainsworth smiled at him and he felt better.

She couldn't compete with Bert's new-found blonde in looks, of course, but from a glance at her you knew she was a product of the Magic Valley and would have its vitality. (Vitality which is a little too pushing, perhaps, and which has scant consideration for unobtrusive individuals like her father, however deserving.) She would be wearing that white dress because it was cool and gave her freedom of movement, not because it was prescribed by style centers on which the sun never stares from the zenith.

"Thanks for coming here. I thought this would be the best place to talk."

She sat across the desk from him, her bare tanned arms folded, and regarded him with steady black eyes. "I'm so glad you called me," she said. "I'm ready to help Doctor Lack in any way I can."

Bounty was more self-conscious than she. "I wasn't sure whether you'd be able to go to his house. But I thought you might suggest somebody who would be."

"I'll go, of course. I'm not a registered nurse, you understand, but I've done a lot of nursing. And from what you said over the phone, I think I can manage very well. For a time, anyhow." She straightened her shoulders. "I really feel that I deserted Doctor Lack. You know why I did it, of course. But I've learned things since that experience. It's no good getting the nod of approval from the world and his wife if you have to tell yourself all the time that you're weak for giving in to them. Doctor Lack's alone now?"

"Undersheriff Gus Broddus is on his way out, to stay during the day. Doctor Lack is probably still asleep and I judge sleep's what he needs more than anything else. Doctor Cotillion will be along this morning to examine him. Now I think it's only fair to tell you what happened at Doctor Lack's house last night."

"Christopher Hand told me." Her eyes fell, then rose, steadier than ever. "I talked to him after you called me. I'm concerned for Jimmy Norcott, of course, but Beck's death was worse to me than that blood donor's. I knew Beck, you see, when I worked for Doctor Lack. I thought as much of one of them as of the other. And you have no idea, Mr. Bounty, how lost Doctor Lack is going to be without Beck."

"I'm afraid I have, Miss Ainsworth. I'd like to be the one to break the news to him, if possible. Mr. Broddus can call me for you at any time. If I'm not within reach—well, use your own judgment. As you'll have to do about a lot of things. I'll come out later and explain the situation a little more fully." Bounty hesitated. "There's one matter that has to do with Doctor Lack which I'd like to ask about now, however. Did you know that the contents of his drug cabinet were stolen during his open house?"

She frowned. Her eyes ran quickly over his face and returned to his. "Yes," she said in the same steady, pleasant tone. "I was one of the few people employed by Doctor Lack at the time who knew it."

"You were in the study that afternoon, weren't you?"

"The early part, while we were still laboring under the delusion that we could keep a little formality. About three o'clock I had to go downstairs and help out. Things there—especially around the refreshment tables—had got entirely out of control. I didn't go back up until after almost everyone had gone. You're wanting to know, of course, how the doors of the examining room and the laboratory could have been forced without my seeing it done. There were four hours during which anyone could have watched and found an opportunity."

"You know Las Palmas and the surrounding country, Miss Ainsworth. Were there many strangers? I won't say suspicious-looking characters—"

"Do. I'd call one person out of every ten there suspicious-looking. Many of them I'd never seen before. There has never been any doubt in my mind that a group of men, or men and women, came for the express purpose of robbing that cabinet. You know how much the newspapers carried about Doctor Lack's fine offices and laboratory and about the experiments he was going to conduct." The girl leaned forward. "Is that where the aconite which killed these blood donors came from, Mr. Bounty?"

"I don't know that it did, Miss Ainsworth. I learned of the theft only last night and, knowing that you had been in charge of that study early in the afternoon—"

"And that one of your suspects was with me—"

Bounty shook his head and smiled. "I got you here under false pretenses to question you? No, Miss Ainsworth. Those questions about the cabinet were an afterthought. As to suspects, I have 'em galore. Everybody within the bounds of Hesperides."

"But only one closely associated with the Norcotts. Oh, Chris told me about you questioning him, Mr. Bounty. He was worried. Not because he has a guilty conscience. Nor because he's afraid of circumstantial evidence. He's worried as to what people may think. That doesn't matter to me any more." There was a purposive set to her mouth as she took up her handbag and held it out of Bounty's sight while she opened it. "What I *am* concerned about is the suspicion which you must have of Chris. I can't prove that he didn't rob that cabinet of Doctor Lack's, though I'm prepared to swear there was little enough time when he wasn't with me—or with Bert Larrick. He and Bert were together there a great deal, Mr. Bounty—"

"I know, Miss Ainsworth. Bert is the stoutest defender Chris has had."

"That's admitting Chris has needed one. Well, I'm not going to let him make himself more suspect by going through a lot of heroics about last Saturday night. Chris was with me, Mr. Bounty. He came and got me a little after ten-thirty. We drove to Brownsville and returned the next morning. We stayed at the States Hotel as"— she laid her left hand palm down on the desk—"husband and wife."

Bounty looked at the ring on the third finger and grinned. "I thought so," he said.

"You thought so! Haven't we kept it a secret?"

"Oh yes, but . . ." He wriggled a little. "You see, Mrs. Hand, this is the way it always turns out in a story. And I read lots of stories."

Her sudden laugh showed that she had been under greater tension than he realized. "So this is what a visit to the sheriff's office is like! Chris is outside, waiting for me to scream, I suppose, so he can dash to my rescue. He wouldn't come in and disapproved of my coming in. He's been here with Bert Larrick and I got the idea you had guns and rubber hose and cuspidors everywhere. And that you'd talk out of the side of your mouth. Instead I feel that you ought to have chintz curtains at those windows. Mr. Bounty, Chris is taking his father home after he drives me to Doctor Lack's. But if I make him come to see you after he gets back, will you talk to him? Or rather get him to talk to you?"

"I'll serve tea."

"You won't find Chris very good company at first but you will see that he couldn't any more commit cold-blooded murder than could Bert Larrick." She removed the ring, dropped it into the bag and clicked the clasp shut. "Mr. Bounty, I had the misfortune to fall in love with a snob. I'm still in love with him. We were married last fall—secretly, for no other reason than that Chris couldn't bear to have a wedding that wouldn't get as much space in the papers as those of the young men who were marrying society girls. We intended to announce it about Christmas. But then Mr. Norcott came along with his offer and Chris saw all his ambitions being realized. I know the thought that came to him: if he'd waited a little longer he could have made a better match. He was afraid to tell Mr. Norcott because he might not approve. Which is nonsense, of course. I've known Mr. Norcott a long time. There's nothing lord-of-the-manor about him. But that's the way we went along—shilly-shallying—all winter. I've stood for it because I know Chris loves me and there's no one else here who can make him as happy as I. But I can't endure being idle. I got a job in spite of Chris' objections. When Doctor Lack came I got a better one with him. Chris didn't mind that so much because of Doctor Lack's social position."

"What's he going to say to this arrangement of ours?"

"He'll have to like it. I said I was sorry I quit my place as Doctor Lack's secretary. Well, when Doctor Lack recovers I'm going to ask him if he doesn't want me back. That may call for a showdown between Mr. Hand and me." The girl shrugged, rose and thrust the bag under her arm. "But why am I telling you all this? Isn't that the remark to make now, Mr. Bounty? Besides, I'm neglecting my job."

"Why don't you—" Bounty stopped, the tips of his ears beginning to turn pink.

"Why don't I what?" she asked.

"Don't you ever read stories about—about how these difficulties are solved? It's always done the same way, so it must be—uh—effective. A little drama seems to help when you break the news. Uh—I really must answer this phone, if you'll pardon me."

She looked at one of his ears and then the other and smiled. "Thanks, Mr. Bounty. I should have come to the sheriff's office sooner," she said softly and went out.

Now what the devil did I have to say that for? Bounty wanted to know of himself as he picked up the receiver. His "Sheriff's office!" was spoken in his gruffest voice.

"This is Mr. Palladay, Mr. Bounty." The hotel manager's voice sounded both prim and aggrieved. "I was merely wondering if I were going to have the use of my office today."

Bounty had completely forgotten Mr. Palladay and his locked office. "Sure, sure, Mr. Palladay!" He became genial. "I was just on my way over there. I want one more look at that office, as a matter of form, then I think we can turn it over to you. Wait a moment!"

Bounty always said that his morning coffee took effect at that instant. He wasn't talking to Mr. Palladay over the telephone but over the counter in the lobby of the Sutherland. It was the evening before. Hieronymus stood a few feet away. Fred Winters was at the cashier's window, waiting to get a check cashed.

"Mr. Palladay," Bounty announced, "I have news that may interest you. Las Palmas is to be host to the Texas Sheriffs' Association at its next meeting. A big affair. Lots of banquets and all that. I thought we might possibly make the Sutherland our headquarters."

"What's that? A convention!" You could see the manager's face (the lower part of it, that is) brightening. "By all means, Sheriff. There is no hotel in Texas better equipped to handle a convention. We can guarantee—"

"Well, I'll talk to you about it later. The decision rests with me, so . . ." Bounty made his pause brief but significant. (It was a foregone conclusion, of course, that the meeting would be held at the Sutherland but he hadn't got around to consulting with Mr. Palladay yet. He wished he had thought of this means of winning the manager's favor last night.) "What time does your cashier make his bank deposits?" he asked.

"As soon as the bank opens, at nine. But about this convention, Sheriff. If the decision rests with you—"

"I wonder if you'd have the cashier hold everything until I get over there to see him?"

"Why—why, certainly, Sheriff. As I told you last night, we ran short on cash during the weekend. The deposits will consist mostly of checks. If you're thinking of that check your deputy endorsed, please don't worry about it. We were only too glad to oblige you and him. Can you have lunch with me today?"

"Sorry, Mr. Palladay. Some other time. But I'll be over to see you as soon as I can. In the meantime tell that cashier to hold onto all the checks he has in his till." Bounty hung up as he heard a key turn in the lock.

Bert Larrick came in. He had changed from his workaday tweeds to tropical worsted that was dazzlingly white in the sunlit room. It made him taller and broader and darkened his skin. He didn't look as if he had missed any sleep, but his carefully shaven face was grave and there was a hard set to his jaw.

"Good morning, son."

"Good morning, Peter." Larrick deposited his panama and a piper sack on the desk. "That's the cup from Palladay's office," he said, stepping behind Bounty's chair.

"Thanks, son. You look like a million dollars."

Two big hands bore down on Bounty's shoulders, sending his knees up to crack against the edge of the desk. "Peter Gustave Toutant Beauregard Bounty," Larrick pronounced slowly. "I want you to do something for me, Peter. Boot me—and boot me hard—for the way I acted last night at the hotel."

"Not when you've got those ice-cream pants on, son," said the happiest man in Hesperides.

"Peter, I hurt you. When I talked back to you—and when I didn't want you to go up to the Winterses' room with me. If you'd gone, things would've been different. I don't know what got into me. Something Mallory said when she first saw you, I guess. That's why I want her to know you now. And you to know her. We'll get together today—"

"Forget it, son. Have you told Miss Winters yet about her cousin's death?"

"Not yet." Larrick sighed and released his grip on Bounty's shoulders. "Look! I brought you a present. Chew 'em up." As he went to his chair he tossed onto Bounty's desk a penny box of wooden matches. "I called Mother from the hotel," he said, sitting down with another sigh. "She told me Mallory wasn't up yet, so I thought I'd take my time about getting out there."

"Where's Doctor Cotillion?"

"I had breakfast with him, then took him out to Doctor Lack's. Gus had just got there and was standing around with his mouth open. He said he hadn't heard a sound from Doctor Lack's bed-room, so I left Doctor Cotillion there and came to see how you were. When I parked out front I saw Chris Hand, waiting for Carrie Ainsworth. I stopped and talked to him till she came out." Larrick stretched out his legs. "Peter, if there's anything to the stars being in a man's favor, they were in mine last night. Maybe the moon. First I met Mallory— By the way, I'm going to marry that girl."

"No, son," Bounty said firmly. "You're going to medical school this fall. In about five years the right girl can come along."

"She's here, I tell you. After you meet her you'll want to be my best man. Maybe I'll let you and maybe I won't. But listen to what happened this morning. Doctor Cotillion and I didn't talk much last night, we were both so tired. But at breakfast, when he got some coffee in him, he livened up. He seems—Peter, he seems to have taken a liking to me. I felt awkward with him at first, but now I don't. He's given up his teaching post and is establishing a clinic in Chicago this fall. A pretty big affair, I judge. He said something about the University of Chicago and I told him how I'd like to go there. We talked about my credits and chances of admission, but I supposed he was just showing polite interest. On the way to Doc-tor Lack's, though, he asked me if I wouldn't like to assist around the clinic in my spare time and earn my way through school. I told him I'd be glad to do anything, of course. He said to go ahead and send for my entrance blanks. If I could get in he'd see I was taken care of. Just like that. I was so flabbergasted I almost ran into a lamppost."

"Doctor Cotillion came out with that offer without you hint-ing?"

"Of course," Larrick said reproachfully. "Much as I want to go to school, I wouldn't ask anybody for favors. You don't seem very enthusiastic."

"Sure I am, son. Send for those blanks and I'll talk to the doc-tor. But I don't see that a wife fits into this scheme of things."

Larrick frowned and stared out the window. "Well, I'm afraid Doctor Cotillion feels the same way. I asked him what he thought about me getting married before I started in. He advised me to go slow. At that stage of the game, he said, a man never knows what turn his life's going to take. I was bold enough to ask him when he got married. He admitted it was while he was in medical school."

"You didn't know the first Mrs. Cotillion was dead and he'd remarried?"

"No, or I wouldn't have asked that question. I was awfully embarrassed when he told me. But I'm betting that you and he both are going to be convinced I'm right, once you meet Mallory."

Bounty worried a second match to pieces. "Son, let's let this slide for a while. What did Chris Hand have to say about Miss Ainsworth going to Doctor Lack's?"

"Not much. He asked me if I thought it'd start the old gossip again. I told him I didn't think so. I let him see that I didn't consider it any of his business what Carrie did so long as they weren't engaged or anything. I'm beginning to change my opinion about Chris, though. Or else he's changed. He told me why he went to the police yesterday rather than to you. Norcott left it up to him and he thought he'd only give me a chance to act uppish if he called in the sheriff's office. He's sorry now he didn't. He admires you a lot but he's afraid you don't have a very good opinion of him. I told him if you didn't I was to blame."

"I understand his father's leaving the hospital."

"Yes, Angelo told Chris he'd have to take the old man out this morning. I guess he was pretty insulting about it. At least Chris took it that way."

"Has Chris said anything about what he expected to happen when Jimmy Norcott became twenty-one?"

"Well, he told me he didn't think Jimmy was happy. He didn't believe Jimmy really wanted to take over the estate but was only planning to do it so as not to disappoint his uncle. Jimmy likes to study foreign languages, literature, things like that. He wants to go on with them at the university, but Roger Norcott takes it for granted he'll study agriculture and animal husbandry. Chris says Jimmy never talks to him much about it and he can't bring the subject up for fear it'll look as if he were influencing Jimmy to give up ranching. Chris thinks Doctor Lack is the only person Jimmy has ever confided in. He hopes that after Jimmy gets well the doctor will sort of mediate with Norcott."

"Chris' future looks brighter and brighter, then. What ideas does he have on these murders?"

"He says he thinks E. Matthew Rone tried to poison you. I'm not sure that's what he actually does think, though. I don't myself. I'll tell you the real reason I wanted to see you this morning, Peter. It's no go: this business of appointing Gus and me guards over Doctor Lack and Doctor Cotillion. As long as there's any doubt about who that poison was meant for, you're the one who's going to be guarded. I mean that. I shouldn't have left you last night. I won't again."

"Thanks, son," Bounty said, very pleased. "Maybe before night we can have this all cleared up and nobody'll need a guard. Let's talk of poison now. I haven't told you about Doctor Lack's drug cabinet, have I?"

As Larrick listened perspiration broke out on his face and he got up to lower the Venetian blinds on the east windows. "Good God, Peter!" he exclaimed, resuming his seat. "This would start a panic in town if it became known. Carrie never told Chris, I'm sure, or he'd have told me."

"It does look like an organized robbery, son. And we've had only petty dope peddling in Hesperides, I'm almost positive. Brownsville is the logical outlet for the Valley. I called Sheriff Cosgro this morning. He's in close touch with the state and federal narcotics men. He said that about three weeks ago they raided a well-known joint and got a big haul. The head man escaped and they never found where the stuff came from. From across the river, they'd supposed. But they're checking with the list Beck gave me and will let me know the outcome. There was aconite, Cosgro knew, but he couldn't say how much. So, while anybody in Hesperides may have swiped the stuff at Lack's open house, I'm going on the supposition it was taken to Brownsville to be sold through regular channels."

"Somebody from here may have bought it there."

"True, though I'll think it unlikely if aconite to the amount that Doctor Lack had was confiscated in Brownsville. That isn't stuff the ordinary peddler keeps. There remains a check on the local places. That can be done easily enough. But let's leave the matter of the aconite for a moment. I think it's going to be much easier to trace the nitroglycerin that was used to blow up Hieronymus' store."

Larrick groaned. "I was forgetting that. What theory are we working on now—that he blew up his own store or that he didn't?"

"That he did. I've thought all along that if he did buy the nitro he bought it in Brownsville. He lived there before he came to Las Palmas, remember, and he'd probably want to make his purchase outside this county. I gave Cosgro a description of him and asked him to check on sales. We'll have to do something for Cosgro to pay him for going to all this trouble. He's doing something else for us. There's a fingerprint expert down there, attached to police head-quarters. Cosgro knows him and has promised to have him come up today. Can you tell me, son, the things we must have examined for prints?"

"Let's see." Larrick crossed his legs. "There's that paper cup Hieronymus drank from. The drawer of your desk where the whisky bottle was. The bottle itself. And the paper it was wrapped in."

"And do we expect to get the prints of the murderer from any of them?"

"No."

"But we have to be thorough." Bounty picked up the sack which Larrick had brought, untwisted the paper at the top and dumped a sanitary drinking cup upon his blotter. It was an ordinary ivory-colored cone with a band of blue flowers below the lip. It had been but slightly crushed.

"I shouldn't be surprised," Larrick said, "if you found my prints on that."

Bounty looked around quickly. "What's that, son?"

"I used a paper clip to handle those cups that were in the con-tainer below the water cooler. Neither Doctor Cotillion nor I touched any of them till after we'd found the one that had had aconite and whisky in it. I had a sack ready and was going to drop that cup in it. But it slipped and without thinking I grabbed it. About the middle. I only hope I didn't ruin the prints of Hieronymus."

"I don't suppose you did, son. Looks like a dunce cap, doesn't it?"

"What's the matter with you, Peter?"

"Just talking to myself," Bounty said, staring with sleepy eyes at the cup. "I'm going to have to take mental treatment after this business is over. Now, son, I've told you how our investigation stands at present. Let me ask you a few questions about that whisky. I'm taking it for granted you never saw anyone have the bottle out of the drawer or so much as open or shut the drawer."

"I'd have said something about it if I had."

"Well, there's no use going into the question of who had access to it. Anyone who knew it was there could have found an opportunity to pour in the poison. But how many people knew it was there? I never told anyone. Gus says he didn't."

"And I certainly never did."

"You mean until last night, son."

"Oh, sure, I told Fred Winters. He was the first."

"A point that's liable to come up, son, is this: why did you ask me to leave it at the desk for him rather than for you?"

"Well, what I was really intending was that Mallory and I should shake Fred and go on to dinner by ourselves. I thought it might be easier to do if I told him the whisky was waiting at the desk for him."

"I see. Now I've tried to think of all the reasons why that liquor might have been poisoned while it was in this office. Anyone who knows me knows I don't drink. True, it was in my desk and some was gone. Anybody who didn't know me might make the obvious conclusion. I suppose someone might have poisoned it on the off chance that it would reach you or Gus. But I know you have the reputation of being a teetotaler now and I think Gus has. So I believe we're safe in saying that the aconite wasn't meant for any of us three."

"Of course not."

"Next," Bounty said with a little smile at his deputy's defiant tone, "there's the possibility it was planted there in order to get our office into hot water. If one of us gave a visitor a drink and poisoned him, we'd have a hard time explaining."

"Isn't that exactly what happened?"

"We're on the defensive, yes. And it may have been coincidence that picked out the Norcott blood donors to receive the poison. But I don't think so. I can't. Let's assume that the stuff was poisoned after it left this office. Our first stopping place along that route is the desk of the Sutherland. And I think we've got to grant that during the confusion someone could have seen the package with the name of Fred Winters on it, abstracted it long enough to pour in the aconite and then returned it. I think it must have been pretty evident from the shape what was in the parcel. But"—Bounty raised a finger—"that person must have had aconite handy."

"Sure," Larrick said. "He'd been trailing Hieronymus, ready to poison him the first chance he got. Hieronymus sees him in the lobby. Maybe that's what scares him into a fit. When Hieronymus keels over the man comes up close and—lo and behold!—spots the name of the other donor he's after on the package."

"That would mean he knew Hieronymus and Winters were prospective donors. And, to the best of my knowledge, six people here knew that. Doctor Lack and Beck were together. Roger Norcott and Doctors Angelo, Cotillion and Ainsworth were together. Unless there's some juggling of alibis, none of them could have been in the lobby."

"Doctor Ainsworth! Why—"

"He's not one of the six I mentioned. I'm not sure how much he has known of what's going on, but my guess is—very little. Chris Hand could have been in the lobby."

"Wasn't he with the others at dinner?"

"The time's close there, but by his own admission he arrived on the scene just after we carried Hieronymus to Palladay's office."

"Oh, none of those men did it. There's someone else we don't know anything about. You said last night another donor might show up. He may have been living right here in town all the time. Or he may be a stranger who's come. Say, what about this nephew of Doctor Lack's?"

"He's the big question mark. His life and those of Winters and Hieronymus touched once that we know of: in Chicago. Let's try now to reconstruct what happened there. First, do you know whether Fred Winters had to undergo a transfusion when he had streptococcus?"

"He didn't, I know. At least he said he didn't. I asked him because I thought we might get on the track of some more donors that way."

"And did he ever give another transfusion except that one in Chicago?"

"I asked him that for the same reason. He said no."

"Very good, son. All right. Winters and Hieronymus—and maybe Lack—made a pact of sorts after they'd worked their extortion game on Doctor Cotillion. If one heard of a streptococcus case where transfusions of B blood were needed, he'd notify the other. Didn't I understand you to say a telegram had come to Winters' New York office? That would be from Hieronymus, telling of the Norcott case. Winters wired Hieronymus in return, telling when and how he would arrive. Hieronymus went to the airport to meet him Saturday night. Miss Winters took her cousin by surprise but he managed to give Hieronymus the high sign and to tell him what hotel he'd be stopping at."

"You're satisfied, then, Peter, that Miss Winters didn't know anything about the racket?"

"If you are, son. Now I'm presuming that Hieronymus was at that time trying to pull an insurance swindle on the side. He prepared the nitroglycerin for an explosion before he left his store. He phoned Norcott to pave the way for his extortion attempt and to start the ball rolling about the plot against the blood donors, so he'd be able to give a satisfactory explanation of why his store was blown up."

"And there was no plot against the donors?"

"Up to then, at least, I don't think so. Hieronymus' little fiction may have proved a boomerang by giving somebody an idea. But he was a liar on so many scores that I'm tired trying to pick out the truth from his stories. We know he came to the Sutherland after Winters had registered, looked at the register, went to the fifth floor, skipped out half an hour later. Presumably he went to Winters' room. Winters denied it to you last night, of course. But I wonder if his cousin could tell us whether he had a visitor?"

"Their rooms adjoined. I'll ask her."

"Well, let's continue to presume that's where Hieronymus went and see what we get into. Say Winters agreed to lie low and give him first shot at the Norcott bank roll, since he'd been first on the scene. If Hieronymus had returned to his store, pretended fright when he found it in ruins, spun his yarn about threats and called on Norcott for protection—we'd have clear sailing. But return he didn't. He skipped out of town. When, as I see it, it would have been to his advantage to stay close to the spot where the demand for his blood was."

"Maybe he and Fred drew straws again and Fred got first chance at the transfusion."

"But in that case, even if he had wanted to keep his activities from Miss Winters, he would have got in touch with Roger Norcott, wouldn't he? And we have no grounds for thinking that he did. For one thing, if Norcott knew that he had one donor to depend on, at whatever price, he would slow down his efforts to find others. And one honest man, with the right type of blood, would have ruined any extortion scheme. No, Bert, neither Winters nor Hieronymus acted as one would have expected them to act if they had had their meeting. Therefore I don't think they did."

"Well, what room could Hieronymus have gone to Saturday night, then?"

"He may have gone to a certain room or he may have met someone in the corridor. You remember I spoke last night of the five hundred dollars Hieronymus had on him when he came back to the hotel yesterday afternoon. I asked you if it gave you any bright ideas."

"I thought about that later. Was blackmail what you had in mind?"

"Perhaps. If someone did want Jimmy Norcott to die he could accomplish his purpose by bribing donors to leave town and stay away as well as by killing them. He'd let himself in for blackmail, of course, which would be right up Hieronymus' alley. Hieronymus returned to Las Palmas to do some more dickering, to collect the rest that had been promised him or maybe to see Winters."

"And that fits right in with my theory of the whisky being taken from the desk in the lobby and poisoned. Whoever it was foresaw that Hieronymus might come back, or else that Winters might arrive, and had the aconite ready."

"I think we're on the right track anyway, son. And I had my bright idea when I remembered the difficulty Fred Winters had getting a check cashed. Not the difficulty about the endorsement," Bounty explained hastily, "but about the amount. Palladay told me their funds had run low. That must mean somebody cashed a big check after the banks closed Saturday. I'm going over to the hotel now. It'll be interesting to look over their checks and to find out which were cashed Saturday night during that half-hour Hieronymus was in the hotel."

18

MALLORY WINTERS STOOD on a hooked rug in Mrs. Larrick's bedroom and studied the framed photographs that hung on the wall. Below them was a low cedar chest and on it a cushion, so that Mallory thought of this as a prie-dieu on which Mrs. Larrick knelt sometimes.

There were five photographs in a row. Bert as the usual bare and sprawling infant. Yet unmistakably, Mallory felt, Bert. Bert somewhere in his early teens, scrubbed and sullen-looking and growing out of his clothes. Bert in what must have been his heyday, clad in a track suit and grinning cockily because he knew you were impressed by his leg and arm muscles. Bert in high-school cap and gown, solemn but probably a little perspiry in the sunlight which beat down on the Larrick lawn. A larger recent photograph of Bert as he was now, bronzed, clear-eyed, with that irrepressible grin touching his lips.

Beyond was space for more photographs. Mallory's eyes moved over the faded wallpaper and she wondered what those photographs would be like, if ever they hung there. The next would be, say, Bert as a bridegroom. And the next—if one were taken after a year of married life? What would that be like? Fred had had the same sort of youth behind him when he married Sue. He had been as safe, as strong, as clear-eyed as Bert. Or had he been? People couldn't change as completely as Fred had seemed to her to change. . . .

The telephone rang in the hall, just outside the bedroom door. Bert answered it at once. He must have been reconnoitering out there, quietly, to see if she were up.

His voice was hushed—as near hushed, that is, as he could ever make it. "Yes, Peter," she heard him say. "Why—why, no, I never made any blood tests myself. I think I know how it's done, though. But, Peter, why under the sun do you want that? Huh? Doctor Ainsworth? All right, if you say so. But still I don't get it. What!" His voice rose. "You're crazy, Peter. Crazy. Why would he do a thing like that?"

19

THE DARKLY TANNED young man was still sitting on one of the ledges beside the front steps, engrossed in his newspaper, when Peter Bounty came out of the John Belton Lack Hospital, another of the town's Monterey-type buildings. The fellow looked as if he had done his share of knocking about the world. The band of his hard straw hat was frayed, his white linen suit was badly in need of cleaning and pressing, the toecap of one of his tan shoes had come unsewn.

Bounty was wrinkling his nose like a rabbit. He assumed a similar posture on the other ledge, knees drawn up, back against a pillar, as he pulled down his hatbrim and prepared to wait for Bert Larrick in sunlight which might not be pure but which didn't smell of disinfectant.

Four automobiles were parked in front of the hospital and Bounty had an interest in each: his deputy's rattletrap of a roadster, a streamlined dark blue roadster of the same make as Dr. Lack's limousine, two dusty and outmoded coupés which had carried Bounty himself and Dr. Hugh Ainsworth over most of the roads of Hesperides.

After a time he became aware that the young man had put down his paper and was looking at him. While he felt in no mood for idle talk, Bounty turned his head in that direction.

The fellow who was regarding him with such friendly interest in his gray-blue eyes was thin and flat-chested yet didn't strike him as being a weakling. His homely face looked weather-beaten, seared and dessicated by the sun, almost like parchment. His large lips were chapped and deep lines about his mouth gave him a prematurely aged appearance.

Suddenly he smiled, showing a great deal of goldwork on his teeth, and said with a little lilt: "Baby?"

Bounty glanced back at the door but saw no one. "Were you speaking to me?" he inquired of the young man.

"Yes, you look as if your wife were having a baby."

"Oh. No, no baby."

"What about a cigarette?" The other pulled a crumpled package from his pocket.

"Thanks, don't smoke."

The young fellow lighted up and tossed the empty package into the shrubbery. "I don't suppose I could help you any?" he said.

"I'm afraid not. Thanks just the same. Say, do I look as bad as all this?"

"I'd say you were brooding too darned much over something. Get your mind off it. Here, would you like to read this paper?"

"No, thanks." Bounty watched a buzzard wheel across the hard blue sky, which was already getting its brassy summertime look. There's mesmerism in following a buzzard's movements.

Several moments had passed in silence when the young man asked: "Do you live here?"

Bounty nodded.

"There seems to be considerable stir about what's happening to these blood donors."

"Considerable stir, yes."

"In this morning's piper there's only a last-minute bulletin about the death of that one in the hotel lobby last night. But I heard them talking in the barbershop, and the taxi driver who brought me out here told me some more had been killed during the night. Nobody seems to know anything but everybody thinks the sheriff is to blame. Some say he was negligent and didn't protect his prisoners. Others believe there's more to it than that. None of it makes sense to me. I wish you'd tell me what you think."

The buzzard dipped and Bounty closed his eyes, his head swimming. "I'm probably more confused about it than anyone in town."

"The taxi driver said the county commissioners were meeting this morning and they'd probably take action against the sheriff. Have you heard whether they did or not?"

"Not yet."

"What about this sheriff—what's his name, Bounty? Do you know him?"

"Urn-huh."

"You do!" The young man sat up and turned around on the ledge. "I heard about him once, from a man who didn't know him. This man said a friend of his had told him Bounty represented the best there was in this Magic Valley. He had the lack of sham and the free-and-easy way of dealing with people that you find in places which still have some of the frontier about them. But he wasn't coarse or homespun. And he must be a lot deeper and more of an idealist than his fellow citizens, because it was an open secret that he'd given Hesperides its name. That meant he saw this movement to establish a new and perfect community as something more than just the raising of bigger and better citrus fruit. That's the way this man I'm speaking of wrote. He's an idealist himself, though, so I take everything he says with a grain of salt. He's probably met Bounty by now and got disillusioned again."

Bounty was facing the young man now, his eyes wide open. He looked at the close-cut white hair in front of the rather prominent ears and asked in a quick undertone: "Who was this who had so much to say about Bounty?"

"Oh, just an uncle of mine," the other answered carelessly, tossing away the short butt of his cigarette.

From the vestibule came voices, an exchange rather of thick gutturals. Christopher Hand held open the screen door and ushered out a hulking old codger whom Bounty knew instantly to be his father. Bounty had a vague recollection of being buttonholed by him on a street corner one Saturday afternoon and treated to a long monologue on the subject of weather and crops.

Apparently the recognition was mutual, for the dark eyes lighted and the older man exclaimed: "Hi, there!"

"Howdy," Bounty responded distractedly, watching Christopher set a huge cowhide gladstone on the cement porch between him and his vis-à-vis.

Both Christopher and Jacob Hand wore, apparently without comfort, white tropical worsted suits and panamas like Bert Larrick's. Christopher straightened, shot back a shirt cuff and said stiffly: "Good morning, Mr. Bounty." He turned to the young man on the ledge and Bounty saw his eyes taking stock of the other's appearance. "Like to earn a tip?" he asked in an insufferably patronizing tone.

"What? Oh." The young man had been staring at Bounty with eyes whose blueness was shot through with milk. One side of his mouth moved in a cocky grin as he looked up at Hand and said, "Sure."

"Carry this bag out to my car. That blue roadster."

"Bet your life." The young man grasped the handle of the gladstone and went jauntily down the walk.

"Mr. Bounty," Christopher said, "I should like to present my father. Father, this is Mr. Bounty."

"Bounty, eh? The sheriff." A knotty stub-nailed hand reached clumsily for Bounty's. "Law, son, I know this man but I didn't know his name. He can tell yuh right smart about farmin'. Sheriff, when yuh comin' out like yuh said an' look at that bull calf of mine?"

"We must be going, Father. You'll pardon us, Mr. Bounty?" Christopher hesitated. "I should like to have the pleasure of calling on you sometime."

"Any time, Chris."

Christopher was looking at the second roadster. "Bert's inside?" he asked in surprise.

"Yes. I'll be out to see that bull calf one of these days, Mr. Hand."

"Do that, Sheriff." Jacob Hand made a whinnying sound. "I'm gettin' away from this place 'fore they cut my gizzard out."

"Come on, Father." A metallic face didn't hide the fact that Christopher knew his father's departure for what it was, ejection, and that he was covering the shame of it by this flaunting of colors.

Bounty was on pins and needles as he watched the pair go down the walk, one marching, the other shambling. The son opened the door of his roadster for the father. Then, going to the rear, he unlocked the luggage compartment and by a nod of the head ordered the young man on the curb to stow the gladstone within. That done, he reached into a pocket, brought out a coin and tossed it through the air.

The young man caught it on his palm, looked at it and said: "I don't have any change."

"That's all right. Keep it." Christopher Hand got behind the wheel, waved at Bounty with a flourish and the car slid smoothly from the curb.

The young man returned slowly, pitching a dollar at the cracks in the sidewalk and grinning a little. "Thought cartwheels were extinct," he said to Bounty, who had advanced to meet him. "That fellow must hoard 'em, so his pockets will make a noise. And was it welcome! After breakfast, a shave and taxi fare, I was down to three cents and a tax token. Just smoked my last cigarette too. Know where I can buy some around here, Sheriff Peter Bounty?"

"You're Malcolm Lack."

"You make that sound like an accusation. But at least you didn't say 'John Belton Lack's nephew.'"

Bounty was getting back as steady and keen an appraisal as he gave. "I wonder," he said, "if you know how Doctor Lack described his nephew to me?"

"I know exactly. He said I looked like him. He's been saying that so long that I think he actually believes it. Uncle Johnny may be one of the finest men in the world, but he certainly is the most possessive. For years he's been trying to tie a nice red ribbon around my neck. I won't let him. Yet I rather think I love the old fuss-budget. Don't tell him that, though." Malcolm Lack cocked an eye at the dollar and slipped it into a pocket. "Don't tell him about this either. He wouldn't see the joke and I don't want to throw him into a conniption lit right at the start. By the way, we haven't shaken hands yet, Peter Bounty. Shall we—or has Uncle Johnny blackened my character too much?"

Bounty's thoughts were busy. "And Doctor Cotillion told me that you were pale as your uncle," he said as their hands met. "But of course he saw you after you'd been ill."

"Yes, and shaky in the knees, to boot, at the prospect of giving a blood transfusion."

"And now?"

"Oh, the soul of courage." Lack stared at the hospital door, the milky suffusion slowly leaving his eyes and with it most of the resemblance to his uncle's eyes. At the same time a little of the doctor's incisive nervousness came to the fore. "How is this Norcott boy?" he asked.

"I haven't heard this morning. It seemed certain last night that he couldn't live through another day without a transfusion."

"Where's Uncle Johnny?"

"At home, ill."

Lack looked around quickly. "I called his house and got no answer. Is he seriously ill?"

"I don't think so. When did you call?"

"About eight, just after I got in on the bus."

"Damn!" Bounty said.

"What's the matter?"

"Just cussin' the way things happen. Do they know in the hospital that you're here?"

"No, I didn't give my name. I asked the girl at the desk if Doctor Lack was in. She said no, but didn't volunteer any information. Then I asked for David Angelo but he wasn't there either. So I thought I'd sit outside and wait awhile." Lack's hands went into his coat pockets and came out, their fingers twitching a little. "See here, Mr. Bounty. Why don't you take me to get some cigarettes and tell me a few things? Or are you supposed to wait on someone?"

"That doesn't matter now. I'm taking you into custody."

Lack blinked as if a hand had been fanned past his face. "Things are as bad as that, are they? Well, your custody suits me fine, Mr. Bounty, so long as you let me get some cigarettes."

"Let's go then. Where's your luggage?"

"I checked it at the bus station. Say, I wonder why Beck didn't meet me? Or why he didn't answer the phone at Uncle Johnny's? You know Beck, don't you? Uncle Johnny's man."

They sat together in the coupé but Bounty said before he started the motor: "Did Beck know you were coming?"

"Uncle Johnny did. At least I sent him a telegram last night from Corpus Christi."

Bounty regarded him sleepily. "What time did you send the telegram?"

"About seven-thirty."

"Did you tell what bus you were arriving on?"

"Yes."

"Was anyone you knew at the bus station?"

"No. Of course I don't know anyone here except Uncle Johnny and Beck and David Angelo. But wait, there was a reporter there looking for me. From the Hesperides *Sun*, is that it? When I got off the bus he was standing by the steps, calling my name. I answered, thinking he was someone Uncle Johnny had sent. But when he grabbed me and said he wanted to take me to the newspaper office, I thought it was time to call a halt. So I acted bewildered and said there must be some mistake, my name was Black. He cussed and started paging Lack among the other passengers. I skipped." Lack took off his hat and passed a handkerchief across his forehead. His tow-colored hair was close-cropped and looked as if it had had too much water on it recently. "Let's get those cigarettes now, Mr. Bounty," he said with some of his uncle's sibilance. "And if something has happened to Uncle Johnny, I wish you'd tell me."

"At last account Doctor Lack was sound asleep," Bounty said, driving slowly down a broad street which, like all the principal streets there, had a row of palms running down the center, to justify the town's name. "It's a case of nervous exhaustion but he's being well taken care of, and I give you my word, I don't think there's anything to worry about. We'll go see him after a while. But tell me what this reporter looked like."

"Oh, he was a big tall fellow, looked like a college student. I've forgotten what he said his name was."

"What was he wearing?"

"A white suit, like that mug's that I carried the gladstone for."

Just for an instant Bounty's fixed frown deepened. "All young fellows wear those suits down here," he said then. "Did he say how he came to know you'd be on that bus?"

"No. Mr. Bounty, you mean that Uncle Johnny didn't get my telegram?"

"He didn't get it, Lack," Bounty said thoughtfully. "But somebody did."

"And was looking for me." Lack's breath came and went quickly.

"We'll probably find it was only a newspaperman's game to get a scoop," Bounty said. "But tell me where and how news of this streptococcus case reached you."

"I was working my way up from Panama to New Orleans on a fruit boat. I'd intended to hang around New Orleans awhile, then come on down and surprise Uncle Johnny. But when I heard about this case over the radio I managed to transship and landed at Corpus Christi yesterday. I didn't know till I saw a paper there that Uncle Johnny had charge of the case. I suppose he has messages following me all over everywhere. But then he usually does have."

"What was the name of your boat?"

"The *Moquete*. Oh, in case you're wondering, I had to forfeit most of my wages when I left it. I'm really not a tramp or a remittance man. And neither"—Lack put emphasis on the words—"am I dependent on Uncle Johnny. I'll get him to cash a check for me here and I'll be all right."

"I understand you play variations on your uncle's name. What was the one you used on the *Moquete?*"

"Malcolm Lack. My seaman's papers and passports have to be made out that way. I don't really use Uncle Johnny's name scrambled. I just like to tease him by telling him I do." Lack chuckled as Bounty drew up in front of a drugstore and honked. "Easy come, easy go. I might as well squander this dollar. What can I buy you?"

"Nothing, thanks."

"Let me." Lack laid a hand on his shoulder. "Peter Bounty, who named Hesperides but wouldn't claim the prize. It was Uncle

Johnny wrote me those things about you, just after he came down here. But he was merely quoting Beck."

"Bring me a candy bar," Bounty said to the curb-service boy. "A big one, with lots of chocolate and nuts."

"And five packages of Camels. Uncle Johnny will try to make me quit smoking," Malcolm Lack told Bounty, "so I want to enjoy my last moments of freedom."

"You were with your uncle before he came to Hesperides?"

"Yes. What home I've had since my parents died has been with Uncle Johnny. I usually drop in on him, stay until I feel freckles breaking out on me, then move on. He sent me to Chicago from Boston this spring, to give a blood transfusion. Otherwise I suppose I'd have come on down here with him. But once I got out from under his wing I decided I'd like to see the West Coast again. I went out to Frisco and then on down to Panama."

"You had your own bout with streptococcus in Boston?"

"Yes, I got it while I was up in Maine. But of course I went right down and put myself in Uncle Johnny's hands. My case wasn't very serious. I had to have only one transfusion. Uncle Johnny located a donor for me out in Washington and I got all right."

"Remember that donor's name?"

"Miles, I think. An anthropologist. I didn't see much of him. He flew right back to the coast. I wonder if Uncle Johnny has been in touch with him again?"

"I couldn't say."

Malcolm Lack took his purchases from the boy. "Keep the change," he mimicked Christopher Hand as he gave him the dollar. "That was once Uncle Johnny almost succeeded in hobbling me," he said, tearing open a package of cigarettes. "I hadn't realized how much he cared about me and how lonesome he was. He stayed with me day and night, doing most of the nursing himself. After that, I couldn't just up and leave him. He was all fired up about this Hesperides move and, as I said, I'd probably have come with him if it hadn't been for that Chicago case."

Bounty had made no move to start the car. "Did you know these donors, Winters and Hieronymus?" he asked, munching candy.

Lack blew smoke through his nose. "I couldn't say I knew them."

"But you met them?"

"Yes. This reflects credit on Uncle Johnny rather than on me, so I'll tell you. When I left he told me what he knew about Doctor Cotillion. He was a hard-working, brilliant man who'd gained professional recognition by his research but not much financial return. He had to teach at this little college outside Chicago and grind out textbooks when he ought to be free to do original work. Uncle Johnny gave me a big check and said I was to help him. That's Uncle Johnny's way, bless him. You know how generous he is."

Bounty's mouth was full and he made no comment.

"I didn't see much of Doctor Cotillion," Lack went on. "But I knew he wouldn't want any doctor with a private income sticking a check at him. So I decided to lend a helping hand in another direction, on my own account. I'd got out of my streptococcus ordeal cheaply. This Seattle donor wouldn't accept any compensation, just his expenses. So I figured I'd look up Doctor Cotillion's donors. If he hadn't taken care of their expenses yet, I'd do so on the q.t. They were leaving the hospital the morning I was there. Maybe I wasn't very diplomatic in inquiring about their financial condition because as soon as they learned who I was they acted suspicious or sarcastic or something. I decided they could go to hell. I suppose they thought I was the rich playboy who let them give their blood and then barged in when it was safe to do some strutting."

"I imagine they saw you putting a kink in their plan," Bounty said and went on to tell of the extortion game which had been played once with good results and which he believed was to have been played again in Las Palmas with better. He watched Malcolm Lack as he talked and saw the cold gleam of John Belton Lack's eyes come for an instant into these gray-blue ones.

"They got what was coming to them," Lack said. "Though it'd been tough on the Norcott boy if I hadn't got here when I did. I wish you'd tell me more, Mr. Bounty. There won't be any use asking Uncle Johnny for particulars of what's happening. He wouldn't know it if there was a hurricane. I'd like to be here when the first one hits. I can see Beck entering and saying, 'Sir'"—he mimicked the valet's tone so perfectly that Bounty winced—"'a hurricane is raging without.' Up will jump Uncle Johnny and go out and order it to stop. Like King Somebody-or-other and the waves."

"Beck died last night, Lack."

"God!" The young man's cigarette fell to his lap and there was the stench of scorched cloth in the air before he snatched it up and tossed it out the window. In the eyes which he turned to Bounty scarcely any blue was discernible in the milk. "Beck!" He gave it a reverence which he hadn't given the name of the Deity. "So that's what's the matter with Uncle Johnny! I've got to see him."

"Let me tell you what happened first," Bounty said, glancing into the mirror and starting the car.

It's no great distance from that drugstore to the telegraph office on the main street of Las Palmas, but they were some time on the way, for Bounty wasn't so occupied with his narrative that he didn't observe an excess of caution.

He did tell, with few reservations, what had happened. Malcolm Lack smoked avidly, inhaling deeply and blowing the smoke through his nostrils. He stared ahead and his face aged steadily.

"Beck committed suicide, I'm sure," Bounty said. "I didn't begin to realize the seriousness of the situation until he asked me for my gun. I didn't know how much of Angelo's spiel to believe, but his statement about Beck's previous act did ring true. And when I found Beck had taken a knife from the examining room while I was outside, but tried to get my gun as a surer method probably, I knew I had to do something. I didn't take time to explain to the undersheriff. For one reason, I thought he'd keep a closer watch over Beck if he thought the man was arrested on suspicion of murder. My idea was that if I kept him under guard until Doctor Lack was himself again I could patch things up between them. Or get Beck another job, another interest in life. That's really what I had in mind."

"Don't blame yourself, Mr. Bounty. You couldn't have done anything with Beck. He'd come to the end of another existence, as I'll make you see later. You wouldn't have been able to stop him from going out in one way or another. Maybe this was best. There's just one thing I wish we could do for Beck now," Malcolm Lack said in a hard voice as Bounty parked in front of the telegraph office and was preparing to get out. "One thing I wish we could save him from."

"What's that?"

"There'll be an autopsy, I suppose, performed by David Angelo?"

"Not by Angelo, I'm ready to promise."

"Good. I couldn't bear to think of him—cutting on Beck."

"Don't talk about that, please," Bounty said and fled.

While he transacted his business inside he kept an eye on the car. He saw Malcolm Lack wipe his eyes and blow his nose before lighting another cigarette. He saw Lack pick something from the cushioned seat behind the wheel, hold it between his fingers and stare at it before he flicked it away.

Not during his waking hours of the last thirty-six had the sheriff's face been so sleepily inexpressive as when he re-crossed the pavement. For the first time he was ready to acknowledge that this case was more than he and his office could handle.

"*Extra! Extra!*" newsboys were screaming down the Street in the vicinity of Yznaga Park.

"You and I have got to do some talking, Lack," Bounty said as he slid behind the wheel. "I'm taking you home with me."

"Who's there?"

"No one. Except my cat. My housekeeper is off having another grandchild."

"Your men in the habit of dropping in on you?"

"They're busy."

"I wonder if you're as sure as you seem to be," Lack said with his eyes on Bounty's face, "that that poison was intended for those blood donors?"

"I'm sure enough."

"Of course you don't have a man on your force who'd like to step into your shoes?"

"Nary a one."

"I don't seem to have much to say about going," Lack observed dryly as Bounty was driving away.

"For a fact you don't," Bounty said. "How did you address your telegram?"

"Just John Belton Lack, Las Palmas."

Bounty nodded. "Our hospital is known as the John Belton Lack. A telegram was delivered there about eight-thirty last night and signed for by Angelo. I didn't get to see a copy of it, but my guess is that it was yours."

A sideways glance told him Lack was frowning and had stopped in the act of putting his cigarette to his lips. "I can't see why Angelo didn't tell Uncle Johnny," Lack said.

"Can't you?"

"Why, no. He's always been a troublemaker, of course."

Bounty told him something of Angelo's actions the night before and of Beck's theory of murder to provide a misleading motive for contemplated murder.

Lack shook his head slowly and none too decidedly. "All Beck told you about Angelo was true," he said. "I can see now why he wouldn't want Uncle Johnny to know I was coming till he got himself established in the house. Though at that, I'd have sent him packing in no time. But I think Beck's imagination was running away with him when it concocted any such scheme for Angelo. The man's subtle enough, of course. And if he ever killed anybody it would be with poison. But . . . Oh, I don't know, I don't know." The tanned and nicotine-stained fingers twitched as Lack lighted another cigarette from the butt of his last.

Bounty had slowed down the car and signaled to a newsboy. He reached into a pocket and brought out a nickel. "Oh, say, Mr. Bounty," Lack said quickly. "That doesn't happen to be the nickel, does it, that Beck had last night?"

"No, I don't think anybody picked that up from the floor."

"I want to get that nickel. Uncle Johnny is going to carry it for the rest of his life. A sort of albatross."

Bounty made his purchase and glanced at the headlines: SECOND NORCOTT BLOOD DONOR MURDERED. A "reign of terror" was proclaimed, of course, and in smaller type he saw: POISON CLAIMS ADDITIONAL VICTIM BY ACCIDENT.

It would be a matter of time before it became known that Beck had been under arrest when he died. And then . . .

"Look that over," Bounty said, handing Lack the paper and driving on. "See if there's anything in it about you."

"Here it is!" the young man exclaimed almost at once. "In a box on the front page. 'Lack Kin a Donor?'" he read aloud. "'Monday's hoax in the Norcott *Streptococcus viridans* case appears at the time of going to press to be no hoax at all. Yesterday, it will be recalled, the *Sun* refuted the widely circulated rumor that the "donor in a thousand" for whom search is being made was a convict in the death cell at Huntsville State Prison Farm. Saturday it was the Emperor of Japan.'" He paused and murmured: "So that's the way it's been."

"That's the way," Bounty said, turning left at the courthouse corner. "A circus."

"'Therefore,'" Lack read on, "'scant attention was paid at first to the report from an unconfirmed source that the man upon whom the life of James Norcott now depends is a relative of Dr. John Belton Lack, the Norcott physician. A search through the files of a Boston newspaper, however, revealed the fact that less than three months ago John Malcolm Lack, age twenty-seven, a nephew of John Belton Lack, recovered from the dread infection. Young Lack is said to have blood of the rare type B. Dr. Lack could not be reached for a statement early this morning but it is understood that his nephew's arrival is expected hourly.'"

Malcolm Lack put down the paper. "That's once," he said with a nervous laugh, "I didn't want to see my name in print. This where you live?"

"Me and my cat." Bounty looked a little more wide awake as he parked in his driveway, got out and glanced up and down the street. "You'd better let me go in first and take her back to the den," he said as they crossed the small flagstone terrace. "She gets terribly frightened when visitors come."

"What's her name?"

"Carmen. She's part Persian."

Carmen was in the hall, excited, Bounty thought, by his home-coming at this hour. To his amazement she eluded his hands when he attempted to pick her up. She stared at Malcolm Lack through the screen door, began mewing loudly and went toward him, waving her tail.

"Shucks!" Lack said, opening the door. "She's not afraid of me. Are you, funny face?"

"Well I'll be darned!" Bounty exclaimed fervently as he took his visitor's straw hat. "This never happened before. She likes to kid herself for being a fraid-cat and have me chase her. She wants you to chase her now."

"Here we go then!" Lack got down like a sprinter on his mark, Carmen bounded toward the rear of the house and Bounty met them in the living room, when they had completed the circuit. Carmen rolled over on her back, played at fighting off Lack's hands, then allowed herself to be lifted into his arms. "Are you sure," the young man asked, "that you meant to name her Carmen?"

"I thought she ought to have a pretty name—as a sort of compensation," Bounty said, watching Carmen raise her eyes confidingly to the gray-blue ones. "This never happened before," he repeated.

Lack leaned back in a chair. He stroked the brindled fur with a large calloused hand, looked at Bounty and smiled. "You haven't been quite satisfied about me, have you, Sheriff? While you were in that telegraph office you wired to New Orleans to find out if I was telling a straight story, didn't you?"

Bounty admitted that he had. "If I'd brought you home with me first," he said, "I'd probably have saved the county some money. I'm willing to take Carmen's word for it that you're all right. Make yourself at home while I do some phoning. And don't chase her any more," he added as Carmen leaped to the floor. "If you let her, she'll run you to—"

"To death," Lack finished huskily. "And you'd never convince anybody how I died. In case you don't know it, Mr. Peter Bounty, it took a little nerve for me to come with you when I remembered the last donor you'd had in custody was murdered. Any idea what made me trust you?"

"I decided I'd suddenly grown a very honest face."

"No," Lack said, lighting a cigarette and holding out a hand for Carmen to return to his lap, "it was those cat hairs you have all over you."

Carmen was sprawled at Lack's feet, however, when her master came back several minutes later. Lack was bending over her, an expression of concern on his face. He looked up and asked: "What's she making those funny sounds for?"

Bounty explained to the best of his ability, the while he paced the floor and told himself he had to stay calm. "I'm afraid I haven't been careful enough about her diet this summer," he said. "I'm going to take her down to a pet hospital in Brownsville as soon as I get time. I dread to think of making the trip with her, though. She'll be so frightened. The world didn't treat her right when she was out in it and she feels safe only inside these walls."

"Like Uncle Johnny," Malcolm Lack said. "Why don't you have him look at her?"

"Why, he wouldn't—"

"Of course he would. Ask him and see how tickled he is." Lack was observing Bounty closely. "I don't think you know Uncle Johnny very well," he said. "I don't think you're telling me the truth about him. I don't think you want me to go to his house for some reason or other."

"Not just yet," Bounty said, standing at one of the windows that faced the street and yanking the curtains out of shape. "I called and talked to Miss Ainsworth, his nurse. She said he was awake and Doctor Cotillion and the oculist were with him. It's going to be a shock seeing you and I want to get Doctor Cotillion's advice before I let you walk in on him."

"It won't shock Uncle Johnny to see me."

"It might," Bounty answered evasively. "I called the Hesperides *Sun*, too, and asked how they came to know about you. It seems an unknown man rang about seven-thirty this morning and gave 'em the dope, including the hour your bus arrived. They must have got around to calling your uncle's house for confirmation just after I left. The fellow who met the bus was one of their reporters, all right."

Lack lighted another cigarette. "You think it was David Angelo who called the paper?"

"I feel sure it was." Bounty ducked his head, glanced down the street in the direction of the court house and ascertained that the approaching car was Bert Larrick's. He wasn't aware just how closely Malcolm Lack was observing him now. "What would be Angelo's idea in telling the town I was coming?" Lack asked.

"Angelo had to tell the town," Bounty said as he moved toward the front door, "in order to tell one individual—*an individual whose identity he doesn't know.*"

"Throwing me to the wolves, eh?"

"To the wolf."

"QUESTION!"

The commissioners of Hesperides County, in regular meeting assembled, looked at the head of the table, where their chairman, Rolf Jester, sat and swore under his breath and plucked at his stubby red mustache. Jester was known as a warmhearted soul. He was known also for having his own way, even if he had to ride roughshod over a few rules of order to get it. But he had met his match in Sam Spicard and the scowl he gave that individual was an ugly one.

Spicard, as gaunt as Jester was lusty, had an ax to grind here, everyone knew. His partner in the trucking business had a son, Tom Lynch, who had campaigned for E. Matthew Rone in the county's first sheriff's race, under promise of a deputy's job. Tom still had no job.

"Question!" Spicard called again, looking straight at Jester and smiling a little.

Jester let out his breath so forcibly that he sent papers sailing down the table. He rose and almost shouted: "The motion has been made and seconded that Sheriff Peter Bounty be suspended from office pending an investigation of the death of the Norcott blood donors. God damn it to hell! Everybody in favor signify by saying 'Aye.'"

"Well, son?" Bounty asked tensely, leaning over the door of his deputy's roadster.

Larrick sat hunched over the wheel, staring blankly into the shimmer of the heat that rose from the paving. He shook his head slowly, back and forth, and said: "You were wrong, Peter."

Bounty's eyes went shut for an instant and his shoulders sagged. "You're sure, son?"

"Sure." Larrick's voice was hard, almost without intonation. "I did as you said. I went by the morgue and got specimens of blood from Fred Winters and from Hieronymus. Doctor Ainsworth met me at the hospital and we tested them. Both men had blood of group B."

"Did you tell Doctor Ainsworth what blood it was you were testing?"

"No, I just told him I wanted him to show me how it was done. There wasn't any trouble about using the laboratory at the hospital. Everyone seemed to know that he was going to be the next head."

"Was Angelo there?"

"No sign of him."

"Well, this leaves us up the creek without a paddle, son," Bounty said, getting into the car and attacking a match. "I've staked everything this morning on Doctor Cotillion being the murderer."

"I don't see that you had any case against him. He cashed five hundred dollars worth of travelers' checks soon after he registered at the Sutherland Saturday night. Hieronymus had about that amount of money on him. So what?"

"Aside from that, son, he's been the only one I could make out a satisfactory case against. He's seemed to me to be an odd number from the beginning. Doctor Lack didn't ask him to come, yet he interrupted his honeymoon and flew clear across the country."

"He was grateful to Doctor Lack for having sent his nephew to give the first Mrs. Cotillion a transfusion."

"I'm a cynic, I suppose. That didn't seem reason enough. And I had it all worked out so beautifully this morning. When Hieronymus came to the hotel Saturday night to see Winters, the passengers from the Chicago plane were registering. Cotillion saw Hieronymus, in the lobby, in the elevator or in the fifth-floor corridor. Since Chris Hand would be with him, he signaled to Hieronymus that he wanted to talk to him. Or else Hieronymus spotted Cotillion and followed him to his room. At any rate I felt sure they met and talked after Hand left Cotillion."

"Why would Hieronymus have wanted to see Doctor Cotillion?"

"To get his identity established before he interviewed Roger Norcott. Norcott wouldn't shell out any money unless Hieronymus could prove he was a blood donor."

"But that's all supposition," Larrick argued. "And in spite of what you said at the office Hieronymus could have gone to see Fred Winters. I asked Mallory. She didn't know whether Fred had had a visitor or not. But she said he could have had and she wouldn't have known it."

"That leaves the money unexplained, of course. As I saw it, Cotillion was ready to commit murder only as a last resort. He told Hieronymus he'd pay him to skip out. But he'd come down without time for much preparation, being in a hurry to get here before Hieronymus and Winters were found and their blood tested. He probably spent only the night in Chicago. The plane he came on leaves there at 9 A.M., so he wouldn't have had time to go to the bank. He cashed what checks he had with him, gave Hieronymus the money and promised to pay the rest as soon as he could get it transferred on Monday. In the meantime Hieronymus was to go to Brownsville and lie low."

"But the man outside Doctor Cotillion's door who said this wasn't a healthy place for doctors?"

"I called that a red herring, son. Then, as I saw it, Hieronymus went to Brownsville but came back—for any of the reasons I outlined at the office. Maybe he planned to set Norcott and Cotillion to bidding against each other. He got a paper in the lobby to see if another donor had appeared. Anyway, when Gus picked him up he was between the devil and the deep. But I took him back to the hotel and he saw a chance to talk to Cotillion in private. He pretended to fall ill and refused to have a local physician. That left only Cotillion."

"But Hieronymus *was* scared."

"Maybe only of the law, son. I figured he put it up to Cotillion: he was in a scrape and the doctor had to get him out. Cotillion wouldn't use any halfway measures then. In his pocket he had aconite that he'd brought from Chicago. And we played right into his hands with that whisky. He'd just learned Winters was in the hotel—and, incidentally, tried to make Hand believe the Winters he'd met couldn't be the Fred Winters who was a blood donor—and there on the desk in Palladay's office was a pint of liquor going to Winters. Cotillion asked Hieronymus if he didn't want a drink. While pouring it into a paper cup he slipped in the aconite. Or else he poisoned the bottle first. Strong as he is, he could easily hold Hieronymus down and keep him still while the poison got in its work. When he made an excuse to go to the cigar counter he could have got rid of the container. When I remembered how ready he'd been with a suggestion about the cup I decided he'd seen to it that Hieronymus' prints were on it."

"Why were you so interested in that cup?"

"Because of the shape, Bert. If it had been flat-bottomed, the theory that Hieronymus poured himself a drink after Cotillion went out would have been acceptable enough. But you have to hold one of those cone-shaped cups in your hand while you pour the drink. Then you can't very well hold onto it while you cork a bottle and wrap it up again. You drink and throw the cup away, then do your wrapping. It seemed to me, from what I'd heard about aconite, that it'd be cutting the time rather short to say Hieronymus drank, threw the cup into the receptacle, wrapped up the bottle, then went and lay down and died—without making himself heard in the next room."

"That argument would never hold up in a court of law, Peter. The action of poisons depends on too many factors."

"I know. But when I saw that cup I got suspicious. I wasn't suspicious of Cotillion last night, or I'd never have let you stay with him. As eminent a man as he seemed beyond suspicion if anyone was. But I got to thinking how he acted after Hieronymus' death. Of course his explanation was plausible. But another would be that he delayed telling the cause of death as long as possible because he knew that once I learned it was aconite I'd tumble to the whisky and prevent Winters from drinking it. As it was, he delayed just long enough. And, the way I looked at it this morning, his interest in getting this donor from the Aleutians was in itself damning. Doctor Lack didn't try, because he was depending on the Chicago donors being found. But Cotillion employed an agency, because he knew those donors would never live to give transfusions."

"But what ever made you figure out such a motive?"

"It was slow in coming, son. But it kept coming. Cotillion was married. His wife died from streptococcus after being given two transfusions. A couple of months later he marries again. From a college professor, none too well off from all I've gathered, he steps up into a clinic in Chicago. He looks over Doctor Lack's house with a view to establishing a winter home here. He talks of putting you through school. It all pointed to a second marriage with money."

Larrick threw himself against the back of the seat and scowled at a passing car. "You didn't think Doctor Cotillion meant to help me through the university?"

Bounty sighed. "It was an even bet with me whether he did or whether he was soft-soaping us. I gave him the benefit of the doubt. I didn't see him as a deep-dyed villain, but as a man who'd made up his mind what he wanted and was determined to get it. He'd reconciled himself to murder but his conscience needed a salve. I pictured him," Bounty quoted, "as a middle-aged man who'd gained professional recognition by his research but little financial return. Ahead of him he saw years of the same routine, teaching and grinding out textbooks. I pictured a drab wife, the one he'd married while in medical school. Then along comes an orchidaceous heiress who gives him a come-on look. Because I imagine the man would be physically attractive to a lot of women. Maybe the money is incidental. Maybe it's love with a capital L—"

"Then you admit there is such a thing?"

"Oh, sure, son. But it can wear off sometimes. And I thought that's what he was warning you against. There's this wife, standing in his way. She gets streptococcus—"

"You read too many stories, Peter."

"Yeah, but his dilemma would have made such a corking good plot for a story. Up to that point, a story of the tribulations of married life. Afterwards, a murder story. The doctor saw a way to kill the wife he'd looked at over breakfast eggs for twenty-odd years. A way to kill her safely and without any spattering of brains—"

"Peter!"

"I wasn't thinking of real life, son," Bounty explained hastily. "He was her physician but his care of her had to be above question in the hospital. Then the problem of donors arose. As one of the foremost specialists in the country, he personally tested the blood of volunteers. His grouping would be accepted without question. If anybody came who already knew he had blood B, Cotillion would have dismissed him on the pretense that he'd lost immunity to streptococcus. But I doubt that anyone did, before Malcolm Lack arrived." Bounty paused. "I don't suppose there's any doubt that Winters and Hieronymus did have immunity at that time, is there, son?"

"I don't know about Hieronymus, but Fred had just recovered from streptococcus. So he must have had."

"Well, I give up then. More likely, according to my theory, Cotillion selected the first two volunteers who hadn't had or given transfusions and who consequently didn't know what group their blood belonged to. He pronounced it B and used them as donors. To the nurses who assisted him, to his associates, everything would be open and aboveboard. But it wasn't the kind of blood his wife needed and she died."

"But he wouldn't have let Winters and Hieronymus get to him for five thousand apiece, would he?"

"I accounted for that by saying that the security of his position rested there, as it has rested here, on avoiding suspicion. He had to be the husband who'd made every effort to save his wife. Once somebody smelled a rat, even if nothing were proven, his professional reputation would be damaged."

"But wouldn't he have known that there'd be another case where these donors would find out about their blood?"

"You know better than I do, son, what slight chance there was of another *Streptococcus viridans* case, in which the victim needed blood B, developing in the United States within the next few months. He watched for reports of one, though, just as Winters and Hieronymus were watching. And on his honeymoon comes this telegram from Doctor Lack. He hurries to Chicago and finds that the superintendent of the hospital has dug up newspaper files and sent Lack the names of Winters and Hieronymus. Though Cotillion has taken the precaution of destroying all records of them in the hospital. Cotillion flies here then, knowing that he has to keep Lack from testing their blood in case they are found. It seemed to me last night that there wasn't any need for him to volunteer so insistently to help Lack make those tests. I figured this morning that he wanted advance information of the donors so he could prevent them from going to the hospital."

"But those were to have been tests to see if immunity to streptococcus had been lost."

"There was the likelihood that Lack would have tested for blood grouping while he was at it. Or taken blood from Winters and Hieronymus for comparison with that of other donors. Even if he hadn't, he would have known something was wrong after he gave the transfusions, wouldn't he?"

"Yes, he probably would have."

Bounty sat forward and looked at the windows of his house. A curtain moved, he thought. "So there's the case against Cotillion as I prepared it this morning," he said. "It all hinged on the question of whether or not Winters and Hieronymus had blood B. If they didn't, Cotillion had murdered his wife, Winters, Hieronymus, Beck. But they did, so he's not our man. I'm still betting on the orchidaceous heiress, though," he added obstinately.

"Doctor Cotillion doesn't know you had any suspicion of him?"

"Oh no. I haven't seen him today. But I've been worried about you, son. I was afraid he'd go to the hospital while you and Doctor Ainsworth were there and find out that the game was up."

Larrick was silent for a time. "Then as things stand," he said in that hard toneless voice, "you don't suspect anybody in particular?"

"It's an open field. Not only do we not know who the murderer is, we don't even know whom he intended to murder."

"What do you think the commissioners will do if you fail to solve the case?"

"Nothing. Provided, of course, this killing of donors doesn't go on."

"Did you see that extra? It says Malcolm Lack is expected."

"He's in the house."

Larrick turned his head quickly. "He is?"

"I met him at the hospital while I was waiting on you and Doctor Ainsworth. I've been keeping him from going to his uncle's till Doctor Cotillion left there. Now I expect we'll go on out."

"But even if your theory had been correct, Lack's life wouldn't have been in any danger from Doctor Cotillion, would it?"

"No, but I wasn't quite sure what Lack's relations had been with Winters and Hieronymus. He seems on the level, however. I don't know what the arrangement will be about a transfusion. But I'd like to have you at the hospital when it takes place, son."

"All right. Let me go home and see Mallory now. I barely had time to break the news to her about Fred before I left. She took it very well. We wired Fred's wife in New York. From what Mallory said, I don't think it'll be any great shock to her. Their marriage doesn't seem to have turned out very successfully."

"You might make a note of that, son," Bounty said as he got out of the car.

"Peter!" Larrick spoke suddenly and clapped a hand over his eyes as if the light had grown blinding. "Remember that case you had in Brownsville where you were looking for a murderer who'd already died? It didn't strike me till this morning how queer it was that Beck didn't catch on to the whisky being poisoned before he drank it. I asked Gus when I was out at Doctor Lack's. He told me he thought Beck committed suicide. Now I don't know what all you found out about Beck. But I know you were suspicious of him when you went there last night. Did he have any motive for killing these donors?"

"I'd say not, son."

"But you rigged one up for Doctor Cotillion. Why couldn't you do the same for Beck? He may have been in the lobby of the hotel when you had Hieronymus there. He may have taken the whisky from the counter and poisoned it. Did he know why you arrested him?"

Bounty was frowning. "I'm not sure," he answered after a moment.

"Suppose he thought you had evidence against him and were arresting him for murder. He didn't know the liquor he'd poisoned was in the pocket of the car till Fred and I came up. But he let Fred drink. He'd accomplished his purpose then. So he drank himself—to escape the electric chair. How's that for an ending?"

In the house the telephone was ringing. "Neat enough, son," Bounty said, stepping from the curb onto the grass.

"Can you suggest a better one?"

"Right at the moment I can't."

"Well," Larrick said and drove away.

Quickly as he went to the house, Bounty kept his head turned and stared sleepily after the roadster.

He made his way back to the den without passing through the living room. Gus was on the wire. "Chief"—the undersheriff's voice was excited—"somebody just called here and wanted to talk to Doctor Lack. I made him tell me who he was. He said he was the doctor's nephew, callin' from your house. I told Carrie Ainsworth. She talked to Doctor Cotillion and connected the fellow with Doctor Lack's bedroom. I got to thinking about it and decided I'd better call you and make sure."

"Just a second, Gus." Bounty went into the living room, where he found his guest leaning back in his chair, blowing smoke rings. Carmen, curled up on his lap, contemplated her master sleepily.

"I hoped you'd hear the phone," Lack said. "I didn't want to go to the door and call you."

"You called your uncle?"

Lack nodded and grinned, rather sheepishly. "Guilty, Sheriff. It wasn't that I lost my trust in you. But I didn't like the idea of this house becoming a meeting place as soon as I got here. And it did seem a little strange that there should be so much difficulty about Uncle Johnny and me meeting each other. But I find that everything's lovely. Uncle Johnny has made you the guardian angel of the Lacks. I'm to hold onto your hand until he gets here."

"Is he able to be up?"

"He was in bed when I called but he said he was getting up. And from the tone of his voice I judge it'd take a strait jacket to hold him."

Bounty returned to the telephone. "O.K., Gus," he said. "Guard duty's off. You might wait and come over here with Doctor Lack, if he comes. Is Doctor Cotillion handy?"

"He just left in a taxi for the hospital."

"Let me talk to Carrie Ainsworth then."

"Hello, Mr. Bounty," came the girl's cheery greeting in a moment.

"What's the word on our patient, Miss Ainsworth?"

"He was a patient until his nephew called. The oculist said there was no injury to the eyeball. He put a bandage over the eye, though, and said it oughtn't to be exposed to the sun for a few days. Doctor Cotillion prescribed a complete rest for Doctor Lack and Doctor Lack agreed. He seemed no more than half alive, utterly indifferent to everything. His nephew's voice did wonders for him. He insisted on getting up and performing the transfusion himself. Doctor Cotillion said it would be better to let him do it than keep him in bed fretting. So Doctor Cotillion has gone to make preparations at the hospital and Doctor Lack is dressing."

"That's fine, Miss—"

"Mrs. Hand, if you please. Your little expedient wasn't necessary. On our way over here I informed the Honorable Christopher that I was going to get my old job back. The upshot of our conversation was that I'm to stay here only as long as Doctor Lack is ill. Then we're to start in housekeeping. That's the way your stories end, don't they, Mr. Bounty?"

"It's the place to end them," Bounty said. Returning to the living room, he decided Bert had been more foxy than he realized in suggesting last night that he call Dr. Ainsworth's daughter.

"Hope I didn't gum the works for you," Malcolm Lack said, stroking Carmen's left ear and calling forth from her the grating sound that passed for purring.

"Oh no," Bounty told him. "If I'd known what I know now, we'd have gone straight to your uncle's house. Did he know about Beck?"

"About his death—Doctor Cotillion had told him, I judged—but not about the real circumstances. I want to tell him sometime. But not now." Malcolm Lack stuck a finger through a smoke ring. "He warned me by all means not to get out of doors. That would be his agoraphobia at work. Mr. Bounty, I've got the feeling that you're of two minds about Uncle Johnny. I'm not going to try to defend him but I'd like to explain him a little, if you don't mind. Because he's going to need someone to lean on now."

"Aren't you going to stay with him?"

"Not for long. The same thing would happen as did in Boston. I'd get to feeling sorry for him and before I knew it I wouldn't be able to break away. And I've got to get over to Europe this summer. I promised a fellow I'd meet him in Paris in August. But I want Uncle Johnny to adapt himself here. If he's ever going to get over that agoraphobia, I figure it'll have to be in flat open country like this, where he can come to feel himself safe yet not be shut in by anything. And if the poor sap would only tell people and let them help him! But he won't, he's afraid of ridicule, and as a result they think he's goofy. Did he tell you about the agoraphobia?"

"Beck did."

"Just as I thought." Lack lighted another cigarette. "Well, it all goes back to his childhood, of course. My grandparents were to blame. They were overly conscientious, to put it mildly. Uncle Johnny was the older son and they thought it their duty to discipline him and harden him to manage the family fortune. My father got off more lightly, but at that he left home the first chance he got. Uncle Johnny was a high-strung kid and I suppose he did have a pretty violent temper. My grandfather didn't whip him but he did what was probably worse. Every time Johnny had a tantrum he was shut in a dark closet and left there until he subsided. I remember hearing one of his old nurses tell my father about it. Poor Johnny would scream and go into convulsions until he wore himself out and cried himself to sleep. And Grandfather never would relent. That went on for years and he thought he was gradually getting Johnny subdued. The boy became quieter, a regular Little Lord Fauntleroy, but he wanted to stay in his room all the time. They thought he was reading. But what he was doing was sitting in a dark closet. He'd got used to it, see, and it was a refuge for him. They'd pick out playmates for him but, when he didn't slip back into the house and shut himself up, they saw he always started one game: jail. With himself as the prisoner. That explains the fascination jails have for him today. You've probably noticed it."

"Up until last night I never exchanged more than half-a-dozen words with your uncle."

"You'd never guess it from the way he spoke of you over the phone. Or from the way you've spoken of him."

"I've been taking him a great deal on faith," Bounty said. "I believe my undersheriff did say that Doctor Lack had asked once to go through the county jail."

"It wouldn't be a place of constraint for him. I've heard him swear, sometimes when he was at his worst, that a lifetime in solitary confinement was the only solution for him. And all because of that closet. My grandparents finally discovered that at night he was moving his bedclothes into it and sleeping there. Then they had to start in breaking him of that habit. But the harm had already been done. They tried to make him spend more time out of doors. Sometimes he'd fight against being taken out, sometimes he'd go and then, when he got in a park, break loose and run home and beat against the door to get in. When he was old enough for tutors he got along better, because he could stay in his room. And once one of them gained his confidence, he'd throw himself into his studies."

As Lack felt in his pocket for a package of cigarettes he disturbed Carmen, who protested plaintively. She fixed her eyes on Bounty and he thought there was reproach in them.

"Just a little while, Carmen," Lack said to her, "and you'll have the best doctor a cat ever had. You were surprised, Mr. Bounty, at the thought that Uncle Johnny would stoop to examine a cat. You'll see. There never was anyone kinder. And there you have the great tragedy about him. The passion to be a doctor, a humanitarian, got hold of him and helped carry him through prep school and college and medical school. By that time he knew his weakness and by gritting his teeth could conquer it. His father's death really bucked him up, too, because it gave him responsibility and power. It was while he was serving his internship, I think, that he began to lose his nerve. He'd been sheltered in the classroom and laboratory. Now he had to get out and deal with people. He threw over everything, went home and shut himself up. When he came out at last, it was to go into research. But he was never satisfied that he wasn't shirking his duty. He went back, finished his internship, then joined a clinic. There it was, at a crucial moment with him, that he met Beck."

"In connection with the death certificate and legal formalities, Lack, it'll probably be necessary to find out the man's real name. Do you know it?"

"John Allton Beck is his legal name. What his original one was, I don't know. I know next to nothing about his life before he and Uncle Johnny came together. His ambition had been to be a musician of some kind. He'd studied and practiced and deprived himself of everything with that one goal in view. And then he was told that he was wasting his time and money. He could never be even a second-rater. He simply wasn't a musician. You noticed his hands?"

Bounty nodded. "And compared them with your uncle's."

"Then you had the substance of their relationship. On getting the verdict, Beck went to his room and shot himself. Uncle Johnny happened to be at the hospital when he was brought in, dying. He did die, that much I know, and Uncle Johnny brought him back with adrenalin. When he regained consciousness he begged to be allowed to die. He tried to tear off the bandages and told the nurses he'd do the same thing over again as soon as he got out. When Uncle Johnny came in Beck cursed him. Uncle Johnny had him moved to a private room and said he wanted to be alone with him. He came back day after day and sat with Beck. What they said to each other during that time no one'll ever know. But for the first time in his life Uncle Johnny must have found someone he could open up to. And Beck, I think, made Uncle Johnny a substitute for his music. Because they say it was almost miraculous, the way he recuperated. When he left the hospital he went with Uncle Johnny. From that day to this I don't believe those two were separated for more than a few hours."

"Fourteen years," Bounty said slowly.

"Fourteen years. I suppose, from what you saw of them, you think Uncle Johnny simply made Beck his servant. That wasn't it at all. Their relations weren't very well defined at first. But what Uncle Johnny wanted was a companion and friend, somebody he could lean on. Beck tried to fill the bill, I think, but he couldn't. And after he got well I think it was a distinct anticlimax. Both of them became self-conscious. You know how it is when two men have been on a drunk, sworn undying friendship and all that. They meet each other the next day and feel silly. And by the way, Mr. Bounty, you don't happen to have a drink about your house, do you?"

"No, I don't, Lack." Bounty grinned feebly. "And if I did I don't think I'd dare give it to you."

"Oh." Lack gulped. "That's right. Well, to go on with Uncle Johnny and Beck, it was Beck who deliberately fixed his own status as servant. In that way he could be with Uncle Johnny constantly but there'd always be a barrier to intimacy between them. And don't fool yourself, it was Beck who kept Uncle Johnny in his place, not the other way around. Uncle Johnny would try, very timidly as a rule, to establish the companionship he wanted with Beck. Beck would become the perfect servant and hold him off. Now Beck probably wanted the same thing, but was afraid to unbend. Then, too, some obstinacy may have entered in. Uncle Johnny could have anything in the world that money could buy. But what he wanted most of all, friendship, Beck wasn't going to let him have. Ironic, wasn't it?"

"I suppose so. And your uncle, on his side, bore resentment against Beck."

Lack gave Bounty a keen glance. "Exactly. I said I wasn't going to defend Uncle Johnny and I'm not. He has a mean streak in him. You probably saw plenty of evidence of it. Yet he grew more and more dependent on Beck, had to have him with him all the time. The reason he had Beck come back from the airport night before last was that he couldn't stand being alone any longer. Beck knew that; that's why he called. He helped Uncle Johnny devise ways that would mean their being together. That reading aloud, for instance. Uncle Johnny couldn't bear the thought of lying alone in the dark, dropping off to sleep and being helpless. But you were wrong about one thing, Mr. Bounty. You seemed to think Beck wanted privacy and Uncle Johnny wouldn't respect it. He didn't want privacy for its own sake. He had made every effort not to have a life of his own but to live Uncle Johnny's. But there were times—such as when he was shaving and when he was eating his meals in the kitchen—that he couldn't keep up his barriers against Uncle Johnny. I know he would never eat with Uncle Johnny. He'd serve him very formally and then Uncle Johnny would follow him out and sit down with him while he ate."

"And Doctor Lack never paid Beck any wages?"

Malcolm Lack gave a deep sigh. "Not that I know of," he answered. "And there's the thing that always made me want to give Uncle Johnny a swift kick. I used to wonder if way down in his heart he wasn't afraid not to keep Beck dependent on him. Honestly, though, I don't think that was it. I asked him once why he didn't fix Beck up with an annuity, if he didn't want to hand him a monthly paycheck like an employer. He got sore, said every penny he had was Beck's for the asking. That was absolutely true, I have no doubt. Uncle Johnny would have asked a hundred and one questions, because that's his way, but he'd have taken actual pleasure in fulfilling Beck's wish."

"Thus adding to his own stature. Did you ever know Beck to come out and ask Doctor Lack for money?"

"I don't believe so. Of course I don't remember an occasion when Beck needed money. I never thought he cared. But there's where I was mistaken, evidently. He's been sensitive about money all this time."

"Sensitive to the extent that he wouldn't, if he could help it, ask your uncle for any. And it probably galled him to have to let Christopher Hand know he was without a cent in his pockets. But I'd hazard a guess that when he resorted to a subterfuge to repay the nickel he was really wanting to spare Doctor Lack the agitation that would come from knowledge that a man of his had had to borrow—and from that particular individual."

"To shield Uncle Johnny from reality, just as he shielded him from the out of doors. He always tried to do that. I've got in scrapes and Beck always kept Uncle Johnny from knowing about them." Malcolm Lack stared into the street.

"And what finally broke Beck," Bounty said, "was the exhibition of your uncle's—oh, picayunishness. Beck must have been trying all those years to make himself believe that John Belton Lack and John Belton Lack's work really were a substitute for his own lost music. But no man can be a hero to his valet. And at last Beck had to admit to disillusionment. Doctor Lack had disappointed him. After that, he had nothing to live for."

Bounty could hear the ticking of the clock in his bedroom. The noon blanket of hot desert silence was settling upon the town and stifling, briefly, its activity. Siesta time and Bounty had to yawn. . . .

"It had to come," Malcolm Lack said, "sooner or later. I told you maybe it was better this way. That doesn't mean I don't feel Beck's death. I do, because he's been a part of Uncle Johnny so long. But I can't think of him as an individual. Though with me he came as near to being one as he ever came during the last fourteen years, I suppose. I hate to say this, but I've always thought of Beck as a crutch that Uncle Johnny leaned on. As long as Uncle Johnny had that support, he was never going to walk by himself. As long as Beck was there, ready to sleep across his door, he would dread what lay beyond that door. And now . . ." Lack yawned and looked at his watch.

"Is there any danger of your uncle following in Beck's path?" Bounty asked. "I've had that in mind all morning. That's one reason I've wanted someone near him."

Lack was sunk in thought for a moment. "No," he answered, "Uncle Johnny would never commit suicide. His feeling of duty to humanity would be too strong. He'd bear in mind that he was destroying the skill and knowledge that could save lives and case suffering. Though he has doubtless been tempted to suicide here, since this Hesperides move has proved a failure. He's gone to the furthermost limit of the United States now and hasn't been able to shed his old skin. He'd just got over his last disappointment, some kind of a brotherhood-of-man community out in California that would have swindled him out of a quarter of a million if Beck hadn't put a stop to it. I'm especially sorry about this, because I urged him to come. He saw all those ads, you know, that your Chamber of Commerce ran in the Eastern papers. He sent for literature and read all about this brand-new country—"

"Alabaster cities' and 'man and nature ever smiling.'"

"I knew what all that meant, of course, but I'd been in the Valley and I did think Uncle Johnny might snap out of it here."

"So you've been in the Valley before?" Bounty observed interrogatively.

"I was through here about five years ago, after working in the oil fields down at Tampico. I fell for this country. It's like the ocean, a man can see. Maybe I'll spend next winter here, if Uncle Johnny stays."

Bounty rose and took a turn about the room, his hands in his pockets. He had to shake off this lethargy, he told himself, and do something. All this stress on the urgency of getting a blood donor and here was the donor, lolling in a chair and smoking cigarette after cigarette while Jimmy Norcott's life flickered out. . . .

"Lord, what plans Uncle Johnny laid! He swore that this time he was going to succeed. From the minute he set foot in Hesperides he was going to be like other men." Malcolm Lack talked away for the same reason, perhaps, that he smoked. He grinned a little. "Now Uncle Johnny has his share of vanity. And while he's the most un-worldly soul you ever met, he's fully aware that he's a rich man. He saw himself coming here and becoming a sort of godfather to the town. He saw himself looked up to and loved by everybody, friends popping into his house to ask his advice and help when they were in trouble, people stopping him on the street to call him by his first name and shake his hand. And he was anxious to do good, too, mind you. He's always got along better with children than with adults. Reading about the year-round sunshine and fresh sea air here, he planned to buy up land and turn it into permanent camps, where he could bring children from the tenements. He didn't want kids to grow up in dark little rooms, as he had. I think that's really the picture that brought him here: himself walking into a playground and a flock of kids running to hold his hand and ask him to play with them. I didn't expect to find things had worked out that well. But I didn't think he'd make a complete failure. What in the dickens happened?"

"He thought he was coming to Utopia," Bounty said, "and found he'd come to an ordinary American town. Inevitably we let him down. As he let Beck down. If he'll stay—"

"You and I'll have to make him stay, Mr. Bounty. He hasn't any place to go, except back to Boston. If he does that he admits he's licked and I don't think he'll ever make another attempt. He'll shut himself up and shrink and shrink till he's an old redheaded mummy. You'll continue to live at his house, won't you? If you don't, I'm afraid I won't be able to get to Europe. I can't just go off and leave him alone."

Bounty was at the window again, yanking at curtains. "You'd better reconcile yourself to becoming a Texan then," he said. "I notice you keep referring to your uncle's hair as red. It's salmon rather, isn't it?"

Malcolm Lack chuckled. "I understand. I've heard that question debated before. I'll tell you the awful truth. If that hair were on the head of an ordinary man, it'd be called red. Plain old red.

But since it belongs to Uncle Johnny people think they have to give it fancy names. I shouldn't be surprised if he hypnotized you with it."

"Hypnotized me?"

"Into seeing its color in everything. One of the principles of hypnotism is involved, I think. You concentrate on that red hair—" Lack half rose from his chair, so suddenly that he let Carmen slide, clawing, to the floor. "Who's that?" he demanded, trying to inspect the car which had turned into the driveway.

"That," Bounty said, "is your redheaded uncle. And the under-sheriff."

"Undersheriff," Lack muttered as he crushed out his cigarette. "Sheriff maybe, you don't know. I heard talk this morning that the commissioners might put him in your place."

"If there's one man in Hesperides who's not suspect, Lack, it's Gus Broddus."

"Then in a murder story— Wait!" As they went through the hall to the front door the young man grasped Bounty's arm. "Look," he said, nodding. "The old boy's fighting his enemy. That's a good sign."

Dr. Lack wore a black suit, black hat and dark glasses. He had left Gus Broddus sitting in the latter's sedan and was walking to-ward the terrace, slowly and stiffly, his head up, his eyes fixed pre-sumably on the roof line of Bounty's house. Only when he came to the flagstones did he look at the door, quicken his steps and say, with heaving chest: "Malcolm."

So disheveled was the man that Bounty's thought was of an accident. His necktie hung untied from his collar. His coat was buttoned unevenly. The lace of one shoe was flapping. As he passed through the screen door that Bounty held open, the latter stared at his face. It was of a deathly pallor and all over it were little cuts, some encrusted with drying blood, some white with talcum pow-der, a few covered by strips of court plaster.

A man who has dressed and shaved himself for the first time in fourteen years . . .

Malcolm Lack's hands were gripping the narrow shoulders and he was drawing his uncle to him while he laughed. "Uncle Johnny, you old ragamuffin!"

"Malcolm."

Bounty went outside and to the sedan, where Gus Broddus sat with the door open and one foot on the running board. He had always wondered what a person looked like when he looked aghast. Seeing the undersheriff, he knew.

"I didn't know whether I ought to come in or not, chief," Gus said, with his attention on the house. "The doctor told me he wanted to walk to the door by himself. I knew you'd see him and there wouldn't be any danger of him gettin' away—"

"Getting away? What do you mean?"

"Why, he's the man! The murderer."

"Nonsense! You must be crazy with the heat."

"He told me he was, chief."

Bounty blinked his eyes and stuck his head into the shade. "Let's have this, Gus. Quick."

"Well, I was in the hall when he came downstairs. He shook hands with me, just as nice as could be, and said he supposed I was goin' to take him to your house. I told him I'd be glad to. I could tell he'd dressed in a hurry so I asked him if he wouldn't like for me to tie his tie for him. It didn't seem right, somehow, to let him go out on the street lookin' like that. But he said no—bitter-like—there was no reason why I should treat him different from any other murderer. You could've knocked me over with a feather. I just took him to the car and didn't say anything."

"Was nothing more said on the way over?"

"Well"—Gus held his mouth open for a moment—"yes. He asked me all of a sudden what you wanted more than anything else in the world. I told him. Maybe I shouldn't have. I thought afterwards maybe he was fixin' to bribe you."

Bounty mopped his face. "What did you tell him, Gus?"

"Exactly what you do want most, chief: to send Bert Larrick off to school. Though I've said and I'll say again that I think it'd be a waste of good money. Bert would flunk out—"

"Oh, Gus, never mind that," Bounty said distractedly. "Doctor Lack didn't mean what he said about being the murderer."

"He *is* off his nut then? I thought he acted like it."

"No, Gus. Forget all this, will you? Or at least don't mention it to anyone." Bounty consulted his watch. "A fingerprint expert will be at the office at one. I'd like to have you meet him and get his report on some things." He detailed the services which he wished the man to render, then with difficulty sent the undersheriff on his way. Gus seemed convinced that he was leaving his superior in the company of a madman. "You're too trustin', chief," was his parting shot.

For an instant, coming upon Dr. Lack seated cross-legged on the living-room floor, Bounty did experience a misgiving. He glanced at Malcolm Lack, who was straddling the arm of a chair and grinning. The young man winked and gestured toward the sofa.

Dr. Lack was leaning in that direction, with both hands extended. "Come to me, Carmen," he ordered in the identical voice, divorced from all passion, which Bounty had heard Beck use the night before. Two dark paws and the tip of a dark nose emerged from under the sofa.

Bounty looked at those white, finely shaped hands and thought of them as he had grown accustomed to think of Bert Larrick's: wielders of delicate instruments. "Let me get her out, Doctor," he said. "She'll be scared and might scratch you."

"No, Bounty. I want her to come to me voluntarily. If something is wrong with her I may have to hurt her. She won't be so frightened then if she trusts me. Come, Carmen."

Carmen came, her eyes fixed on the dark spectacles, the right lens of which concealed a small bandage. She nudged Dr. Lack's right hand with her nose and began talking to him as she talked to Peter Bounty. The head with its red, crookedly parted hair bent over her and after a few moments Dr. Lack began laughing. It was wild loud laughter that had a trace of hysteria in it.

"Oh, Bounty, you innocent!" he managed to articulate. "The man I thought knew all there was to know about life. Didn't it ever occur to you that—that you might be going to have a family on your hands?"

"Oh," Bounty said and stared at Carmen, who had given Dr. Lack a long smug look, then set in to wash the freckles from the back of one of his hands. "Why, yes, Doctor, it did occur to me. But I don't know how it happened. I have the back door fixed so she can go out if she wants to, of course. But I never knew her to venture outside. She's always been so very timid."

"She found a way to live her own life. She had to." Dr. Lack began to sob; his sobs sounded much like his laughter. "Men have to live their own lives. I denied a man that right—after I'd denied him the right to die—"

The telephone rang and Bounty tiptoed quickly away. Behind him he heard Malcolm Lack saying: "Up, up, Uncle Johnny. I want to do some repair work on you. And remember you've got another patient here."

"Sheriff." Dr. Cotillion was on the wire. "I wish you'd tell Doctor Lack that I've just examined young Norcott. He isn't going to live through the afternoon without a transfusion."

22

Peter Bounty held a handkerchief to his nose as he stood in the corridor on the top floor of the John Belton Lack Hospital. "I thought you might like to explain why you cashed five hundred dollars worth of traveler's checks as soon as you arrived in Las Palmas," he said to Doctor Cotillion. "It doesn't take that much to keep you in chewing tobacco, does it?"

Dr. Cotillion had the plug in his hands and was creasing and uncreasing the tinfoil. He took his bloodshot eyes from it and glanced up and down the corridor. "Sheriff," he asked, pitching his voice low, "did you ever hear of a buried treasure in the desert on the other side of the Rio Grande?"

So nonplused was Bounty that he lowered his handkerchief. "Did you say treasure, Doctor? Why, there's treasure buried under every square inch of the desert on both sides of the Rio Grande."

"That's legendary. This isn't. On the plane coming down from Chicago I got to talking with a man who used to be an engineer in Mexico. An old Mexican named Pedro, who once worked for him, had sent him word that he was dying and wanted to give him a secret he had been keeping for years. He'd discovered a treasure out in the desert but was afraid to touch it."

"Don't tell me there was a spirit guarding the treasure!"

"So Pedro believed. But he said if his former employer would come down and see him he'd show him the location. The man needed money for digging operations and offered to give me a half interest in the treasure if I'd advance him five hundred dollars. I didn't have that much on me but he said he was staying in Las Palmas overnight and would look me up. I told him he could get in touch with me through Doctor Lack or Mr. Norcott. Evidently he stopped at the Sutherland, too, because he came to my room just after I'd registered. I went downstairs, cashed some traveler's checks and gave him the money. He's to come back in a day or two and report."

Bounty was getting pale. "And you're planning how to spend your half interest?" he asked through his handkerchief.

"I've been making some plans, yes. Goodman tells me—"

"Goodman?"

"Yes," Dr. Cotillion said. "My partner's name is Frank Goodman. I felt sure he was telling me the truth about having been in Mexico because he was so tanned."

23

HUGH AINSWORTH had a new spring in his step, Peter Bounty observed as he sat on the same ledge in front of the John Belton Lack Hospital and watched the physician come up the walk. His dark sober clothing was still not far from shabbiness but he wore a bright necktie and a matching handkerchief peeped from the breast pocket of his coat. His face was still mild and homely but a smile had chased away its apologetic expression. For the first time Bounty saw him, not as a country practitioner ready for the discard, but as a man little older than he, who perhaps had been in the position of the tortoise among the sleek spectacular hares of the Magic Valley. And who now, from all indications, was about to touch the goal which he had never made a goal.

"Good afternoon, Mr. Bounty."

"Good afternoon, Doctor."

Dr. Ainsworth stopped, with his heels together, and pushed back his stooped shoulders as he looked up at the front of the hospital. He looked at Bounty and asked: "Wouldn't you like to wait in—my office?"

Bounty grinned, rose and stuck out a hand. "Congratulations, Doctor. I knew your appointment was a foregone conclusion but I'm glad to hear of it just the same. When does it take effect?"

"At once. I'm still a little dazed by it. There were so many better qualified men the commissioners could have chosen—"

"Listen to one of my political speeches sometime and you'll learn that's no way to talk." Bounty got out a match. "I'm afraid a goodly amount of work faces you at the outset," he said reluctantly. "Three autopsies. I don't think Doctor Angelo has made even a beginning."

Carrie Ainsworth had her father's eyes, if no other feature. The hot bright sunlight didn't weaken the steadiness of his gaze. "The work is welcome, Mr. Bounty, if such work ever is. I shall be glad of an excuse to avoid a meeting with my predecessor while he is removing his effects. And the only serious case in the hospital at present is that of young Norcott. Doctor Lack and Doctor Cotillion are attending to it. I can start on the autopsies at once. Bert Larrick told me something of the deaths. But don't you want to come inside?"

"Can't stand the smell, Doctor. I want to thank you for cooperating with Bert this morning."

"Glad to have him call on me. I've always known the lad had the makings of a physician. He tells me he plans to continue his medical course this fall. I hope he'll come around the hospital often this summer, to get his hand in."

"I'll see that he does." Bounty hesitated. "I suppose there was no doubt about the grouping of those blood specimens he brought?"

"No, none at all." Dr. Ainsworth looked surprised. "Did you want a written report on them? I understood Bert to say he was merely experimenting."

"That was all. I thought this was a good chance for the boy to learn how to make those tests."

"Mr. Bounty," the physician said hastily as Roger Norcott drove up and parked behind Larrick's roadster, "my conscience has been troubling me about last night. About our concealment from you of the identity of that blood donor at the Sutherland. I'm not trying to slide out from under responsibility. But I hadn't been in touch with Mr. Norcott or Doctor Lack. I didn't fully understand what the sudden agitation was about. It wasn't my case—"

"That's all water under the bridge now, Doctor. I'm not holding anything against anyone."

Norcott's cigar was cocked at the sky. There were dark pouches under his eyes and the leather of his face was wrinkled and old. He strode up the walk, shooting glances right and left, and Bounty saw at once that he carried a gun on his hip.

"Hello, Hugh. Bounty" he barked out. "Doctor Lack just had one of the nurses call me. Why wasn't I told about his nephew? I'd have been here sooner. I'd have had Christopher wait to take his father to the country. What guards do you have posted, Sheriff?"

"Bert Larrick's upstairs."

"That all?"

"Why, yes," Bounty answered blandly. "I understood you to say last night you believed I was the one whose life was threatened, not your nephew."

"I still think so. But . . ." Norcott turned to Ainsworth. "Have they begun the transfusion yet, Hugh?"

"I don't know, Roger. I only just arrived and haven't taken charge yet officially."

"Heard about your appointment. It was time."

"The transfusion is under way," Bounty volunteered. "Doctor Lack had to give his nephew a blood test and physical examination first. I stayed inside till I learned he was a satisfactory donor."

"Thank God!" Norcott took a deep breath. "Has Doctor Cotillion had any more word from that donor up north?"

"A telegram was forwarded to him from the hotel a few minutes ago. This man Miles had reached Unalaska and chartered a plane to take him to Juneau. From there he can get another to bring him to the States."

Norcott frowned. "All that chartering of planes will be rather expensive, won't it?" he said.

"Rather. I understand the expedition is advancing Miles the money. On the strength of the inquiry agency's credit, I suppose. And they on Doctor Cotillion's."

"I was wondering"—Norcott looked at his cigar—"if we'd need Miles now. Doctor Lack's nephew might be able to give enough transfusions."

"I wouldn't advise you to make that suggestion to Doctor Lack," Bounty said dryly. He glanced at Dr. Ainsworth as the latter moved toward the door and suspected that the new county physician had turned away to hide his contempt.

Norcott threw away his cigar and followed.

"Roger," Bounty heard Ainsworth say, "do you remember the time you imported cattle from Indo-China to improve your stock?"

Bounty resumed his seat, his own gun thudding against the ledge. He watched a buzzard, perhaps the same one, wheel through the cloudless sky and wondered if it were laziness which induced his feeling that this case, like a fever, had run its course. . . .

Gus Broddus' sedan wheezed to a stop in front of the hospital. The heat was playing hell with his bunions, Bounty knew as soon as the undersheriff climbed out. At the office Gus kept carpet slippers to wear at this time of day.

"Chief, did you know you had a lateral pocket loop?"

"Huh?"

"On your right thumb. And I've got a tented arch. Here's a telegram came to the office for you."

Bounty grinned and tore open the message. "How did you and the fingerprint expert get along?" he asked after a moment.

Gus sat on the other ledge. "He did the talkin' and I did the listenin'. Let's see." He tabulated on his fingers. "Your prints were the only ones the fellow got from that drawer of your desk. Yours and mine were the only clear ones on the whisky bottle. Mostly smudges on the wrapping paper but he identified some as Bert Larrick's. That's all as it should be, isn't it?"

"Yes. And on the paper cup?"

"Prints of Bert and Hieronymus."

"And that's as it should be, I suppose. Sheriff Cosgro called me just before I left the house. He's found the place where a man answering to the description of Hieronymus bought some nitroglycerin last Saturday morning. He compared the list of the contents of Doctor Lack's drug cabinet with the cache they confiscated. It all tallies except for morphine and some of the easily disposed-of stuff. The entire amount of aconite that Doctor Lack had was there. So, for the present at least, I'm dismissing that drug cabinet as a false alarm."

"Things seem to be fallin' our way then, chief."

"Like hell," Bounty said, staring at the buzzard again. "Anything new at the office?"

"Rolf Jester came in to tell you what the commissioners did. And—oh yes—Palladay called from the Sutherland, wantin' to speak to you about this sheriffs' convention. He said he'd been thinkin' it over and got afraid there might be gunplay. I felt like kiddin' him but didn't. I promised all the sheriffs would leave their shootin' irons at home."

Bounty attempted nonchalance. "I heard the commissioners put Doctor Ainsworth in Angelo's place."

"Yeah, and it didn't take 'em long. But they did more that, chief. Sam Spicard forced Jester's hand and they had to take action on you." Broddus unlaced his right shoe. "Speakin' of Angelo, I hear he's started on another big toot. Jester called his apartment, thought it only fair to give him a chance to answer the charges against him, but he said Angelo was already so drunk he could hardly talk. Guess we won't have any more trouble out of him— unless he gets to whoopin' it up."

"I think Angelo has shot his wad so far as this case is concerned. He's Malcolm Lack's problem now and I rather think the young man can handle him." Bounty's eyelids had drooped a little. "What action did the commissioners take about me, Gus?" he asked after a moment.

"Huh?" Broddus unlaced his left shoe. "Oh, they gave you a vote of confidence, chief."

Bounty looked around. "Sure enough?"

"Sure enough. Jester was grinnin' from ear to ear. He said to tell you they'd named a committee to draw up a resolution. Old J. B. Sizemore's head of it, though, and you know how long-winded he is. So Rolf said it'd probably be several days before they got it finished and typed and presented to you. He said you'd have readin' material for all summer."

Bounty swallowed several times. "I wish they hadn't gone that far, Gus."

"Why, chief? This'll knock E. Matthew Rone's ears down for good."

"I don't care about knocking anybody's ears down, Gus. I want to solve this case. And I can't. I'm at a dead end. As soon as I get Malcolm Lack safely disposed of, I'm going to go to the chief of police and eat humble pie. Then I'm going to call Austin and ask for some state men to help me."

There was a long silence, during which Gus stared at his wriggling toes. "Chief," he said hesitantly, "I've got a sneakin' suspicion you know who poisoned that liquor."

"I know, Gus. Sure I know. But I could never make a charge against him stick, the way things are now."

"Was it E. Matthew Rone?"

"No, no. I repeat: it's too farfetched a theory to say someone took that means of killing one of us. Or of giving our office a black eye."

A blue roadster approached, exceeding the speed limit, and joined the line of parked cars. Christopher Hand jumped out and cut at the double quick across the grass. "Mr. Norcott left a message for me at the hotel," he said, panting. "Have they given the transfusion yet?"

"It's being given now, Chris."

"Thanks," Hand said and hurried through the door.

"Was it him, chief?" Broddus asked.

"No, Gus. Nobody wants Jimmy Norcott to die. If he did, he wouldn't use this indirect method of killing him. A direct one would be less dangerous, if only because it didn't necessitate repetition."

"Is it some donor who wanted to be able to boost his price?"

"What donor, Gus? He's waited too long now to appear."

"This Malcolm Lack."

"He hasn't put any price on his blood. Besides, that telegram was from the New Orleans police. They interviewed the captain of the *Moquete*. Lack couldn't have got here before this morning."

"I know you don't think it was Doctor Lack. But—"

"Doctor Lack had no motive. When he called himself a murderer he meant he'd driven Beck away from him and to his death. Only one man had a motive that seems to me logical. He had the opportunity. Damn it, Gus! He did it."

"Bad news, Bert?" Both of them had looked around as Larrick barged out, letting the screen door slam behind him.

Larrick's face was quivering. "No," be said in a choked voice as he went down the steps. "The transfusion was successful. They think Jimmy Norcott will live—if he keeps getting them. But, Peter, I've got to talk to you. Come out to the car."

"Steady, son, steady," Bounty repeated in an undertone all the way out to the roadster. When they sat side by side, Larrick pressed something into his palm, then bent over and covered his face with his hands. Bounty looked down. He held a deputy sheriff's badge.

"I couldn't go through with it, Peter. I could have, I think, if it hadn't been for you—"

"Let me tell it, son." Bounty laid a hand on his deputy's broad back. As he talked he eyed the entrance of the hospital.

Roger Norcott and Dr. Cotillion came out, followed by Christopher Hand. Norcott bit off the end of a cigar and lighted it while the physician began removing tinfoil from his chewing tobacco, apparently searching for an unbroken corner. Hand propped a foot on the ledge beside Gus Broddus, glanced at Bert Larrick's roadster, then stared eastward, in the direction of the Gulf. Dr. Ainsworth emerged, a black case in his hand, and fell into conversation with Norcott and Dr. Cotillion.

"Put that badge back on or I will boot you, son," Bounty said, getting out of the roadster. "Just sit here and let me handle this."

As he went up the walk Dr. Lack came shepherding his nephew out. Malcolm Lack was grinning. John Belton Lack's voice was loud and excited: "Gentlemen, have you all met my nephew? Mr. Hand, you haven't met my nephew. John Malcolm Lack. He has come to make his home with me."

Christopher Hand stared. "Why, you're the fellow I tipped!"

"No," Malcolm Lack said, "his name was Black."

Bounty halted a few feet from the steps and called: "Doctor, I'd like to see you."

There was a pause, during which the group looked at him and at the man whom he had addressed.

"Certainly," the physician said, coming down the steps.

"Let's go to the car. I want you to take a drive with me."

"May I ask where we're going?"

Out of earshot of the men on the steps, Bounty said: "To the county jail. You'll be its first occupant."

"I suppose you know what you're doing?"

"I wouldn't have made this move if I hadn't."

"I wonder. I doubt that you have enough evidence, even circumstantial, to take before a court."

"I'll risk it," Bounty said, getting behind the wheel. "At least I have enough to ruin you. That will be some punishment."

"And that evidence is?"

"Blood."

"I see. Perhaps I made an error. Everyone is apt to err occasionally."

"Not you, Doctor," Bounty told him as he drove away.

"Thanks, Sheriff," the physician said. "I believe you do know what you're doing. I've seen this coming but it was worth the gamble. Here's an envelope with a few commissions I'd like you to take care of for me. In return I'll do something for you."

"Don't say you'll give me your share of your buried treasure. That was quick thinking, Doctor. I almost believed you had been taken in for a sucker."

"No, I've heard how proud you are of never having had a prisoner in your jail. I won't mar your record. Turn left at this next corner. Take me to the morgue."

And Bounty snatched too late at the broken plug of tobacco from which Dr. Clive Cotillion's teeth had extracted a capsule.

24

Twenty-four hours later Peter Bounty sat nodding behind his desk. Through the open door of the inner office came the regular snores of Gus Broddus. The sheriff's force had nothing whatever to do.

The telephone rang. Bounty roused himself and picked up the receiver. "Sheriff's office."

"Mr. Bounty, this is Mr. Touchstone, the jeweler."

"Yes, Mr. Touchstone," Bounty said briskly, envisaging robbery.

Mr. Touchstone's voice was lowered. "I have a rather delicate matter to bring up with you, Sheriff. Your deputy, Bert Larrick, is here and wishes to buy a ring."

"A ring?" Bounty's voice rose in alarm. "What kind of a ring?"

"It is to be an engagement ring, I believe, Sheriff. He wants it charged to his account. Now the young man has no account with us—"

"Let me speak to Larrick."

Bounty had seen his deputy only briefly since the death of Dr. Cotillion by aconite. There had been no need to discuss further Bert's falsehood about the results of the blood tests conducted by Dr. Ainsworth. Bounty understood all too well the lad's temptation. Disclosure of the truth (that neither Winters nor Hieronymus had had blood of group B, but one of A and the other of O) meant the substantiation of Bounty's theory, the arrest of the man who promised to be his benefactor and the end of his ambitions to complete his medical course. It had been so easy to prevaricate and to advance a specious theory against a dead man, knowing that there

257

was slight chance of a checkup by Bounty with Dr. Ainsworth, knowing that Dr. Cotillion constituted then no menace to anyone. . . .

"Hello, Peter." Bluff as was Larrick's voice, it betrayed the constraint which he felt. "I didn't know Mr. Touchstone would call
you. How are you?"

"All right, son. What's this about a ring?"

"Well." Larrick laughed. "What would be your guess?"

"Son, we've been over this again and again and again."

"But this time it's different, Peter. Sure enough it is. Why,
you've never even met Mallory yet. You're going to eat dinner with
us tonight, remember. I promise you that afterwards you'll say I'm
right."

"You haven't broached the subject yet, have you, son?" Bounty
asked hopefully.

"No, but I'm not worried about what she'll say. I'm driving her
up to Corpus Christi in the morning and I want her to wear the
ring. Peter, I've got it all figured out. We can be married next
month. We won't be able to have much of a honeymoon, but that
doesn't matter. We can go on to Boston, or wherever I go to school,
and get an apartment. Under this scholarship of Doctor Lack's we'll
have plenty to live on."

"But, son, Doctor Lack won't want—"

"Oh, it's all right with him. When he had me over at his house
this morning I told him what I wanted to do. He said it was up to
me to make my own decision. He told me it was my own life and I
had to decide how I wanted to live it. Better to make mistakes, he
said—"

"Oh, all right." Bounty spoke crossly. "Let me talk to Mr. Touchstone again."

"Thanks, Peter. Say, Carmen's having a big time over at Doctor
Lack's. He says he bets she won't want to leave."

"We'll see about that. Call Touchstone, son."

To the jeweler Bounty said: "Let my deputy have the best ring
you've got in the store and charge it to me."

"Yes, Sheriff. The one he has selected is the best one I have."

Bounty hung up, pivoted about and, until the telephone rang again, stared at the vacant chair beside his.

"Sheriff's office."

It was a call from a rural line. "Sheriff," a voice came to him indistinctly, "this is A. B. Blackburn, thirty-two miles south of town, second farmhouse on the right as you turn toward Cruces. We've got a first-class little crime wave out in this community."

"Crime wave," Bounty said as he jotted down the directions.

"I should say. Yesterday somebody swiped a crate of oranges from one of my neighbor's trucks. And this morning two of my prize pullets were gone. We want you to come out and investigate. We hear you're good at that sort of thing."

"Not much good, Mr. Blackburn, but I'll be out."

Bounty went to get his hat. "Wake up, Gus," he called, "and attend to business. I'm going out on another case."

COACHWHIP PUBLICATIONS

COACHWHIPBOOKS.COM

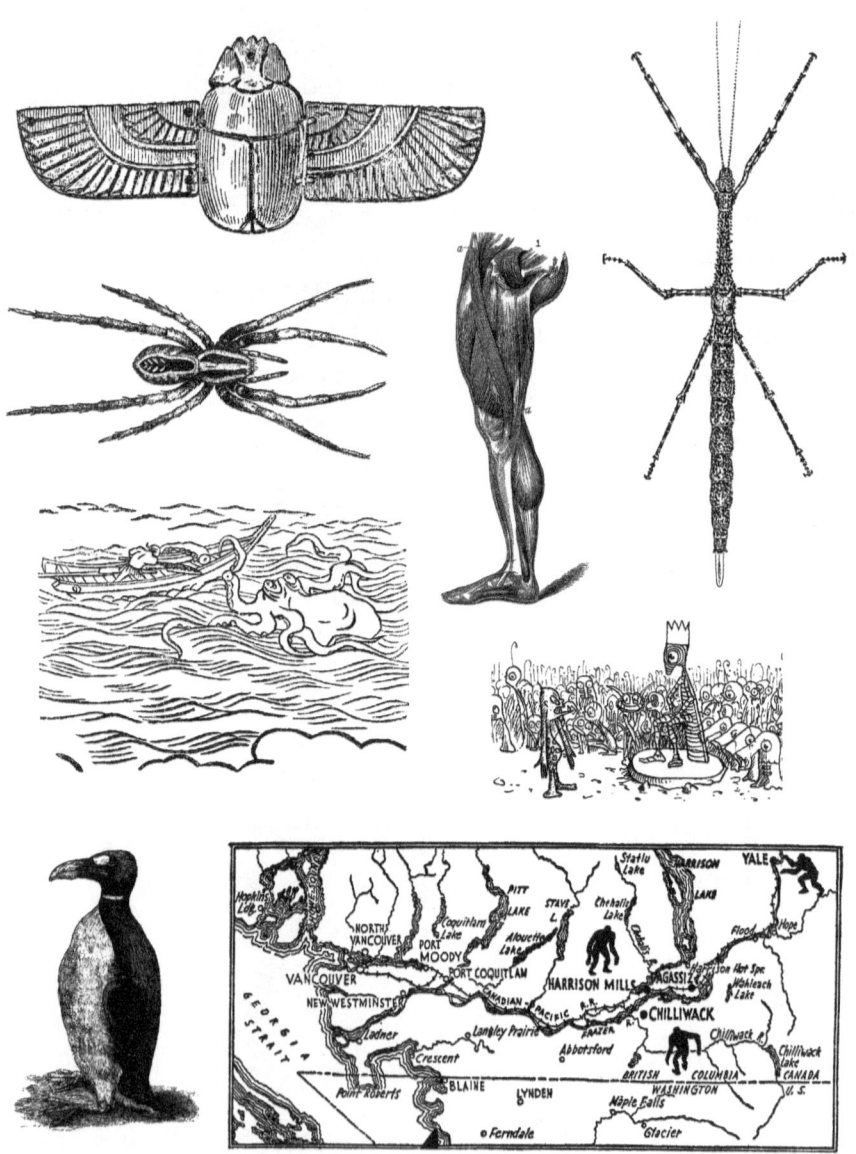

THE CAT
SCREAMS
A HUGH RENNERT MYSTERY

TODD DOWNING

The Cat Screams
ISBN 1-61646-148-9

VULTURES
IN THE SKY
A HUGH RENNERT MYSTERY

TODD DOWNING

Vultures in the Sky
ISBN 1-61646-149-7

Murder on the Tropic
ISBN 1-61646-150-0

The Case of the Unconquered Sisters
ISBN 1-61646-151-9

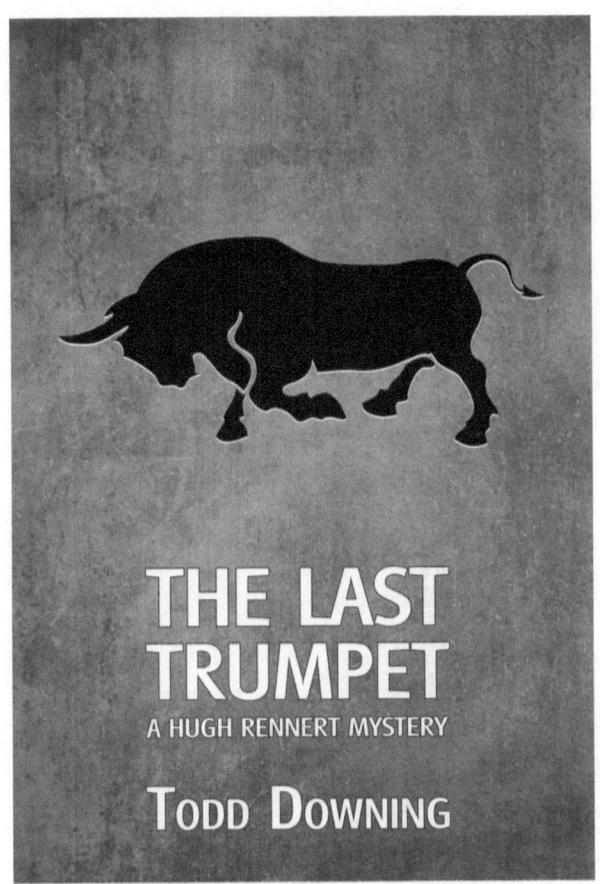

THE LAST
TRUMPET

A HUGH RENNERT MYSTERY

TODD DOWNING

The Last Trumpet
ISBN 1-61646-152-7

NIGHT OVER
MEXICO
A HUGH RENNERT MYSTERY

TODD DOWNING

Night Over Mexico
ISBN 1-61646-153-5

Clues and Corpses: The Detective Fiction and
Mystery Criticism of Todd Downing
Curtis Evans
ISBN 1-61646-145-4